THE DEVIL'S ADVOCATE

GHERBOD FLEMING

First edition October 1997.

White Wolf Publishing
735 Park North Blvd.
Suite 128
Clarkston, GA 30021
www.white-wolf.com

CONTENTS

PROLOGUE

Anno Domini 1093

The creature paused on the moonlit hillside, clawed fingers and toes kneading at the exposed rockface. Wolfish nose twitched, revealing canines too long for the once-human form. There was a scent on the winter breeze, a new scent, not far away. Distracted by an itch, the beast scratched behind an ear with its foot, then picked a louse from the toenail with its teeth. More sniffing the night air. Definitely a new scent. Not sheep or boar or the blood-rich stench of peasant. Something else.

Owain stepped from behind a boulder and with the momentum of three powerful strides thrust his spear into the back of the crouching Gangrel, raising the creature to its feet by the force of the blow. For a brief moment the skewered beast grasped at the spear protruding from its chest, then the last strength fled from its body. With a snarl of pain and rage, it dropped to its knees and then collapsed to its side.

"Forty years since I've hunted these hills, and still I'm able to track you three nights running before you notice my presence." Owain fairly spat the words as he stood above the impaled, convulsing figure. "And you *Gangrel!* What elder would choose you as progeny?" He noticed blood splattered on his dark cloak; the stain would not show, but still he raised the cloth to his lips and licked the damp patch. "Was your sire's mind fouled with tainted blood, or maybe the years have caught up with him? More animal than man by now?"

The Gangrel struggled to speak, but could only gasp as blood gurgled in its throat.

"Where is your sire?" Owain asked leaning down close to the Gangrel's face. "The deep cave a league to the west by the birch stand?" The surprise and the fear—the elder Gangrel was not an understanding master, then—in the Gangrel's eyes told Owain that he was right. "Yes, you led me there last night." Owain smiled and patted his prey roughly on the cheek. "I'll mention you to him."

Finally the Gangrel forced out stuttered words: "B-Bl-aidd…will t-tear…"

Owain stood and placed a booted foot firmly against the Gangrel's face, pinning its head to the ground. "Blaidd. Wolf. How quaint. What the peasants call him, no doubt. And he's going to tear me apart? Limb from limb? Perhaps." Owain drew his sword and with one fierce blow rent the Gangrel's head from its body.

"And so it begins," Owain said solemnly to the night. *I've been away from Wales for far too long*, he thought as clouds obscured the moon and a mist of rain began to fall. *Far too long.*

☥

Morgan ap Rhys strode briskly into the great hall, all but deserted at this late hour of the morning, and found red-haired Iorwerth. Morgan called to his older brother, the lone occupant of the hall, who hardly looked up from where he sat oiling his boots. "He's dead, Iorwerth! Robert of Rhuddlan is dead!"

At this, Iorwerth did stop his oiling. "According to whom?" he asked, eyes narrowed.

Morgan ignored his brother's skepticism. "Riders from the north. It was Gruffudd that killed him—raiding at Degannwy and Robert tried to stop three shiploads of Welshmen with only one man, and Gruffudd took his head!"

"Answer my question," Iorwerth pressed impatiently. "What riders?"

Morgan scoffed. "He's *dead*, I tell you."

Iorwerth threw his boot and oiled rag to the floor. "*What riders?*"

Morgan stared back into the hard eyes of the man who would be lord of Dinas Mynyddig, king of Rhufoniog, when their father died—*if* their father ever died. Morgan took a deep breath and replied more calmly. "Cynwrig. And others."

"Did they see it?"

"They heard."

"Hearing doesn't make it so."

Morgan bristled, slammed his fist down on a table. "Do you have to be so damnably thick-skulled?"

Iorwerth stood. He clenched his fists by his sides and looked down at Morgan. "Until I talk to someone who was there, someone who has touched his swollen tongue, he's not dead."

It was more than Morgan could take. House Rhufoniog had supported Robert and his overlord cousin Hugh the Fat, earl of Chester, because it had been the practical move. Morgan had never liked it. He hadn't liked losing the northern lands near Rhos, and moreover he hadn't liked his family swearing fealty to a Norman. And now that the situation was changing, his brother was too damned slow-witted to see it! Morgan grabbed Iorwerth by powerful shoulders. "Robert is dead, and Gruffudd is on the move! They can't hold Degannwy; they can't hold Rhuddlan. The Normans will be running back to Chester."

"Gruffudd has *been* on the move," Rhys ap Ieuan, their father, corrected Morgan. The old man had shuffled into the room unnoticed among the shouting.

Morgan released Iorwerth. The two brothers stood only a foot apart, the tension between them palpable. They watched in silence as their father came closer. He was older than a man had a right to be, especially a Welsh lord whose sons waited for their inheritances.

Rhys placed a hand on either son's shoulder. He spoke through one side of his mouth, a concession to the rotting teeth that pained him. "Didn't I tell you when news arrived of Gruffudd's escape that either he or Robert would soon be dead? I knew it." Rhys patted Iorwerth on the cheek. "Gruffudd ap Cynan is not a patient man, not a man to let twelve years of imprisonment go unavenged."

Morgan had always felt that both sons were reduced somehow in the presence of their father, much as Morgan sometimes felt lessened in comparison to his brother, who had once killed three cattle thieves single-handedly. Did greatness recede so much with each birth?

Rhys patted Morgan's cheek also; Morgan pulled away from the gesture meant for a child. "No," Rhys continued, "Gruffudd is not a patient man.

Neither is he a man on whose behalf one should act rashly. Robert *may* be dead." Iorwerth, vindicated, smiled. "But there is no cause, just yet, to act."

Morgan could feel his color rising. Their father was taking Iorwerth's side. "But this is our chance to push the Normans out of Wales!"

Rhys grunted contemptuously, as if disgusted that a son of his could be so dense. "And then what? Fight the Normans? So that instead of paying a reasonable tribute to Robert, or to the earl of Chester, we are under Gruffudd's yoke? Think, my boy."

Morgan had no response to this. *At least Gruffudd is a Welshman*, he thought, but that would carry no weight with his father. Besides, it would be Iorwerth who would someday rule House Rhufoniog. Morgan was resigned to his fate of holding a *cantref* or two to the south, guarding against incursions from Powys. He would own land, but the real decisions would be made by his father, and by Iorwerth.

"Even if Robert is dead, the Normans aren't turning tail for Chester just yet, I'd wager," Rhys crooned through the stench of decay. "Hugh will come, or he'll send someone else. Before Hugh, William the Bastard sent Gherbod the Fleming. There will always be someone. The trick is to be ready for him. Not to throw in our lot before we know which way the wind blows." He jabbed a gnarled finger at Morgan's chest. "You're not the risen Rhodri Mawr here to unite all of Wales."

Neither are you, thought Morgan. *Neither are you*.

"When the time comes," said Rhys, "we will act."

☥

Owain stood in the rain and the darkness just beyond the earthworks that had been maintained and expanded over the years. Would the young noble—young compared to Owain's true age, at least—respond to the message delivered by his ghoul Gwilym? Owain thought so. He had watched the noble, as well as all the other members of House Rhufoniog, for many nights. Owain could pick out the sounds of their differing heartbeats—calm and regular, angry and pounding, fluttering with the flush of sex—and he fancied he could fairly read their thoughts.

And Gwilym was dependable. He had led the loaded mules to the empty summer hunting lodge that was exactly where Owain had said it would be. Surely the ghoul could deliver a simple message.

Owain's prediction was borne out as Morgan ap Rhys, wrapped in hides and furs against the cold and wet of the night, cautiously picked his way through the muddy defensive works of Dinas Mynyddig. Owain did not feel the cold.

At length the vampire moved, allowing himself

to be seen by the mortal, who had been peering ineffectually into the dark. Morgan seemed faintly surprised to see someone where a moment before he'd seen no one, but if he found this disconcerting, he hid it well as he sauntered over to Owain.

"Your man said you'd be here."

"He did, and I am." Owain kept his wide-brimmed hat pulled low. No need to reveal too much too soon. Morgan eyed him suspiciously. *As well he should*, Owain thought.

"And that you had news of Robert of Rhuddlan," Morgan continued.

"I can only confirm what you have already heard," said Owain. "He has died the death from which none may return." Even through the gloom, Owain could see Morgan's eyes narrow as he weighed the value of information from an unknown source. "No. You have no reason to trust me," Owain answered the unvoiced question, "but I would earn your trust if you will allow me. I bring a token of my good intent."

Morgan's hand instinctively shifted to the hilt of his sword. "Yes?"

Owain smiled at the haughty attempt at intimidation. *Time enough for that later, my boy*. The vampire, with exaggerated caution, handed over a small bundle. Morgan gingerly unfolded the rag to find a fang half the size of his middle finger and coated in still-moist blood.

As Morgan held the rag, the rain began to wash away the blood from the tooth. "Who are you and what do you want?" Morgan asked sharply. "Your man called you *arglwydd*. Are you a lord? What's the meaning of…" he vacantly waved the bloody rag and tooth, "all this?"

"All this," Owain imitated Morgan's gesture, "is my way of proving how I can aid your people, this land, you." All hint of facetiousness left Owain's voice. "There is a beast that prowls your land. Blaidd, the villagers call it—wolf. This tooth is from its spawn which is dead, but if you do not kill this Blaidd, there will be more, and your people will die."

Morgan considered this for a moment. "But there have always been tales of the wolf."

"And you have believed them while others have not. 'Tales of dodderers, and of mothers to frighten their unruly babes,' your father calls them."

Morgan tried unsuccessfully to hide his surprise at hearing his father's words parrotted now. Owain had eavesdropped on Morgan teasing a serving girl he bedded about her fears of the wolf. Later the vampire had also listened as the young noble had mentioned the peasants' fears to his father and had been admonished. Owain wondered for a moment if he had given away too much, set the younger man too keenly on guard, but then realized that it didn't matter. The moment Morgan had ventured out into the cold night, into the rain-soaked unknown to meet with a complete stranger, at that moment the hook had taken hold, and now was the time to pull it true.

"Listen carefully," Owain said with great urgency. After giving terse instructions, he slipped away before a protesting Morgan, merely feet away, knew the vampire was gone.

The clouds gave way to stars and moon during the night, and the morning dawned bright and chill. As Morgan gnawed a cold biscuit and waited, as he had been instructed, at the edge of the forest for Gwilym, the second son of Rhys ap Ieuan couldn't help but wonder what manner of man was the stranger, who had vanished so quickly and completely into the night. The man's audacity had angered Morgan, especially since, as far as Morgan could tell in the deep shadows and with that hat, the stranger had looked so young. But his words had not been those of a young man; they were spoken with an inherent authority, with the expectation that they would be obeyed, much like…Morgan's father.

Morgan had been prepared to disregard the arrogant words, to ignore the stranger's instructions, but had changed his mind for two reasons. The stranger had quoted, word for word, Rhys's rebuke of Morgan for his concerns about the wolf. How was that possible? The stranger didn't seem the sort of man with whom Morgan's father would consort.

And there was the tooth.

"Dry it off and expose it to the sunlight," the stranger had said, and when Morgan had done so early this morning, the tooth had crumbled to dust in his hand. Mere trickery? Perhaps. But worth investigating, and if Morgan could rid his family lands of the beast...

So he waited with spear and torch as instructed. "It fears fire," the stranger had said. "Also, the beast will be sluggish during the day, even in its cave. Attack it at noon and you will have a chance. Drive your spear through its heart—it must be the heart—and then wait for me to join you at nightfall."

What manner of man, indeed? Morgan wondered.

Eventually Gwilym arrived. He was a short, stolid man, probably from southern Wales, Morgan guessed from the accent of the few words the servant uttered. He led Morgan to the east, away from Dinas Mynyddig, out of the forest, up into the unforgiving mountains. For several hours they kept up a brutal pace without speaking, sweating even in the cold, steam rising off their bodies. Just before noon, they stopped.

"My *arglwydd* commanded me to go no farther," said Gwilym. His breath hung in the air before him.

"There is the cave." He pointed up the hill to a small opening near a stand of weather-beaten birch trees.

Morgan doubted he would ever have noticed the entrance on his own. He proceeded alone, stopping before he reached the mouth of the cave to light the sap-soaked head of the torch. Flame sputtering, spear lowered, he entered the cave.

Morgan was a born hunter. He had brought down all types of game and, on necessary occasions, had tracked human prey. But this was different—he sought a beast he'd heard stories of since his childhood. Morgan adjusted his grip on the spear. The torch cast dancing shadows on the cave walls. Once beyond the entry and the whistling breeze, he could feel that the air in the cave was slightly warmer than that outside. The cave's damp, musty smell was familiar to Morgan, but there was something else as well—an odor similar to the kennels at Dinas Mynyddig, except with a fouler edge, less aired-out, and the farther Morgan advanced into the tunnel, the stronger the smell.

A stillness descended around Morgan. The only sounds were those of his measured footsteps, the distant dripping of water, and the pounding of his heart. It wasn't fear that caused sweat to trickle down his back, but rather the intense alertness that he'd only ever experienced when death was at hand. Morgan was thinking that he must be close, as overwhelming as the odor had become, when he heard it—growling from around the next turn.

His mouth went dry.

There was no way to surprise the beast; the torch had certainly given him away already, but there was no getting around that. Spear levelled before him, Morgan stepped around the corner and came face to face with the beast—Blaidd, wolf, the monster of his childhood, the bane of the peasants of Rhufoniog.

For a moment they regarded one another. The beast looked much like a wolf—pointed snout, bared fangs, ears laid back, hackles raised—yet it stood on two legs against the back wall of the cave. Its glaring eyes were thick with sleep, but it looked anything but sluggish.

One heartbeat passed, and the creature pounced.

Morgan thrust the torch at the wolf and it veered away from him with an angry snarl.

He attacked immediately, but the beast countered with inhuman speed and strength, almost tearing the weapon from Morgan's hold.

Again the wolf charged and Morgan warded it off with the flame, and again his counterattack was easily turned aside. Each time the creature struck the spear, the force of the blow sent jolts of pain up Morgan's arm. His hand tingled.

Morgan thrust with his spear and the beast's downward slash almost ripped the shaft from his hand, this time wrenching his smallest finger to the side with a loud pop. He howled with pain and dodged to the side as the wolf's jaws snapped shut inches from his face.

Morgan lurched off balance. The ancient beast swiped sideways at the torch and connected, burning its own hand but knocking the firebrand from Morgan's grasp.

Morgan lunged for the torch—more potent than any shield—but the wolf had expected that. Its claws dug into Morgan's flesh just below the neck and tore down across his chest and belly.

He felt shock more than pain as he stumbled backward and fell.

Now it was Morgan's turn to anticipate his opponent's next move, and his ability to do so saved his life.

As the beast surged forward with a roar of triumph, Morgan hastily braced his spear under his arm against the stone floor, jerking the point upward in line with the charging creature's chest instead of its stomach. With the terrible, bone-shattering force of its killing lunge, the beast crashed onto the spear, imbedding itself well down onto the oaken shaft.

As the dead weight of the wolf yanked the spear from Morgan's quivering hands and blood welled up in his wounds, the torch on the floor sputtered and there was darkness.

Owain arrived shortly after sunset to find Gwilym caring for the half-dead Morgan just inside the cave entrance. "The Gangrel?" Owain asked.

"Staked." Gwilym nodded toward the inner cave. "In its lair."

"And young Morgan?"

Gwilym's expression remained neutral. "Got himself cut pretty badly. Lost a lot of blood. If the claws had gone much deeper, he wouldn't have made it this long." Owain saw that it was true; the heap of blood-soaked hides and rags with which Gwilym had been able to stop most of the bleeding attested to the fact. Gwilym looked up with an unusually intent expression. "Was it this way with me, *arglwydd?*"

It was the only time Owain could remember Gwilym asking about his transformation into a ghoul. "You were worse, I think." Gwilym nodded, apparently satisfied.

Owain knelt down beside Morgan. The vampire forced himself to ignore the enticing scent of so much blood. He drew his dagger and with a forceful jab pierced his own right palm. Blood flowed freely. "From the stigmata the fallen are given eternal life. Eh, Gwilym?" Gwilym frowned. Owain smiled, still amused that his ghoul had not yet shed the ingrained piety of his former life. "I shouldn't blaspheme, should I? Who knows what torments

Gherbod Fleming

the powers of heaven might devise for us?"

He lowered his bleeding palm and after a moment of blood dripping into Morgan's slack mouth, the unconscious noble began sucking at the wound, weakly at first, then more forcefully, greedily. Gwilym pulled back the bloody rags and watched with Owain as the torn flesh of Morgan's chest and abdomen miraculously knitted itself back together, closing over the exposed bone and muscle below.

Satisfied that Morgan would survive, Owain pulled his hand away. It, too, was already healing. Owain chuckled, "Physician, heal thyself," again to Gwilym's obvious discomfort.

Owain headed deeper into the cave. As he advanced, the smell of wet, dirty beast that dominated the cave became atrocious. *How far from humanity some Cainites have fallen,* Owain thought. This was no occasion for compassion. Having been defeated by a mortal, the beast had earned its fate.

When Owain emerged from the depths of the cave, he was ruddy-cheeked with the blood and power of a vampire of elder generation. Morgan was awake now, sitting up against the cave wall. Owain dropped the head of Blaidd at the noble's feet. "You did well."

Morgan blinked, dumbfounded. "I should be dead."

"You're a quick healer," said Owain dryly.

Morgan was in no mood for trifling. "Who are

you? *What* are you?"

"All in good time, dear Morgan. All in good time." Owain raised a finger for silence as Morgan began to protest. "For now, the night is young and you are a hero. You must return to Dinas Mynyddig and present your father with this trophy." He indicated the severed head and waved away Morgan's question. "You're too weak still to journey alone, so Gwilym will aid you. Do not mention me. I want none of the glory. We will speak again." And for the second time, Owain stepped away from Morgan and disappeared into the night.

☥

Owain, too, would return to Dinas Mynyddig, but not yet. Instead, he turned east and passed over mountain and through forest with the speed and grace of a stag, the strength of a bear. None saw his passage as leagues fell away behind him. He travelled until he reached a hilltop above the abbey of Holywell. From above, he could see within the outer walls—the spring, the shrine—and he knew that she was there, but he went no closer that night.

☥

After covering the distance back from Holywell, it was no great task to slip past mortals into the manor house at Dinas Mynyddig. Owain was but a shadow in the night to them. He could hear the celebration in the great hall. Morgan had staggered in and pulled from a sack the head of the beast. He was met first with confused silence, then with whispers of awe, and finally with cheers of triumph at his heroic deed. This night would be remembered for many years to come. *Oh, yes. It will be remembered*, thought Owain.

The revelry continued without sign of abatement, but not all would drink and cheer and sing until dawn. Owain entered a particular bedroom and waited.

When Rhys ap Ieuan returned to his room, Owain was on him before the door had completely closed. With preternatural speed and iron grip, the vampire clutched the old man from behind, wrenching his head to the side so his ear was within inches of Owain's lips. "Do you remember my voice, Rhys?" Owain hissed. "Has it haunted your dreams for these forty years, or have you slept peacefully at night?"

Owain could see Rhys's eyes bulging.

"Do you still have a tongue, old man?" Owain twisted Rhys's head a bit farther, so that the king of Rhufoniog cried out, then threw the old man to the floor.

Rhys, confused and in pain, held his strained neck and licked his dry, cracked lips. "Owain?" He stared unbelieving at the impossible sight.

"But…you're alive? Young?"

Owain laughed. He had looked forward to this moment for decades. "Greetings, brother."

Rhys struggled to speak. "How…?"

Owain lifted Rhys to his feet by the shoulders. "Don't worry. Your assassin didn't botch the job. I'm dead." Rhys's mouth hung open; his eyes blinked rapidly, vacantly. "It was Angharad, wasn't it?" Owain's knuckles were white with rage. "You married her, but I loved her."

"No, no, no…" Rhys stared ahead, mouth agape; reason was quickly fleeing him.

"What size *galanas*, do you think? How large an honor-price do you owe me for forty years of unending death? Hundred head of cattle? Five hundred?" Owain snarled and bared his fangs. Rhys moaned; his eyes fluttered, began to roll back in his head. "I think there aren't enough cattle in all of Wales, dear brother." Owain held the king's face in his cold hands. "You've lived too many years, old man. Your body stinks of rot." The vampire moved his face closer to Rhys's. "And your son Morgan, he has become a great man tonight," Owain whispered, "and he is *mine*."

Rhys began to let out a doleful wail; pus and frothy drool ran down his chin. Owain snapped the old man's head violently to the left—*crack!*—then let the body crumple to the floor.

With singing from the great hall echoing in

Owain's ears, he waited in vain for the relief he had always dreamed would come at this moment.

Morgan was in bed, taken with sudden illness, when he received his brother's summons. Three days ago Morgan had felt the chill grip of death. As he had lain on the cave floor next to the impaled beast, he had prayed to the risen Christ to intercede on behalf of his soul.

Someone else had interceded.

Morgan had awakened to find what should have been an open, mortal wound healed as if it had happened weeks before—the stranger's doing, somehow.

Just as peculiar, as Gwilym the Tight-Lipped had helped Morgan back to Dinas Mynyddig, instead of collapsing from fatigue and physical strain, Morgan had grown stronger and increasingly energetic. Throughout the impromptu feast honoring the death of the beast, he had felt flushed with vigor and praise. Even Iorwerth had embraced Morgan while their father looked on admiringly—enviously in all probability, considering the old king had no such heroic deed to his own credit.

Don't think ill of the dead, Morgan chided himself. Early that next morning, a servant had found Rhys ap Ieuan's body at the bottom of a staircase, his neck broken by a fall.

The next evening, last night, there had been a mass and then a feast in honor of the late king of Rhufoniog—and in honor of the new king, Iorwerth ap Rhys. By the end of the mass, however, Morgan had been beset by spells of dizziness and had almost fainted. The feast barely begun, he had been forced to excuse himself and had retreated to his bed, where he had remained throughout the past day, wracked by vertigo if he so much as sat up to relieve himself in the chamber pot.

Presently, his head was clearing somewhat, and, with the aid of an attendant, he was able to make his way to the study that doubled as an audience chamber on informal occasions.

"Uncle Morgan!" Iorwerth's six-year-old daughter Branwen hugged Morgan; so enthusiastically, in fact, that she nearly upset his fragile balance.

"Hello, Branwen. Easy, child." The room began to swim slightly before Morgan.

Iorwerth sat in a padded armchair by the fire, his glittering hair seemingly an extension of the blaze. Beside him sat delicate Blodwen, cradling their infant son Iago in her arms. Morgan's other two nieces, Elen and Siaun, red-haired like their father, sat at a table nearby practicing their letters on a piece of slate with chalk.

"Morgan," Iorwerth greeted him.

Morgan, trailing behind Branwen, her tiny hand gripping his finger, approached the royal couple.

He felt surrounded by the comforting warmth of family, but distinctly separate from it, an outsider glimpsing that which was denied him.

Against the wall to the king's right stood Brochwel, *penteulu*, captain of the household guard, listening, watching with his fierce eyes.

"Morgan, you've not been well," said Blodwen, the beautiful new queen of Rhufoniog. Her eyes sparkled blue in the light of the fire; her small nose and strong chin framed the smile that induced forbidden stirrings in Morgan. She still radiated strength and vitality, even after giving birth to four children. "You should settle down. Stop your carousing and find a woman to care for you."

"How can I, when my brother has already taken the most lovely woman in Wales for himself?" The words were offered as flattering jest, but struck closer to truth than Morgan would have cared to admit.

"I must speak with Morgan," Iorwerth said gently to his wife.

Blodwen nodded, then gracefully stood. "Come, children." As she ushered them from the room, she turned one last time to Morgan. "Guard your health well, Morgan," she said, and then closed the door behind her.

Morgan saw the way that Iorwerth's eyes followed Blodwen's progress across the room. Whatever differences lay between the brothers, Morgan freely acknowledged that Iorwerth was easily ten times the husband and father that their father had been, and, though Morgan was not a man of great sentimentality, Blodwen and the children held a place close to his heart.

"You have been ill, brother." The eyes which had shown such affection toward Blodwen were more guarded with Morgan.

"I have, but I will survive."

"I will not keep you long," said Iorwerth. "As was Father's wish, you are granted Penllyn and Dyffryn Clwyd. I imagine you will want to take up residence at your new holdings as soon as possible."

The news itself was not a surprise to Morgan. He had expected to receive one or two of the southern *cantrefi* while Iorwerth retained the more central lands of Rhufoniog, but the abruptness with which the grant was presented and the haste in which he was apparently expected to leave Dinas Mynyddig caught Morgan up short. He scrutinized the closed expression of his brother, and then looked over to the more openly challenging gaze of the man-at-arms Brochwel. There was a new facet in how they regarded him, Morgan realized. Now that Iorwerth was king, now that Morgan was a hero, the slayer of the beast, they no longer saw him merely as a younger brother, but as a rival, a possible claimant to the kingship of Rhufoniog; the sooner he was safely tucked away in the isolated lands south of the Hiraethog Range, the better.

Morgan's blood rose at the thought of no longer being welcome in the ancestral lands where he had spent all the days since his birth, at the thought of being hustled off beyond the mountains. "I am loyal to you, brother," he said more tersely than he'd intended.

"I do not doubt that you are."

The two brothers regarded one another for several moments, neither's gaze wavering. Morgan saw in Iorwerth's eyes no hope of reconciliation, no possibility of cooperation. Their father had torn the two brothers apart more completely in death even than in life. Morgan turned and, fighting the vertigo that once again assailed him, made his way to the door.

"There is news from the north," Iorwerth said finally. Morgan stopped but did not turn. "Robert of Rhuddlan *is* dead, and Gruffudd ap Cynan has driven away Hervé, the Norman bishop of Bangor."

"Then we must throw in with Gruffudd," said Morgan quietly, still facing the door.

"We must do whatever I decide we must do," Iorwerth responded.

Morgan left without further comment. *So, there it is*, he thought as he closed the door behind him.

Climbing up the outer wall and easing through the shutter that a moment before had been latched, Owain found Morgan sick in bed, feverish and furious. "So, you've been ordered to the south." The mortal started at the sound of the icy voice. "This is your moment of destiny, Morgan."

Morgan raised himself on his elbows. "Who in damnation *are* you, and why don't you leave me in peace?" he snapped.

"Your question nearly answers itself," said Owain with a wry smile. The vampire, now by the bed, looked down intently at his pale nephew. Though Owain was more than thirty years older, he appeared to be at least ten years Morgan's junior. "But all things in their time. Do you plan to tuck tail and slink off to the southlands like an obedient little brother?"

Morgan opened his mouth to issue a sharp retort, but Owain's glare snatched the words from the young noble's mind. "I…I am loyal to my brother," Morgan forced out.

"As he is loyal to you?" Owain asked with raised eyebrow. "Tell me, Morgan. Does he treat you like a brother? Does he seek your counsel, confer with you as a trusted advisor?" A harsh strain crept into Owain's voice. "Or does he treat you more like a leper, ordering you far away from your home?"

Owain held Morgan's gaze; the mortal's eyes blinked and began to water, but he could not look away. "I…am loyal…." he repeated weakly.

"Do you know why he treats you so, Morgan?" Owain leaned very close now. "Because he fears you—you who destroyed the beast. Your name is whispered in awe throughout Rhufoniog. People will follow you, and he knows it. He harbors ill feelings against you. He sees that he is slighted by your leaving the feast in his honor. He jealously parades his wife and children before you. He fears you."

Morgan opened his mouth but was unable to speak.

"You have proved yourself worthy. Unlike your brother, unlike your father, you are a man approaching greatness." Owain towered over the mortal, knowing that Morgan was incapable of looking away from the mesmerizing vampire eyes, black as death. "You asked who I am, Morgan. I am Owain ap Ieuan, your father's brother."

Morgan lay on his bed, breathing shallowly, hearing the words but robbed, in his stuporous state, of the profound shock that would otherwise have accompanied them.

"Three nights ago you asked what I am. I am accursed by God," said Owain, "but that is just as well, for God has failed me. I am the devil's spawn." Owain turned away, began pacing methodically around the sparsely furnished room. "Forty years ago," he continued, "my brother was to be anointed *subregnum*, king of Rhufoniog, by Edward the Confessor, but Rhys was taken ill and sent me in his stead to Westminster. Looking back over the years, I have no doubt it was an illness of convenience, for Rhys hired an assassin to kill me in Westminster. It was to appear a common robbery, a visiting Welshman caught unawares in the city."

The rage of decades washed over Owain; he flexed his fingers, all lengthy claws now. "What my dear brother could not know was that the assassin he chose was no mortal. He was a vampire of royal blood, and he did more than kill me; he took me beyond death, into the world of the Kindred."

Morgan stirred as the haze began to clear from his mind.

"You see, your father and I had argued about…" Owain paused. "About many things. But it was his fear of me, his fear and jealousy, that condemned me to be what I am."

Owain raised a clawed finger and with one slow motion slashed his own forearm. For the first time— too late—Morgan looked with fear upon the creature leaning over him. A second time, Owain's deep, black eyes took control of the mortal, holding both muscle and will immobile as Owain presented his bleeding arm. Morgan drank. Owain smiled as his cursed blood flowed into his nephew. Shortly, the vampire pulled his arm away and stood. Morgan, seized by a spasm of coughing, fell back onto his pillows.

"Do you feel it?" Owain asked. "Do you feel the

power of the blood?"

Morgan struggled to prop himself against the headboard, took a deep breath. "The power of the blood or the curse of God?"

"They go hand in hand."

"Then I, too, am cursed?"

Owain laughed derisively at the question. "Idealism is the luxury of the young and the foolish, Morgan. Loyalty to your brother, loyalty to God—they do not exist, not in this world or the next." Two powerful strides and Owain was again by the bed, lifting Morgan into the air by his collar. "I have given you what you want, what you all but asked for." Owain bared his fangs; he had no stomach for self-pity, not from a mortal whose suffering could never match his own. "Or would you rather pad away quietly to Penllyn or Dyffryn Clwyd? Is that what you want? To give up all you've ever known? To never again walk the paths or hunt the forests that have always been yours? To bow before your brother?"

Morgan stared deep into the animal eyes. "No," he finally answered in a subdued voice. "That is not what I want."

Owain lowered his freshly fed ghoul back to the bed. "Somehow, I thought not." The vampire smoothed the wrinkles from his cloak as the rest of the trap fell into place. "You have no great love for the Normans?"

"No."

"Good. I am of the vampire clan Ventrue, but with the Conqueror from Normandy have come a new breed of Ventrue wishing to drive before them or rule over those of us already here." Owain gnawed at a speck of blood beneath his now-receded fingernail. "Needless to say, London is no longer so hospitable as it once was. I have returned home, and I never again wish to see a Norman on my soil."

All the old wrongs will be redressed, thought Owain.

Morgan, overwhelmed by all that he had been subjected to, sat quietly.

"By morning," the vampire continued, "your strength will return, more strength than you've ever felt. This is my next gift to you, Morgan. You need not submit to your brother's designs for your fate. Challenge him. Challenge him, and after you defeat him, declare the allegiance of House Rhufoniog to Gruffudd ap Cynan. *You* will be lord of Dinas Mynyddig. *You* will rule Rhufoniog. All of Wales could be at your feet."

Morgan did not protest.

Good, thought Owain. *He will do it. So easy when you give them what they want.* "One matter remains to decide—your brother's family. You must take his wife and children as your own."

At this, Morgan balked. "I will not."

Owain could see the struggle within Morgan,

could remember what it felt like, the struggle to separate family from politics, power from blood. "Blodwen is not an unattractive woman," the vampire pointed out, "and wouldn't you like young Iago to grow with love and respect for his uncle rather than with vengeance in his heart?"

A bit of Morgan's fire had returned now. "I will *not* take my brother's wife as my own."

The vampire sighed. "So, you'll kill your brother but not bed his wife, eh? How noble of you, Morgan." Owain smiled, only partially amused. "Very well, then. That is your decision to make." He returned to the open window. "I have taken shelter in the hunting lodge on the ridge three days to the south. You know which one?" Morgan nodded. "Good. Come to me there as soon as you can. Eventually you will not need to feed so often, but for now we must keep up your strength."

And then the window was again latched, as if Morgan had been without a visitor that night.

All singing and merriment died away as Morgan entered the great hall with a naked blade. The crowd parted before him, all except Brochwel and his second in command, Cynwrig, who stepped forward to block Morgan's way. "What is the meaning of this?" barked Brochwel.

Behind the *penteulu* sat Iorwerth, king of Rhufoniog, at the high table, Blodwen's seat empty beside him. "Yes, brother," said Iorwerth, "what is the meaning of this? Treason?" He did not look surprised, nor particularly worried.

The ties of blood weighed heavily on Morgan—on one side, the undeniable bond with a brother, regardless of any rivalries that persisted over the years; on the other side, the strength and ambition that, magnified by vampiric power, flowed through his veins. Such thoughts had plagued Morgan all night and all day. He had neither slept nor eaten. When he spoke amidst the confusion of the great hall, he heard the words as if from a distance, as if they were spoken by someone else. "I challenge you, Iorwerth. I claim the kingship of Rhufoniog."

Brochwel drew his sword; Cynwrig stood ready with hand on hilt. A worried murmur rippled through the hall.

"Hold, Brochwel," called Iorwerth.

"Such traitorous dogs should be put down," responded the *penteulu*.

Iorwerth ignored his retainer's ire. "Morgan," said the king calmly. "Put down your sword, ride south tonight, and this is forgotten."

"Do you fear me, brother?"

"I fear *for* you."

Morgan bristled at such condescension. "I challenge you, Iorwerth. I claim the kingship of Rhufoniog."

Iorwerth sighed deeply. "Very well, then." He reached out his hand and an attendant brought him his sword. Iorwerth drew blade from sheath with the grace and power of one well versed in the arts of war. He stepped forward around the table. "Brochwel, go make sure that Blodwen and the children remain in their chambers."

"But, *arglwydd*..."

"Do as you're told," said Iorwerth evenly. "And let all know that Iorwerth ap Rhys accepts the challenge of his brother. House Rhufoniog will be led by who survives here."

Morgan had been sure that Iorwerth would accept the challenge. Whether it was arrogance or nobility that forced the king's hand, Morgan could not decide. Either way, the result would be the same. Brochwel stormed out of the room, and Cynwrig, also, stepped aside.

Challenged and challenger circled each other for only a moment, as tables were pulled back and goblets overturned, before Morgan attacked. Iorwerth parried and swiped at his brother's knee, but Morgan easily sidestepped the stroke.

Neither man gave ground as they traded blows. The sound of steel on steel echoed from the rafters of the great hall. They offered no witty banter, only grunts and gasps of exertion as they swung and parried and dodged.

Twice Iorwerth's blade struck glancing blows and

bit into Morgan's flesh—once on the calf, once the forearm—but Morgan felt nary a prick. He pressed his brother relentlessly, attacking at every turn, and as Iorwerth's breathing became labored, Morgan still moved strong and fresh. Iorwerth was clearly the more adept swordsman, but Morgan was skilled enough to hold his own, and his ceaseless aggression was taking its toll. It was soon apparent that fatigue would tell the tale.

As Morgan pressed his increasing advantage, he saw, for the first time he could remember, fear—*real* fear—creep into his brother's eyes. *Is he thinking of his lost kingdom?* Morgan wondered. *Or of the wife and children he will never again hold?*

It was time now for Morgan's blade to strike true. He caught Iorwerth's left side, and then his wrist, and then his bicep. None of the blows were crippling, but they added to Iorwerth's mounting exhaustion, and Morgan was not yet winded.

The king fought on, his jerkin stained with spreading blood. His attacks came less and less frequently, and Morgan brushed them aside with ease. Iorwerth backed away, but Morgan gave him no quarter.

When the final blow fell, a thrust that dug deeply into Iorwerth's belly and left him with blood on his lips, the king seemed surprised. He staggered, then slumped to the floor.

Morgan, standing above his brother as the last

of his life fled, felt none of the exultation he had expected. All he had wanted, all he had dreamed of, was in his grasp now. Dinas Mynyddig was his. House Rhufoniog would stand by Gruffudd ap Cynan, the Welshman, and drive the Normans from Wales.

Blood pooled around Morgan's feet.

He heard his own voice, again from far away, "Cynwrig, fetch Brochwel."

Morgan was only vaguely aware of the murmurings around him of the household and of the few guests remaining after the feast in honor of Rhys ap Ieuan. The victor, the new king of Rhufoniog, could not turn away from his brother's lifeless body, from the eyes that someone should close. He must have stood there for some time, because now Cynwrig was back, speaking quietly in Morgan's ear: "Morgan, come with me."

Morgan, the lord of Dinas Mynyddig, allowed himself to be led from the great hall, away from the shocked silence, to the family chambers of Iorwerth ap Rhys. The king stepped from the corridor into a room of madness.

Littered among Blodwen's modest decor were the sprawled bodies of Iorwerth's loved ones. Elen and Siaun, tangled young limbs, on the floor. Little Branwen crumpled on the bed. Blodwen was propped in a chair, her head tilted back, while Iago, barely a year old, lay limp across her lap. Blodwen's gown was torn, and two red punctures stood out at the top of her left breast.

Off to the side lay Brochwel, his head at an impossible angle to his body. Of all the carnage, there was no blood—not on the floor, not on the clothes, and not, Morgan was sure, in the bodies.

Very well, then. That is your decision to make.

Morgan had not wanted this. But hadn't he known? Hadn't his ambitions set this in motion? Had he actually thought that he would be able to shield Blodwen and innocent Branwen from the fury set loose by his unsheathed sword? Morgan wanted to throw down his bloodied blade, to run far away from the evidence of his crime.

"Is this your doing?" Cynwrig stood behind Morgan, horrified at the thought, wanting to be told otherwise.

Morgan did not turn, did not weep. "Yes," he said. "This is my doing." *As surely as if I slit their throats myself.* "I am king."

Owain had been vaguely unsettled for the past four nights since his brother's death. Not since the first weeks after his embrace had he felt so. *Forty years thirsting for revenge, and now I have drunk of it fully.* Yet still he thirsted.

He had tried to kindle his rage in dispatching Blodwen and the children—*It had to be done. Mor-*

gan will see that in time. Send a message of ruthlessness to the other petty nobles that they'll not soon forget, and no rival claimants to the kingship—but of all the lives taken, only Brochwel's had been at all satisfying, an amusement.

As rain fell again from the dark skies of Wales, Owain, flushed with the family blood that ran in his veins, passed across the countryside more swiftly than an eagle, more silently than a shadow. He sought the one loose thread that still tied him to the past.

Stolen warmth radiated from his body as he stood atop the hill above the abbey of Holywell. He paused not long, what might have been a heartbeat for the living. The outer wall was low, not meant particularly for defense. Within, the power of faith hummed about the spring, so Owain took a wide route around. He had no use for faith.

He found her by scent. She was kneeling in prayer by the bed in her cell. Even as quietly as Owain entered, she heard. She looked in his direction.

"Angharad," he whispered, the ability to speak almost escaping him.

She cocked her head slightly; a bemused smile played across her features. "They said you were dead these many years." Angharad's voice was still musical, though huskier, richer. Like Owain's brother had been, she was old now, nearly sixty, and the years had not passed her by as they had Owain. Her skin was leathery where once it had been supple, though it did not droop overly much. The once-bright eyes were obscured by cataracts. She was blind. "I must finish my prayers," she said.

Owain waited silently while she prayed.

Finally she stood, then sat on the bed.

"You look well," Owain said quietly.

"I may look well," she smiled as she spoke to him, "but I no longer see well. It is good to hear your voice, Owain." She did not see his smooth, young skin, his still-dark hair.

They remained in silence for many minutes. For perhaps the first time in his long life and unlife, words deserted Owain. He had thought to snuff this last smoldering ember of his past, but he no longer knew if he could. After some while, he again found his tongue. "I never wanted Rhys to send you away."

"I know," she nodded quietly. "He needed children."

Again there was silence.

"I always…" Owain faltered. "I always cared for you, Angharad." He realized as he spoke the words that, though the memories lived, the passions were long dead. "But I was loyal to my brother. How the years have changed me." Loyalty dead, love dead; Owain was an empty husk, consumed by insatiable hate.

"Owain?"

For a brief moment, he had deluded himself that redemption might lie with this woman and her infinite capacity for tenderness. *Redemption*, he thought as he looked at the crucified Christ on the wall. *Humanity*.

Owain left her on the bed and slipped from the candlelit cell back into the infinite night.

ONE

The skyscrapers towered on every side, enormous walls to a cell—or coffin—from which Grimsdale might never emerge. He jerked about, the hundredth glance over his shoulder that hour.

Nothing.

But they had to be close. He could *feel* their predatory gazes boring through him like a stake. Grimsdale harbored no illusions. If they caught him there would be no trial, no appeal to the archbishop.

There!

He whirled around at the sound of a deep, raspy cough just down the street. Street person or assassin? No way to know. *Keep moving,* Grimsdale told himself. He dashed across the intersection and hurried down the sidestreet. *Keep moving.* He hadn't come this far to die now.

Downtown Atlanta was mostly deserted this time of night—no crowds for cover, but always plenty of shadows to hide killers. Grimsdale's hearing was sharp, but would that be enough for him to slip out of the city, to get to Chicago? He had avoided New York, Washington, Detroit, but even here they had found him. How much longer could he elude them? How many hours until his luck ran out?

Headlights up the street, coming his way. Grimsdale ducked into an alley until the police cruiser passed. Probably the local authorities were under Camarilla control, but that would be bad enough. Slow him down until his former allies caught up with him. That's all it would take.

Footsteps! Or...no, he was wrong. But he was sure he'd heard them. Almost sure.

Grimsdale felt panic rising, fought it back down. *Stay calm. Think straight. Keep moving.* He had to lose his pursuers and get back to the airport. *The Giovanni hangar. Neutral ground.*

After a full minute of standing perfectly still and hearing no signs of pursuit, he eased back onto the street. Coughing in the distance. Grimsdale had to fight his nerves to keep from breaking into a mad dash.

☥

The hounds strained against their leads. It was all Mike could do to hold them back when they were on a scent like this. He hopped a fallen tree at the bottom of the small ravine and then allowed the dogs to half-pull him up the opposite incline. As the hill levelled off, he saw what he was looking for and covered the earpiece of his headset against the howling of the dogs.

"Arden, I found it—G-7."

The motion sensor lay crushed on the ground, next to it a dead branch, not heavy enough to have merely fallen and damaged the equipment. The dogs sniffed at the branch and erupted in a new frenzy of barking and jerking ahead. Mike, busy scanning the area for an intruder with the light mounted on his Ingram Mac-10 and at the same time struggling to hold back the dogs, missed the staccato transmission over his headset. "Repeat?"

"*Report. Over,*" snapped Arden, his voice taking on an electronic edge.

"G-7," Mike repeated, "disabled. Intruder definite. Dogs on the scent. Over."

"*Pursue. Report new development for 02:45. Over.*"

Mike held his watch to the light. 02:40. Five minutes. "Copy. Over." He let the dogs choose their path and wove along behind them through the trees toward the perimeter of the estate.

The canine howls grew more distant but never far away. Otherwise, the moonlight wound its way peacefully through the bare winter branches casting shadows on the fallen leaves. Then one patch of leaves next to the battered sensor began to quiver, then to churn, as did the earth beneath. Within seconds dirt and debris fell away as a figure rose from the very ground of which a moment before it had been a part.

Nicholas crouched warily. The dogs still barked in the distance—he had left a false trail to keep them busy—but Nicholas was more concerned with the electronic monitors. He held the gadget he had crushed in his hand. "Hmph." Now that he knew what he was looking for, Nicholas had little trouble sniffing out the contraptions and avoiding their areas of effect.

He quickly made his way through the remainder of the wooded area to the cleared space surrounding the main house itself. This last ten yards were undoubtedly criss-crossed with detection devices, probably beneath the thick manicured lawn. He could leap the span of grass and sink claws into the side of the house, but why bother?

Nicholas stepped out of concealment and headed up the main walk. As he approached, the front door opened. A well-dressed red-haired gentleman stepped forward to greet him. "Good evening, sir. Mr. Evans has been expecting you." Everything about the servant was formal—speech, black vest, starched white shirt, polished shoes—the complete opposite of Nicholas' tattered jeans and jacket, flannel shirt, his hiking boots and long hair. "Please follow me."

The servant led Nicholas through tiled foyer and immaculate entrance hall. The polished mahogany and crystal chandelier, the fine velvet tapestries and sparkling brass fixtures all bespoke quiet luxury, but even among the spacious elegance, Nicholas felt as if the house were closing in on him. He longed for the nearby woods, or better yet the North Georgia mountains, even the endless plains of the Midwest, somewhere he could run with the moonlight on his back. *Soon enough*, he thought.

Nicholas followed the servant through lavish dining and sitting rooms to a large wooden door. The servant knocked lightly.

"Yes, Randal," came the voice from inside.

The servant opened the door and deferentially ushered Nicholas into the study. A rather young man faced him from behind the large ornate desk. *Young looking, anyway*, Nicholas thought as the door closed behind him.

"Hello, my friend," said Owain Evans. "What brings you to my home? I have too few visitors these days...unannounced, at any rate."

Evans didn't appear to be troubled that his estate security had just been breached, that an intruder had walked up to his front door in the middle of the night. He seemed attentive yet relaxed. Nicholas was impressed. Before he could respond, Evans casually cut him short. "Oh. Excuse me just a moment, please." Evans pressed a intercom button set into his desk. "Randal."

"*Yes, sir,*" crackled the servant's response.

"Do tell Arden that our guest has arrived. He can rest the dogs."

"*Yes, sir.*"

Evans returned his attention to Nicholas. "I'm sorry. You were saying…?"

Nicholas smiled—the games these city dwellers played, holed up in their fancy houses, so insulated from the instincts that connected them to the night. He reached inside his jacket and removed a thin ivory cylinder, which he placed on the desk. Evans, Nicholas noticed, seemed interested but not especially concerned as his guest reached into his jacket. Here was a man who, whether through confidence or foolishness, had little reason to fear a stranger. Nicholas suspected the former.

Evans regarded the bone case but made no move toward it. Instead, he rose and occupied himself with a decanter nestled within a silver ice bucket nearby, half filling a delicate crystal wine glass with dark liquid. "May I offer you refreshment, my friend?" Evans held the glass forward. "An excellent vintage, if I do say so myself—only the finest Atlanta high society vitæ."

"Many thanks, but no." Nicholas had fulfilled his

obligation, delivered the parcel. He didn't feel like observing all the niceties, kowtowing to some "high society" city Kindred.

Evans sat easily upon the edge of his desk, savored a sip from the glass he had poured. "You are from eastern Europe…not the Balkans, to the north…" He took another small sip, concentrated. "Minsk?"

A smile crept across Nicholas' features. He had underestimated this elder of the city. "Kiev."

"Kiev." Evans nodded. "Of course. Accents are tricky things, and yours is quite faint. You've not been home for quite some time, I'd wager."

Nicholas snorted good-naturedly. Four words, and the young-looking vampire had guessed his home within a few hundred miles. Nicholas' predatory instincts were again as alert as they had been in the forest. He wouldn't let his guard down again, not around this wily Kindred with his disarming manner and sharp mind. Nicholas didn't know much about Owain Evans other than that he was a prominent but unobtrusive member of Atlanta's Kindred community. Obviously he was well-off financially, and he would bear close watching while Nicholas was in town.

But Nicholas preferred to do his watching from a distance. He fidgeted in his chair. The air in the room felt heavy, as thick perhaps as the blood in Evans' glass, and the plush drapes and large furniture seemed to be creeping slowly toward Nicholas, taking up all available space. He wanted to be out of the house, *immediately*, but he forced himself to keep his attention on his host—the hand raising the wine glass; the long dark hair pulled back, not a strand out of place; the strong straight nose; the inquisitive but black black eyes.

Evans chatted on politely about something. Nicholas inwardly cursed his own weakness. He had completed his task. How much longer would this maddening formality go on? Nicholas did not feel he could risk offending this elder by dashing out of his home.

"Well, my talkative friend," Evans continued, "let me ask you one final question."

Final question. That phrase muscled through Nicholas' distress and grabbed his attention.

"I'm curious." Evans sat behind his desk once again and gestured toward the bone case. "You did not bring this message all the way from Berlin purely out of good will. What was your payment?"

The question was like cold water thrown in Nicholas' face. Even though Evans must have known the message was coming and where it came from, how did the cursed Ventrue know to ask about the one thing Nicholas couldn't divulge?

"A favor from a friend's friend," he mumbled. He could feel those black eyes watching him, and wasn't sure if he could meet the probing gaze without losing control, without falling into frenzy. Suddenly the urge to shred the expensive drapes, to rake his claws across the perfectly stained hardwood floor was quite strong. The thought of such savagery in this all too proper room was so appealing that Nicholas couldn't help laughing at the dichotomy.

This seemed to catch Evans off guard. For the first time this evening, the Ventrue looked perplexed, and his obvious puzzlement made Nicholas laugh even harder. The violent nature of his thoughts intensified proportionately, which struck him as increasingly hilarious. Soon Evans joined in the laughing, almost nervously at first, then more forcefully, still not comprehending but not caring, for laughter, like hatred, is contagious.

"What, exactly," Evans forced out between mirthful convulsions, "are you laughing at?"

"I was thinking…a-hem…of ripping your throat out," Nicholas explained gleefully.

Rather quickly, Evans stopped laughing. Shortly Nicholas, too, had regained his composure, and both men looked about slightly embarrassed, not exactly sure what had just transpired.

Nicholas decided prudence called for taking his leave before the room again began to close in on him. "With all due respect, Mr. Evans, I must go."

Gherbod Fleming

Owain had Randal show the visitor out. "To the front gate, perhaps," Owain had suggested. "No need to upset the dogs further."

What an odd courier, Owain thought as he sat staring at nothing in particular and drained the last vitæ from his glass. Just as he finished, his distracted gaze fell upon the ivory cylinder on his desk, the message nearly forgotten amidst the strangeness of the visit. He picked up the tube and inspected the intact seal of his long-time opponent. A pity almost to open it. Often times the anticipation was more titillating than the actual revelation, especially when, like this time, Owain felt sure he knew what the message contained.

He crossed to the small alcove in the study where he kept his Battle of Hastings chess set. It was carved by a wood worker who had seen with his own eyes both Harold Godwin and William the Bastard on the field that black day in 1066. Owain, as always, played the dark Anglo-Saxon defenders so that he might rework history and spare his homeland the indignity and the horror of Norman overlordship.

And *this time*, the Bastard was getting what he deserved!

This particular game had been going on for about three centuries now, moves sent by courier every decade or two. The previous game had bogged down a bit, as Owain had spent most of the Renaissance in torpor, but not so this time. Owain congratulated himself as he surveyed the board. The end-game was nearly played out, his black forces relentlessly pressing the attack. The white king was backed near a corner along with a woefully misplayed bishop. A lone rook, a sorely pressed knight, and a smattering of ineffectual pawns cluttered the center of the board.

Owain's pieces were in a far superior situation, even lacking both of his knights. Otherwise, one bishop and one rook were the only casualties of any significance. Owain's queen whisked around the board mercilessly crushing every semblance of resistance from the damnable Normans. *Perhaps Harold should have taken his wife into battle*, Owain mused.

Surely the end was near. This correspondence might just as well contain a final concession as a move. *Unlikely*. Owain's opponent, he knew, would probably struggle on to the end. *Futile. And not particularly graceful*. Owain grinned as he conjured the image of driving the Normans, mauled and bloodied, back into the English Channel.

It would be a shame, really, to end the game. It was one of the few diversions that held much interest for Owain any more. He was fairly ensconced within Kindred society, and his financial empire more or less ran itself. Occasionally a bit of blackmail, corporate espionage, or murder was required, but nothing overly taxing. Generally, one night was like the next was like the next.

That very fear, of anticipation giving way to boredom, stayed Owain's hand, kept him from opening the cylinder. Even the messenger, that odd Gangrel, had proved entertaining. When could Owain again expect such an intriguing break from routine? A blackness gnawed at him from within. Blacker than the pieces on the chess board, blacker than the night outside his window. *Perhaps it is the call of torpor I hear once again.*

The knock at the study door interrupted Owain's darkening spiral of thought. "Yes, Randal."

Owain's most trusted ghoul stepped into the room. "Sir, our…ah…guest, as he were, has departed, and Ms. Jackson has brought the car around."

"The car? For…?" Owain was still concentrating on the chess board.

"The art exhibit," Randal finished his master's sentence.

"Oh, yes. That," Owain said absently, again examining the ivory case in his hand. "Is that tonight? You're sure?"

"Yes, sir."

"Of course you are. I knew it was tonight. I suppose a man is due a lapse of memory every century or two."

"Indeed, sir."

"And our dear Prince Benison wouldn't take kindly to being ignored, now would he?" Owain sighed and set the tube on the table by the board. Now that he was required elsewhere, his curiosity about the message was piqued. "Oh, bloody hell." He rose in frustration and started across the room. He would need a fresh suit, but first he should shave the stubble that began every night as two day's growth and never grew longer.

Halfway to the door he stopped and turned back to the table. "Wouldn't do to be unfashionably early, now would it?" It would be a rare day when impatience didn't win out over duty. Owain settled into the seat by the chess board. "Well, Randal, let's see what pitiable defense my esteemed adversary has put forward."

A suddenly claw-like fingernail made short work of the seal, and Owain was unrolling the yellowed parchment he slid from the tube. As always, there was no preamble or greeting; the black script flowed smoothly limning the five essential words:

Rook to King's Knight five

and then a sixth:

Check

Even close to a millenium of undeath had not prepared Owain for that instant. But he recovered quickly; only for a moment did his mouth drop open before he assumed a more directed response. "There must be a mistake." The words rasped forth from his suddenly parched mouth and throat, but there was no mistake.

Owain had pinned White's pesky remaining knight and within two or three moves would most likely have maneuvered the king into checkmate. But now this! Not only did the rook place Owain's king into check, the piece's movement revealed a discovered attack from White's king's bishop which also produced check.

"But...how?" Owain weakly whispered. *There was a pawn blocking that diagonal. A white pawn, but I don't remember it moving....* He lowered his face into his hand. Owain's opponent had not, in fact, moved that pawn. Harold Godwin's omnipotent queen had whisked it away to Norman hell. *That was several turns back. Probably...1930.*

The queasiness in Owain's stomach intensified as he studied the board more closely. Not only was Owain's king in check from two attackers, he was trapped. He could escape for one turn, but then rook to king's knight eight, protected by the bishop, every black piece at least two moves away—*checkmate*.

"*Ahhhhhh!*" Owain's fangs slipped down and his claws took shape, so incensed was he.

"Sir?" Randal, who had quietly eased forward to look over his master's shoulder, jumped backwards, nearly knocking a bust of Oliver Cromwell from its marble pedestal. As Randal watched from a relatively safe distance, Owain, his hand quivering with rage, moved the white rook from its former position to king's knight five with a resounding *thump* that threatened to upend the other pieces. Randal, an accomplished gamer himself, examined the board for a brief moment. "Oh."

Owain restrained his urge to take each chess piece, one at a time, and rend its head from its body, before grinding its disjointed form into bits too minute to be recognized. With a supreme act of will, he calmly rose from his chair and left the room. "I believe I have somewhere to be," he muttered through clenched teeth. Randal quietly followed behind.

Grimsdale thought he had lost them when he cut back east and then turned south. For close to an hour he'd neither seen nor heard any indication of pursuit. If he could only make it to the airport, to the neutral ground of the Giovanni hangar, and then on to Chicago to bargain with Ballard, or maybe Capone, whoever offered the best deal.

But it was becoming sickeningly apparent to Grimsdale that, even if he had lost them at some point, it hadn't been for long. Now they were toying with him, like cats with an injured bird. The coughing street person had reappeared too many times for coincidence, and once, as Grimsdale had crouched in the shadows, an inky blackness, colder and more dense than the darkest night, had snaked toward him. He had not been able to control his terror that time and had screamed as he'd fled.

As he leaned against the back wall of the pawn shop, he smoothed down his shirt, more trying to still his trembling hands than straighten any wrinkle. Grimsdale needed to feed, and badly. This night had dragged on and on, a horrible surreal dream, never ending or allowing rest.

He was away from downtown proper now. The immense office buildings and highrises had given way to smaller shops, restaurants, and convenience stores with a liberal mix of boarded up storefronts. There were a few more people about in this part of the city, but Grimsdale couldn't concentrate on hunting while being so relentlessly hunted himself. He closed his eyes for a moment and laughed quietly, desperation taking firm hold. At one point earlier, he had tried to convince himself that he was imagining it all, that there was no one after him, and he had almost believed it until that all too familiar rattling cough had shattered his pitiful little fantasy.

Grimsdale took a deep breath—to calm himself; his body no longer required oxygen. Only blood. *I'll loop around*, he decided. *West, then north and east, then a hard dash south. If I have to, I'll find shelter and ride out the day. Make it to the airport tomorrow night.*

He couldn't let himself give in to panic. Not when there was still a chance. *All I have to do is make it to Chicago, and I'm a made man for the rest of eternity.* Grimsdale smiled despite the cold that he only felt when he had a severe need for blood.

But this was more than a chill.

He tried to leave his hiding place, only to find that his legs would not obey his wishes. Too late he saw the inky blackness, the unnaturally dark shadow that was wrapped around his legs and working its way up his body. Grimsdale cried out, terror again gripping his soul.

"Don't go makin' such a fuss, honey." An African-American woman, not ten feet away, smiled up at him from where she crouched in the shadows.

Grimsdale struggled frantically, but the blackness held fast, pinning his arms to his torso, constricting his chest. From around the edge of the building, another figure emmerged, this one wearing a long bulky overcoat and a wide-brimmed hat pulled low.

"Ain't no use in screamin' now," said the black woman as the second figure moved closer to Grimsdale. His mind raced. *Chicago. I've got to get to Chicago! This can't happen!*

A thickly accented voice hissed out from beneath the hat, "Can have no screaming," at the same time that a gnarled hand grasped Grimsdale's throat.

There was nothing Grimsdale could do as he felt his larynx not crushed, but completely reshaped, molded into a useless mass of flesh and cartilage that protruded from his neck. The pain was of an intensity that he had experienced neither in life nor in unlife. As he gasped, air whistled through the gaping holes in his throat. Indeed, there would be no screaming.

The woman giggled, and the second figure flicked off its hat, revealing a monstrously contorted visage—spikes of flesh and exposed bone protruding along a central ridge on its skull; long spear-like chin that twisted to the left; lower fangs jutting upward piercing jowly skin.

Grimsdale, now even his head immobilized by the cold shadow, closed his eyes, trying to wish himself away from this horror. But he was not to have that luxury. He felt pressure against his eyes, and then his eyelids melted away like hot wax at the monster's touch.

His lungs nearly burst as, again, he tried to scream, but a sick gurgling sound was all he could hear. Gurgling…and laughter. The cruel twittering of the woman, and from the monster, a raspy laughter that could almost be mistaken for coughing.

Muscles strained and tore, but Grimsdale was unable to force the least bit of movement within the confines of the evil black vise. He was completely helpless as the monster set to work on his face, a mad chortling potter crafting living clay. Beneath the consuming agony, Grimsdale wished for the end. He was faintly thankful when the woman fell upon him, biting deeply into his neck. The monster, too, fed at last, sinking its grotesque fangs into Grimsdale's face, ripping away freshly deformed chunks of flesh.

There was a new voice, but Grimsdale could not hear it.

♀

"Save some for your lover, Dietrich." Francesca's words rolled off her tongue, the very sound of her voice enough to drive Dietrich to distraction. He stepped away from his current masterpiece and pushed away Liza as well. The African-American woman hissed, droplets of fresh vitæ spraying from her mouth as Grimsdale collapsed to the ground.

"I don't believe he'll be going anywhere now," Francesca observed.

Dietrich laughed at her words, unable to contain himself. He began bouncing where he stood. Liza licked her lips and wiped her face with her sleeve, watching begrudgingly as Francesca lifted Grimsdale and drained the rest of his blood. Even Liza had to admit there was a certain style, an innate sensuality, about this Hispanic woman. Watching her lick the mangled body gave Liza goosebumps and set her to fantasizing.

"Your shadow it hold him good," said Dietrich.

"Of course it did," Francesca responded. Dietrich edged closer and guffawed idiotically at her acknowledgement of his complement.

Liza had had enough. "I'd love to stay so we could all kiss each others' asses, but I got places to go."

Francesca nodded in her direction. "Your aid was invaluable. It will not go unnoticed, I assure you."

"Yeah?" It was difficult for Liza to mouth off at this woman. "Okay." As Liza turned to leave, she noticed Dietrich's reptillian tongue stretching out and wrapping itself around Francesca's forearm. Walking away, Liza tried to ignore the maniacal cackling spilling out from behind the building.

TWO

The song called.

Antwuan made his excuses to his friends and left. They weren't going anywhere. Nobody Antwuan knew was going anywhere. Nobody but Antwuan. His friends had always ragged on him. Except for Little Johnnie, Antwuan was the only one who'd stayed out of trouble, "kept his nose clean," like his mama put it. Soon he would be old enough to work for his uncle Maurice driving a cab. He was going to save some money, buy his own place. The ladies would like that. He wasn't going to spend his whole life in Reynoldstown. *I seen too many folks get shot down, or go crazy on drugs*. None of Antwuan's friends really thought they'd live much past thirty, anyhow. None except Little Johnnie, and he was just too scared to get himself killed. Antwuan liked hanging out with his friends, but he didn't need them every night.

And it wasn't every night that the song called.

The first time Antwuan had gone had been for other reasons. Taquanna had hinted that he should come, so he'd figured, play his cards right, he might get down her pants. Seemed worth a shot. Since then, though, there was no question. The song called, he was there.

The old church had always been a part of the scenery for Antwuan. It was there, he just didn't mess with it. Nobody messed with it. The place had that feel to it, and people stayed away. Not even the up and coming gangstas congregated there. *Hell*, Antwuan reasoned, *plenty other boarded up buildings to trash.*

As he actually went all the way to the church itself for only the fourth time in his life, he noticed that the building was not in that bad a shape, all things considered. The little dingy white paint that was left was peeling from the bowed, gray wooden planks. The steeple, mostly collapsed, stood precariously above partially intact, soot-covered stained glass that peeked out between the boards over the windows. Could have been worse.

Again as he approached, Antwuan heard the notes that floated through the night and summoned him. He had never heard the song before that first time, but now he heard it every time, no matter where he was. This past summer he'd been down at a Braves' game, and even over the miles, the traffic, and the crowds he'd heard it and hopped on MARTA and gotten back as quickly as he could.

There was no one else around as he walked up the cracked sidewalk into the shadows surrounding the church. But there would be others, he knew. The song would reach out to those who were aware, and many would come. Antwuan was glad he lived so close and could almost always make it. He reached for the door, the lofty, lilting notes pulling him more forcefully now. It was a prelude, as his mama called it when she made him go to their church, only this music was far more alluring than any church prelude, and the service was nothing he would expect from Preacher Rutherford. Antwuan chuckled at the thought, but immediately fell silent as he entered.

She stood at the front of the sanctuary before the toppled, graffiti-carven pulpit—the pale angel. Her skin was white as ivory, made more noticeably so by the dark black hair and straight bangs that framed her thin face, now lifted toward the heavens, eyes closed, lips slightly parted to allow forth the most enticing sound heard to man.

Antwuan walked slowly past broken pews, each step on the faded and torn, moldy red carpet taking him closer to paradise. Others were already there: two older black men, a short middle-aged Korean woman who was always present, and a younger white woman who looked a bit too well-off to live nearby. Antwuan kneeled with the others at the pale bare feet of the angel, only a few feet from the hem of her layered white gown.

Her voice brought them to her, held them there, not that they would want to tear themselves away. Antwuan closed his eyes, let the music ease his mind, carrying away thoughts of trouble, of his mama pestering him to get a job now instead of waiting till he was old enough to work for his uncle, of the long empty days since he'd dropped out of school, of wondering if the gunshots he heard at night would kill a member of his family or one of his friends. The daily concerns were washed away, replaced by soothing music, the closest thing to true contentment that he'd ever experienced.

But even this contentment was not complete. At its heart was a tiny ache, the seed of desire, a rising need. The music did not erase this need, did not carry it away, but rather caressed it, cared for it.

Now the music changed, shifted indescribably. Antwuan knew that if he opened his eyes he would see the others around him, ten or fifteen of them. He felt the familiar presence of Taquanna beside him, her shoulder inches from his. The angel still sang above them; her music reminded Antwuan of a song his grandmother used to sing to him as a little boy, but he couldn't quite fully summon the tune to memory. Besides, that would only distract him from the pleasure at hand.

Slowly the song began to intensify. The easy soothing timbre grew stronger as, parallel, the faintest undertone of urgency was introduced. The ache within Antwuan intensified as well, the seed putting down roots, sprouting, budding, flowering. His desire rose with the song, every need—love, acceptance, security—combined in one irrepressible exigency to be fulfilled here without fail.

God's merciful angel. Tears were running down Antwuan's cheeks, joyful tears for a revelation he could never hope to find elsewhere. He was dancing. They all danced, whirling around, drunk amidst the euphoria, absorbing salvation. Partner to partner, man, woman, black, white, old, young. He touched in friendship those he would never even acknowledge on the street in everyday life.

Still the music rose. In strength, in pitch, in volume. The urgency tore at his chest, a longing not to be denied. A rhythm took hold of him, dragged him to see his innermost self, stripped naked, vulnerable. The angel's sweet vibrato called to him to be true to himself, his desire, his needs.

The pounding in his ears was deafening. His heart raced to keep time with the song. Always there was the song, calling, pounding, spinning.

Taquanna's breast rubbed against his shoulder. His need found direction in her nakedness, her rich brown skin. They touched, caressed, the interlaced harmonies of the song pulling them together.

They lay in the grass. Taquanna's delicious scent surrounded him. All over, she held him. Hands. Loving. Needing. Desiring. He buried himself between her breasts, drank her in, felt her taut arched body, wanting him. She grasped him. Hands all over. The sun warmed him, almost burning, but the pain only heightened their desire, strengthened their need.

He felt her beneath him. Above him. Arms and hands erupted from the moist earth all about, stroking, caressing. She cried out, or was he crying out?

The music.

Song.

Swirling ecstacy.

Crescendo.

Consuming bliss.

Antwuan, warm, near joyous tears, stumbled out of the old church near dawn. His legs nearly failed him as he stepped off the curb. At home, he collapsed into bed and slept very late into the day.

THREE

Liza took a detour through Piedmont Park. She loved the freedom of walking the city at night by herself, something she couldn't do as a mortal. Not only did she revel in her newfound powers, she always looked for a chance to show them off, to convince herself they were real more than to impress anyone else. *Liza don't need nobody else*, she told herself quite often. She hoped somebody would give her trouble, wished that some thinks-he's-tough asshole would try to mug her, or better yet, to rape her. She'd leave him with his dick stuffed down his throat.

I bet ol' Dietrich give Francesca a big hard one, Liza mused. *Probably got spikes just like on his head.*

Strangely enough, it was Francesca that intrigued Liza more. *The way she rrrolls her rrrrs*. The very thought gave Liza shivers. Maybe the two women would meet again, without Dietrich. *The freak*. Who knew when another Sabbat mission might bring them together again? The team had worked well enough: Liza, the Atlanta native, guiding; Dietrich helping herd their prey; Francesca giving the orders and immobilizing old what's-his-name at the end.

To Liza's disappointment, it was a slow night in Piedmont Park. After about forty-five minutes completely unmolested—not even a nibble—she headed toward the High Museum of Art and Prince Benison's exhibit.

The prince's ghouls, Byron and Vermeil, one white, one black, both silent as the grave, guarded the door at the top of the long ramp. This was obviously a private show at which mortals were not welcome. The Camarilla, the vampire sect that controlled Atlanta, claimed every vampire as a member. So Liza, as an Atlanta Kindred, was automatically invited, even if Benison didn't really want her there. Technically, she was an anarch, a rebel who didn't acknowledge the strictures of the Camarilla, at least not all of them. But since the Camarilla claimed her, there was plenty of gray area to use as she saw fit. Liza liked gray area. Gray area meant freedom. Although if Benison, or any of the other Atlanta Kindred for that matter, found out about her Sabbat connections, that would be the end of freedom, not to mention her life. She'd be staked, or beheaded, or left out for the sun, or all three.

Liza strode past the ghouls who held the door for her. "Hey, Vermeil," she said, "how you like bein' Benison's boy? He that good to you?" The ghouls ingnored her. They locked the door and resumed their watch. "You boys let me know you get tired of his shit. I show you a good time."

Another woman, probably a ghoul as well, showed Liza across the lobby—open to a dizzying height, ringed by a descending ramp—to the elevator. *Like I couldn't find the elevator myself.*

When the elevator stopped, the doors opened revealing a world that Liza despised—the prince's court, prim and proper Kindred acting oh-so-sophisticated, sipping vitæ, and attempting to comment insightfully on the artwork. The only reason worth coming was to remind herself how much she hated them, to laugh at them in their hollow arrogance.

Occasionally, Benison had midnight prayer breakfasts at Rhodes Hall, his mansion just a bit down Peachtree Street. Liza avoided those like the plague. No way was she going to go listen to the crazy Malkavian prince spout scripture, pretending that God still cared about the Damned. Liza the anarch had that freedom. She could skip out on any gathering she felt like. Not so for these other Kindred. *Stupid bastards*. Prince Benison frowned on subjects missing his courtly functions. That was another reason to attend this relatively painless exhibit: to rub it in the others' faces that she didn't *have* to be there.

And they were all there all right, Liza noticed: Eleanor, the prince's snobby bitch wife wearing her poofy *Gone With the Wind* dress; Benjamin and Thelonious, resident legal eagle and Mr. Civil Rights, brothers who bought into the white folks' world; Owain Evans, the youthful and good-looking but boring-ass businessman; Hannah, the local Tremere grand wizard or whatever; Marlene, artist wannabe, porn queen more likely.

There were others too, but Liza was distracted by the sight of Alex Horndiller, Benison's right-hand ghoul, leading two young men, mortals, toward the center of the gallery. She strutted over to them, her black tights drawing quite a few stares amidst the formal evening wear crowd. She slapped the ghoul on the shoulder, hard enough that he almost stumbled. "Corndicker, what you got for me?" Without another word, Liza took the forearm of the first young man, tall, blond, maybe in his early twenties, and sank her teeth in.

He flinched only slightly; the collective gasp that arose was from the onlookers. Liza tried not to laugh—she hated when blood ran out her nose—but it was so like the courtly Kindred to be shocked...like she knew they would be. The two men were the refreshments for the evening, common vessels, but of course the prince should have enjoyed the ceremonious first sip.

Liza wasn't hungry, not after feeding on that vampire sap with Francesca and the Elephant Man, but this was almost as much fun as ripping apart muggers in the park would have been. She let go of the first man and grinned at the irate Horndiller, red splotches forming on his face. "Not bad," she said as she winked and pinched the blond vessel's ass. "And I like the Dixie cup."

Before Horndiller could form his indignant sputterings into words, Liza sank her teeth into the second man, stockier and more darkly complected than his counterpart. She had drunk only a little when she felt a hand on her shoulder. *Corndicker's got more balls than I*...but before she could finish the thought, she was spun roughly around, and to her shock, it was not Horndiller who held her. Instead, it was J. Benison Hodge, prince of Atlanta.

Liza stumbled backward in surprise, but the prince's iron grip held her upright, his fingers pressing down to the bone of her shoulder. He towered above her, his massive dark red beard inches from her face, his green eyes ablaze with more anger than Liza had ever seen in them. She tried to speak but could only wince at the pain as he squeezed her shoulder more tightly.

The prince spoke in a low, throaty growl. "I offer hospitality, and you mock it." The words were meant for her, but Hodge's forceful baritone easily carried across the chamber to the onlooking Kindred, about whom Liza had very nearly forgotten.

The prince released her shoulder and quickly drew back his hand to strike her backhanded across the face...but he stopped, spotless white glove raised, arm trembling with rage. His stiffened jaw forced his beard forward. *"I will not tolerate this."*

Liza could do nothing but cringe at this awesome display of barely controlled ferocity. One swipe of his gloved fist would likely crush every bone in her face. She suddenly felt very young and weak and small confronted with this force of nature that was the prince.

Benison took a deep breath, then slowly exhaled. Just as slowly, he lowered his arm. Not for one moment did his severe gaze release Liza from scrutiny. "For one year and one night, I do not want to see you, I do not want to so much as hear report of your name." A savage, psychotic glint flashed across the prince's fiery green eyes, as if he wanted to end it now, as if he wanted nothing more than to strike her down this instant for her affront to his honor, but the brief wavering passed, and though his wrath was undiminished, restraint held the day. "If I do, you will find final death." The prince turned his back to her. "Begone."

It took Liza a second to realize that she had not been struck down, that he had not snapped her neck as surely he could have. She swallowed her wounded pride and slunk away.

Owain probably had never been to a courtly function in a fouler mood. *Three hundred years of strategy and planning abruptly catapulted to hell*, he kept telling himself. It was not a misfortune he could lightly set aside and forget. *How? How could it happen? Overconfidence? Carelessness?*

The art exhibit was hardly a sufficient distraction. *At least it's not one of those damnable prayer breakfasts*. Prince Benison, through his contacts on the board of the High Museum, had commandeered this gallery to show the artwork of one of the Atlanta Kindred, Marlene. Marlene fancied herself something of a sculptor, and though she was Toreador, Owain did not feel that the term "art" accurately described her accomplishments. Apparently ceramics or clay were too subtle media; Marlene had taken to welding together various shapes and sizes of scrap metal and then attaching somewhat grandiose titles to the resulting monstrosities. What her work lacked in vision it certainly made up in magnitude. No mantlepiece collectibles in this portfolio.

As usual at these functions, Owain attempted to stay out of the way. There was much more to be learned from watching and listening than from taking a lead in most endeavors, a fact that Owain had learned well over his centuries of vampiric existence. *And one that anarch rabble would do well to learn,* Owain thought as Liza was shown the door. Her little outburst had been entertaining. Owain had to admit that, although he had been quite guarded in not displaying his amusement at the spectacle. *She won't live long confronting a prince that way.* Owain was surprised by her brazen recklessness, her stupidity. *There are more efficient ways to undermine a princes' position, subtler ways, safer ways.* Owain could only wonder if the prince's treatment of her might have been more irreversibly detrimental had she had time to actually insult the "artwork."

At the time of Liza's little scene, Owain had been standing to a side of the room, near the Tremere chantry leader, reclusive Hannah. He was close enough that most passersby, assuming that he and Hannah were merely pausing in conversation, continued on without disturbing him, but not so close that he actually had to speak to the Tremere. Owain suspected that Hannah appreciated the arrangement as well, she not being one of the more socially ambitious Kindred in the city. For the most part, the only people who expressed more than the most passing of interests in speaking to Hannah were her Tremere lessers from the chantry. Several attempted to toady but quickly retreated having received nothing but coldly polite and formal responses.

Owain also noticed that Chantry Mistress Hannah's reaction to the anarch-prince confrontation was as muted as his own, only a slight wrinkling of her nose indicating her distaste. Owain himself was not a stickler for manners. Over the years he had come to see their value as a stabilizing factor in both mortal and Kindred affairs. He was not offended by the "affront to the prince's honor." Rather he was dismayed by the anarch's idiocy.

Owain shook his head thinking of her misguided actions. *She wanted to embarrass him, to damage his reputation. But Hodge came out looking stronger than ever, and now she's banished for a year and a night.* Owain laughed to himself. *A nice touch that—a year and a night. Hodge does have a flair for the dramatic.* The duration of the punishment was a clear echo of the length of Arthurian quests—a year and a day. Owain was particularly enamored with the legends, as many of the earliest were of Welsh origin. It was clear to Owain that the prince saw himself as some type of crusading knight, protector of moral fortitude. It fit all too perfectly with the prince's other derangements.

No, Owain was not offended by Liza's little show, unlike many of the other gathered Kindred who bought so completely into the aura of southern gentility that Hodge, his wife Eleanor, and his sire Aunt Bedelia so convincingly affected. To Owain etiquette was a means, not an end unto itself. It was sometimes the only keeper of civility between enemies, and more importantly it was a veil behind which to work deceit.

That line of thought reminded Owain that there was business to be conducted this evening. Mostly he was biding his time, making sure to stay long enough not to insult the prince, but not so long as to seem to be attempting to ingratiate himself. Almost no vampire, Owain felt, was worth the time of a social engagement, and very few mortals or ghouls. But if he had to be here, he might as well get something accomplished. He scanned the room until he saw Benjamin, a fellow Ventrue but hardly a friend. As he moved to leave his safe haven near Hannah, however, Owain nearly stumbled over Aunt Bedelia in her antique wheelchair being ushered around the gallery by her childe the prince.

"Goodness, J. Benison. Someone has stepped on me," Aunt Bedelia chittered shrilly. "Who is that?" She squinted up through her half-moon spectacles in Owain's general direction. Her heavy wool dress swallowed her frail form.

"My apologies, Mother," muttered the prince,

gracious and mild-mannered now that civility was restored to the gathering. "This is Owain Evans."

Owain smiled dutifully.

"Never heard of him."

"Of course you have, Mother," Benison patiently reminded her. "He came from Europe during the Great War. He's from Wales originally. He…"

"Never heard of him," Bedelia snapped, testily this time.

The prince lowered his head and sighed. "Of course you haven't, mother. Mother, I present to you Owain Evans, Ventrue of King Road, Atlanta. Mr. Evans, my sire Aunt Bedelia."

Bedelia held her left hand before her. Owain, standing to her right, glanced at the prince who was watching him expectantly, so he stepped around her, delicately took her hand, and kissed it. "The pleasure is all mine, Aunt Bedelia."

"Charmed, I'm sure." Bedelia smiled sweetly, quite content now that she had been paid the proper respect; so content, in fact, that she had apparently fallen instantly asleep, her eyes closed now instead of squinted. She began to snore quietly.

Benison was smiling broadly. "Always good to see you, Owain. Mother and I couldn't be happier that you made it this evening. Enjoying the artwork?" Before Owain could answer, the prince glanced off to his left. "No, I don't think we need to send anyone to follow her," he said, answering a question that no one had asked. Then, without missing a beat, he was smiling at Owain again.

Owain hesitated. This peculiar behavior was nothing new for Benison.

The prince waited a moment. "The artwork?" he asked again.

"Oh yes," Owain assured him. "I've seen nothing like it elsewhere."

Benison cuffed Owain on the shoulder and laughed heartily. "Good, good. Of course you haven't. Our little Marlene is quite the artist."

"She is something," Owain agreed. He wondered what else Marlene was to the prince that she should merit such patronage. Owain had it on good authority that the prince's wife was no paragon of fidelity. Perhaps the indiscretion was reciprocated. Though few vampires retained any type of sexual desire, there were always other…displays of affection that a spouse might guard jealously.

"Well, Mother and I must attend the other guests," said the prince. "Always good to see you, Owain. Enjoy the exhibit." At this, Bedelia perked up. Her gentle snoring ceased abruptly as she blinked herself awake. She squinted up at Owain as if she had just asked him a question and was expecting an answer.

Owain, nodding respectfully at the prince, saw that Bedelia was still watching him expectantly. "A pleasure to see you, madame," he offered.

She continued staring at him, as if oblivious to his statement. "Have we met, young man?"

Benison broke in quickly, "Well, Mother, here's your favorite bridge partner, Hannah," as he wheeled her away.

"J. Benison, why didn't you introduce us?" Bedelia was asking, but the prince continued on their way, greeting Hannah with great enthusiasm and seeming not to hear the protestations of his sire.

Owain gratefully slipped away. He always had gotten on fairly well with the prince. Both were warriors and, even though their wars were of different eras, there was a certain camaraderie in that. Aunt Bedelia was a different matter. Owain was sure her "forgetfulness" was merely an intended slight, a game meant to lessen him somehow. He shrugged off the encounter. *Let the old hag pretend she doesn't know me. I'd rather continue advising the prince than have her approval. Now where has Benjamin gotten to? Must have slipped into a side gallery.*

Owain cut across the center of the main gallery. He nodded politely to the younger Kindred whose actions he took pains to keep abreast of through his network of spies, but to whom he did not deign to speak socially. He also skirted the main work of the exhibit, a behemoth of a piece consisting of three major chunks of curved and twisted metal with numerous smaller additions, suspended in its entirety from the ceiling by chains. It was a work Marlene had crafted several years ago titled "Benison's Ride," in honor of the prince's purging of the Atlanta area of those anarchs and caitiffs who had not paid him the respect of announcing their presence to the court. Benison was quite fond of the piece and arranged for public viewings periodically for the edification of the Kindred in his domain.

A vociferous Brujah had surmised that the sculpture was actually a representation of a whale spewing forth a Volkswagon. The prince felt otherwise. That particular Brujah no longer resided in Atlanta. Other colorful yet more discreet speculations had included but not been limited to: a severely disfigured head wearing a propeller hat, three falcons fornicating, and a ballet dancer engaged in projectile vomiting. At the original unveiling, Owain had limited his response to polite applause.

The thought of Benison's intolerance of visitors failing to present themselves to the court reminded Owain of his guest earlier that evening. Owain seemed vaguely to recall that the Gangrel had been in the city before, and if so he would certainly be aware of the prince's proclivities.

Thinking of the messenger unfortunately dredged up the painfully fresh sting of the message. Owain dug his involuntarily formed claws into the flesh of his palms. If he finished with business, he could return home and examine the board in more depth. *Perhaps all is not lost*, he told himself, not really believing it.

The gallery was quite crowded now as even the latest arrivals made their appearances. Owain edged into one of the side galleries and found the man with whom he needed to speak. Benjamin, an African-American dandy with his impeccable Brooks Brothers suit, tidy short-cropped hair, and wire-rimmed glasses, was relatively young in his undeath but there was power in his blood. Next to the prince's wife Eleanor, he was ostensibly the most influential Ventrue in Atlanta. Owain tended to keep his distance from clan politics; he'd been there too many times before. The fewer everyday entanglements the better, he felt. Both Benjamin and Eleanor, however, held this detachment against Owain and regarded him with suspicion. If they only knew how much older and more powerful he was than they, they would fear him as well.

"Benjamin, we must speak," Owain said as he approached. A young female, whose name escaped Owain at the moment, edged away from Benjamin with only a glare at Owain, a grudging display of deference to the elder.

Benjamin frowned, the expression causing his glasses to slide down his nose. "Yes, Owain, how may I be of service?" he asked in a cool formal tone. Benjamin's slight but noticable English accent always amused Owain. True, the young lawyer had studied for several years at Oxford, but after more than fifteen years back in the States such an acquired accent would normally have faded. Unless, of course, the bearer consciously chose to maintain it as an affectation, a vanity. Owain, after living in Wales, London, France, Spain, and now Atlanta, had studied language and made a concerted effort to acquire an almost accentless English that raised no eyebrows. Speech patterns could give all too much away about a person. Even his current name, "Owain Evans," was a concession to the need to remain unobtrusive and seemed choppy and harsh in comparison to his original "Owain ap Ieuan."

"Owain?" Benjamin's voice snapped Owain out of his woolgathering, a bad habit and one he'd been succumbing to increasingly of late. "How may I help you?"

Owain edged closer to his fellow Ventrue and spoke in a low voice that would not be overheard by the other Kindred milling about. "I need a favor, a simple thing really." Benjamin regarded Owain skeptically but said nothing. "There is a certain case," Owain continued, "that will be heard this week by Justice Chamberlain of the Superior Court. You know Justice Chamberlain?"

Benjamin shrugged noncommittally as he pushed

his glasses back up. "He's an acquaintance."

"Ah. How fortunate. You see, this particular case involves a zoning dispute. Mercator Manufacturing has bought property near downtown with the intention of constructing a regional distribution center. Unfortunately, certain rather reactionary individuals, most notably the Citizens Empowerment Union, have taken it into their heads that such a project would not be a desirable addition to the area. Never mind the jobs it would bring. Never mind the investment in surrounding neighborhoods…."

"Never mind," Benjamin interrupted, unable to hold his tongue any longer, "that the jobs would be non-union minimum wage, or that the people would be working for an international corporation with a history of closing shop when standards of living rise to a point where workers demand raises, then relocating to centers of cheap foreign labor."

"Regardless…" Owain waved away Benjamin's protestations. "I'm not here to debate business philosophy. When the virtuous Fulton County Commission approved the rezoning proposal to allow Mercator to build, CEU filed suit to invalidate the changes. Now, remember your *acquaintance* Justice Chamberlain? This week when Chamberlain hears the case, he needs to approve the rezoning. Isn't that simple?"

Benjamin looked at Owain incredulously. "You

must be joking." He laughed. "Mercator is a slash and burn company. They don't care anything about those neighborhoods except for profit margin." Benjamin set down his drink as he gained momentum, animated gestures punctuating his points. "What the people of southwest Atlanta need is financing to begin their own businesses. They need ownership, not indentured servitude. We've come too far to crawl back into slavery, economic or otherwise."

The two men faced each other in silence for a moment. Around them, the crowd was beginning to thin a bit, but still Kindred hobnobbed, paid respects to Prince Benison, and refreshed themselves sipping from the two vessels that Alex Horndiller escorted as they became less stable on their feet from loss of blood.

Owain smiled contemptuously. He wearied of these games. "I'm not asking for your opinion on the subject, Benjamin."

Benjamin was taken aback by this, half offended, half bemused. "Then why in hell would I help you?"

Owain leaned even closer until he was virtually whispering in his rival's ear. "Because I know what there is between you and Eleanor, and we both know how the prince would be liable to respond if he were to find out somehow. He loves Eleanor too deeply to harm her, but you...? I don't think he would exercise such restraint in dealing with you."

A polite smile masked the venom of Owain's words to any who might be watching.

Owain stepped back. Benjamin could not hide his dismay, his shock, his fear. His every muscle was taut; his glasses slid down his nose again.

"Now that I think of it," Owain went on, "not only will Chamberlain uphold the rezoning, but the Georgia Supreme Court will refuse to hear the appeal." He winked at the still speechless Benjamin. "I'll be in touch."

Owain turned and left the side gallery laughing to himself at the expression on young Benjamin's face. *That should teach him some respect for his elders.* Just as Owain entered the main gallery, a cacophony of gasps, exclamations, and laughter errupted. Owain saw why instantly.

Atop "Benison's Ride" perched Albert, the wiry, bearded Malkavian known to all Kindred in Atlanta. Completely naked. "On, Dasher! On, Dancer!" He rocked back and forth, in his own way reenacting the prince's heroic ride as the massive metal sculpture wobbled precariously beneath him.

Marlene, the self-proclaimed artist, had fainted dead away. The prince, doting over Aunt Bedelia at the other end of the gallery, his back turned, was quite oblivious to the evening's second spectacle behind him.

That was as much as Owain cared to see. He nonchalantly eased around the room—the opposite end from the prince—toward the elevator. Several Kindred were ordering Albert to dismount, but they were unwilling to risk breaking the sculpture by pulling him from his seat.

As the elevator doors closed behind Owain, he could hear Albert singing, "Rollin' rollin' rollin, keep them dogs a-rollin'!" at the top of his lungs, the sculpted representation of the prince towering upward between his hairy legs like a giant scrap metal phallus.

And then dead silence. Owain could picture the prince turning around.

"*Albert!*"

FOUR

Nicholas leaned against the tree. He squeezed his eyes shut tightly, trying to clear his vision. Something was wrong.

Earlier, he had lost track of time. He had been so relieved to get out of Evans' mansion that he had given into his instincts to roam and explore. Atlanta was a very green city. Even with such a stifling concentration of kine, much vegetation had been spared, and not just obscenely manicured lawns that stank of fertilizer to Nicholas. There were numerous pockets of growth—copses of wild bushes, brambles, and the ever-present kudzu. Freed from enclosed spaces, Nicholas had run and sniffed and gloried in his freedom. Before long, he had begun to feel better, to relax. But even in this city, with its merciful abundance of trees, he didn't understand how Kindred could stand it, how they could remain cooped up with the kine and the cars and the airplanes and the buildings and the concrete and the asphalt and the wires...

Eventually, Nicholas had remembered that he needed to present himself to Prince Benison. It was not the Gangrel's first time in Atlanta, and he knew the prince to be touchy regarding such formalities. Nicholas had made his way through the earliest hours of the morning to Rhodes Hall, the prince's main residence, only to be directed by a servant to the museum.

At least if Nicholas had to be indoors again, the museum was open and airy. He had opted to walk up the spiral ramp rather than trap himself within the tiny box-like elevator, only to arrive at the worst possible time. Some Malkavian, who had taken leave of his clothes as well as his senses and run amok throughout the exhibit, was being dragged away as Nicholas arrived. Prince Benison had not been in a pleasant mood and had barely acknowledged Nicholas before stomping off, driving his protesting sire's wheelchair roughly before him.

At least Nicholas had not had to stay long. A brief draught of refreshment, observing the proper forms, and he had been on his way. But just when

Nicholas had fulfilled his responsibilities and was free to explore more adequately, his present problem had begun.

Sudden violent attacks of vertigo had left him disoriented and wandering blindly throughout the city. Twice, he had barely escaped being run down by kine in their automobiles in such a bloody hurry to get somewhere.

The dizziness was not only continuing, but growing more severe. For the first time in his unlife, Nicholas felt nauseated, though if he were sick, it would be blood that splattered all over the ground. He had stumbled to one of the several parks in the city, but could go no farther. The tree that supported him—red oak, he could tell through his fingertips, though his eyes were still closed—was small comfort. He felt as if his blood were boiling within him; blood, the only fluid available for sweat, ran down his side.

The tree trunk was gone. He was staring at the sky and the stars through the upper branches. He didn't remember opening his eyes, or falling to the ground.

More vertigo.

Dislocation.

And Nicholas was no longer in his own body. Nicholas was not Nicholas. He was Jebediah Roney, childe of Pierre Beauvais. *Sire* of Nicholas.

The stars did indeed shine brightly. Pockets of

snow were visible among the gray boulders of the night-time mountains. He was well above the tree-line of firs and aspen.

The brief spell of dizziness receded. Almost immediately, Jebediah forgot it. More pressing concerns demanded his attention. He was in wolf form. The mountain lion he had tracked from the pass was in sight. A mountain lion was not normal prey for a wolf, but Jebediah loved a challenge.

Downwind, he crept forward. Slowly. Silently. He was about to revert to his more human form, better suited for springing upon his prey—wolves, after all, were more efficient as pack hunters—when the mountain lion cocked its head. It had heard or smelled something, something other than Jebediah. Mountain lions didn't easily spook, but this one was gone in a flash, winding around boulders and through crevices. It might as well have never stood on that hillside.

Jebediah did not pursue. He was more intrigued by whatever had scared the animal. But when he heard the first howl, his curiosity turned cold in his breast.

Lupines.

Answering howls followed: four, five, maybe more. Sometimes the Garou shapechangers were willing to talk rather than kill, but Jebediah wasn't about to bet his life on the possibility. He quickly followed a route similar to that of the mountain lion.

He soon realized that the lupines were not interested in the lion. The howls were closer. There were at least five. He was sure of that. There were stories of Gangrel in wolf form mixing with lupines unnoticed, but, again, Jebediah was unwilling to risk discovery. The battle calls of lupines were too insistent, too impassioned. This was no ordinary hunt.

They were practically on him now. Growls and snarls mixed with the howls. Jebediah ducked into a cave. He would have preferred something smaller but didn't have time to pick and choose.

As he melded with the earth, becoming one with the cave floor, large shapes at the entrance blotted out the moonlight. Howling echoed around him.

Nicholas burned. He wasn't sure where he was, but the pain was a certainty. He was half-melded into the earth, a large oak standing above him, *and the sun poking above the horizon*. A thin film of blood covered Nicholas. It oozed from his every pore and sizzled in the morning light.

Quickly he sunk completely down into the soil, and as the saving comfort of the earth took him in, he imagined howls of rage above him.

The grimy smokestacks of the Pankow district always brought out the metaphoric bent in Gisela. The thick billowing smoke and acrid fumes continuously belching forth and the greasy film of soot left unprejudicially covering all within miles made her smile. *She* was such an all-pervasive force, a factor that held sway over all within her reach. Or at least she would be, and soon. Himmler had as much as promised her.

Hunting had been good. She had come across a fat strudel of a man who had smiled at her bulging chest and blonde hair. With a brutal kiss, she had ripped the smile from his face and spit his lips to the ground. *The bloated ox.*

Even after draining him and stuffing his carcass down the sewer, Gisela had still hungered. She was a healthy girl, not one of those delicate western flowers whom she could break like...she reached over and effortlessly snapped the antenna from a nearby parked car.

Gisela's companion for the latter part of the evening, Frank Litzpar, needed no encouragement to join her seemingly random act of vandalism. *"Ja!"* He set to stomping the front fender with his jackboots, and when that was mauled to his satisfaction, he began tearing at a hubcap.

Gisela sighed. He was in fine form, her little *übermensch*, as opposed to the rather grotesque visage he held when he didn't feel like hiding it. Frank had found Gisela tonight shortly after she had rid the world of the strudel man, and they had relaxed by hunting down a puny anarch who had foolishly been cool to Frank's overtures to join the Sabbat several nights ago. She and Frank had drunk together of the anarch after she had twisted his head most of the way around.

Frank, ripping off his third hubcap, used it to smash the windshield.

"Tsk, tsk, tsk," Gisela clicked. "I hope he is insured."

Frank turned toward the nearby housing complex. Some tenants peeked from behind shades; most were more careful, knew better than to get involved. "Let the Turk-loving bastard call the police!" he roared. "Let him tell me he is angry! I would like to see some pig Pakistani stand up to a real German!"

Gisela contentedly drew in a breath and smelled deeply the factory fumes. *Let the Westerners try to tidy up Pankow,* she thought. *It will take them generations, and by then I will be tired of it anyway.* Or maybe she would stop the high and mighty Westerners. Herr Himmler had said she held boundless potential. A girl of her talents could go far in the Sabbat.

But that was for another day, although certainly not too distant in the future. Other matters loomed now. "Frank, dearest, you must come meet my houseguest."

"What houseguest is that?" Frank stepped away from the car; there was not enough left to hold his interest. "You do not tell me you have another favorite, just to drive me crazy?"

Gisela smiled at his flattery. "Of course I have no other favorite. And if I did, no, I would not tell you."

They returned through the wonderfully smoky Berlin night to Gisela's basement haven beneath a fire-gutted apartment building. Her houseguest huddled on the floor in the corner, swaddled in darkness. There was no electricity in the remains of the building. *What a strange one*, Gisela thought. True, he couldn't exactly wander the streets like she and Frank did, unless he were disguised, but he hadn't left that room once since he'd arrived two nights before. Gisela had been kind enough last night to bring him a small child she'd snatched away from a careless mother.

"And how are we tonight, Dietrich?" Gisela asked as she lit the oil lamp on the table. As always, striking the wooden match and then touching it to the oiled wick sent chills of exhilaration down Gisela's spine. Such casual wielding of fire, the deadliest of elements to her kind, never failed to reinforce her sense of invulnerability.

Gisela's words startled Dietrich, yanked him back from whatever twisted Tzimisce thoughts held his interest. As the flame in the lamp danced to life, Gisela couldn't help noticing the changes her guest had wrought upon himself since last she'd seen him, mere hours before. His head leaned at an odd angle, a large bone spur sticking out from the right side of his neck. His fingers were elongated and fused together. As a clan, the Tzimisce prided themselves on their ability to maintain complete control— over their surroundings, over others, even over their own bodies. To Gisela, however, this seemed madness. Crushing those weaker than one's self was demonstration of control, hearing their bones snap and their piteous cries die away, not twisting one's own body like some sick fairy tale.

Still Dietrich didn't quite seem to know where he was; it took a moment for his eyes to focus on Gisela and Frank. He held his knees to his chest and slowly rocked back and forth in the corner.

Grisela pretended to ignore this behavior, which was peculiar even for Dietrich. "Dietrich, this is Frank. He is my friend, our friend…our comrade." Obviously she would not bring anyone who was not Sabbat to see Dietrich—he was not someone who could pass for being other than what he was: Tzimisce, and, in most cases, by extension Sabbat.

Whatever Dietrich's problem, he was coming around now. "Gisela. Frank." He nodded, finally acknowledging their presence. The motion caused a bloody rivulet of sweat to run down his forehead. He wiped the blood away.

"Dietrich," Gisela asked, "can you provide a chalice?"

Dietrich did not answer. He was staring at Gisela but clearly did not see or hear her.

"*Dietrich.*" Gisela was growing irritated with his distracted manner. She fought the impulse to slap him across to face, to shake him violently by the shoulders. "I said, can you provide a chalice?"

Frank was watching this all rather warily. He didn't know what to make of this monstrosity before him, though physical deformity was nothing new to Frank. *Good thing*, Gisela thought, *that Dietrich is German, and not East European Tzimisce.* Otherwise, Frank with his Final Reich thinking would probably go crazy, and then Gisela would be forced to discipline him. Petty ethnic prejudices could not be allowed to stand in the way of the unity of the Sabbat, as Herr Himmler had pointed out. Though Gisela found it unlikely that Himmler would share blood with a Jew. All part of the allowances that must be made for individuals of great destiny, like herself.

After a brief moment of incomprehension, Dietrich raised his fused fingers and began to mold one hand with the other. As Gisela and Frank watched, Dietrich sculpted flesh and reshaped bone. The center of his palm became a small basin, while his fingers, thumb, and what had been the heel of his palm were styled into the sides of the cup. Practicing his art seemed to revive Dietrich somewhat from his inexplicable stupor.

Grinning maniacally, he twisted his hand entirely around three times, forming a decorative spiral pattern along his wrist and forearm, now become the stem of the chalice. A few stylistic flourishes, and he was done.

The artistic display did little to put Frank at ease, but a stern glance from Gisela was enough to keep him quiet. As she placed her hands on the chalice, Dietrich shivered with delight.

"From our earliest days," Gisela intoned, *"the blood has assured our freedom; the blood has kept us strong. Thus we pledge our blood to one another."* Savagely, she slashed her own forearm so that blood welled up, and she squeezed a small stream of it into the chalice. *"To freedom."*

Frank, perhaps a bit less enthusiastically, gashed his hand and added to the cup. *"To loyalty."*

Dietrich raised his free hand. The index finger was now a long, thin spike. He jabbed it into the inner edge of the chalice, causing his blood to gush forth and join the mixture. *"To death everlasting."*

The ceremonial invitation spoken, they each drank, and the Vaulderie was complete.

Liza, hungry and doing her best not to think about her unfortunate run-in with the prince two nights before, was not in the best of moods. She'd finished off a junkie behind the Majestic Diner just a few hours ago, and now she was strung-out and, unbelievably, hungry again. *Must be them drugs*, she decided. Chances were she needed something to take her mind off the second-hand chemicals running through her system more than she needed another meal. But why not take care of both problems together? It hadn't taken long to convince a few of her friends to join in the fun.

It was almost too easy. Liza was a couple of blocks off Ponce de Leon Avenue, not far from the Clermont Lounge. The cars drove by slowly—young studs hanging out the windows and hooting, middle-aged businessmen trying to look inconspicuous, life-long losers tired of their sticky magazines. Didn't matter. They were all interested in the same thing. Liza took a deep breath and pulled the already low neckline of her half-shirt even lower. *Damned if I wouldn't have starved if I wasn't a sister with big boobs.* Sure enough, within twenty minutes a Lincoln was pulling up slow beside her.

"Hey there, honey," Liza called. "Sure looks warm in there."

The guy, a little heavy-set, maybe thirty-five, was leaning over to look out the passenger side window. He nervously licked his lips and straightened his hair, which was combed across the top of his head to try to cover the large bald area. "You sure look *hot* out there."

Liza sneered. No need to hide her contempt with this type. They liked the abuse. "I be hotter with you. Make you real warm. Or you like little boys?"

He grinned. "No. I like girls...women."

Liza ran her tongue along her teeth seductively. "I'm hungry for you, baby." It was true. She was ravenously hungry. "You gonna keep me waitin'?"

His smile faltered a bit now that the moment of decision was at hand, but then he pulled the handle and pushed the door open. "Come on."

Liza slid into the seat. Aside from the man's b.o., she could smell his blood, could almost taste it as it pumped through his body. "Hey there, big boy." She reached over and grabbed his crotch, gave him a little squeeze. "Feels like you ready."

"There's a hotel around the corner." His mouth was dry. He consciously had to swallow.

Liza took his chin firmly in her hand and made him look at her face. Their gazes locked. "Listen up, Mr. White-Man-Wants-Some-Nigga-Ass." It only took a second for Liza to grasp his mind more firmly than she had his crotch. He stared back at her, not in control of himself enough to be puzzled or scared. "We ain't goin' to no hotel. You drive your big-ass car a block and a half that way and turn when I tell you."

They pulled into the alley, and almost before the car stopped moving, two more people were in the back seat and a third standing by the driver's door.

"That didn't take too long," said Aaron from the back. He was a thrift-store hippie, unassuming and devious. Liza had been sizing him up for possible Sabbat membership. In the back with Aaron was Emigesh. Middle eastern, he didn't speak much English yet. He just smiled.

From outside the car, Jolanda stuck her head in and examined the driver from an inch or two away. He didn't pull away or blink or anything. "Leave it to you to get us a ugly-ass white man," Jolanda complained. She was dressed similarly to Liza, except showing more skin, and that was tricky.

Liza didn't feel like putting up with Jolanda's bitching. They'd been friends, more or less, back since mortal days, but every so often Liza wanted to smack the girl. Jolanda would never make Sabbat. She'd get killed the first time she opened her fat mouth. Without waiting for anyone else, Liza grabbed her john's hand from the steering wheel and chomped down into his wrist.

"Hey!" Aaron didn't want to get left out. He leaned up and bit into the driver's neck. Emigesh, still smiling, did likewise on the other side.

"Well, God daaaamn," Jolanda griped. There wasn't much she could do but grab the mortal's other arm, rip his shirt, and try to get a bead on his brachial artery through all that flab. "Shit if this boy don't need a bath."

With all four of them feeding, it didn't take long

to drain the unfortunate john dry. Liza was the last to give up trying to get those last few drops. It was her second feeding of the night, but she felt like she hadn't had a thing.

"Somebody run over to the Majestic and get this sista a straw, " said Jolanda. "She's still slurpin' away."

Liza shot Jolanda a look, and Jolanda knew better than to keep sassing. Liza licked around her mouth, not wanting to miss anything. "It ain't too late," she said. "I bet we could find another."

Aaron shrugged. He was always ready and willing. Emigesh just smiled. "We got time," said Jolanda with her hands on her hips, "but this time *I* do the lookin'. I ain't biting no more ugly, smelly-ass white men."

That was fine with Liza, and the fun continued.

FIVE

Rook to King's Knight five.

Owain stared at the board, as he had stared at it for the past hour, as he had stared at it last night without moving from dusk until dawn. He reconstructed the moves of the last century in his mind, thought through alternate strategies that undoubtedly would have left his opponent helpless and hopeless. But always he was assaulted by the unwavering reality of the board and the pieces that lay before him.

I am doubly cursed, he lamented. *Mocked by the failures of the past as well as the futility of the future.* There was no salvaging the situation, no dramatic move to reclaim the advantage. Two turns were all he had left.

Rook to King's Knight five.

Owain sat and seethed, and, as he seethed, the blackness in his soul, the hollow bitterness that had dogged him all his years called out to him. *Wormwood and gall!* Every so often, his studies of the Bible came back to him, always at the most painful of times, always in the voice of a mocking archangel, always salt upon an open wound.

The thought of my affliction and my homelessness is wormwood and gall! My soul continually thinks of it and is bowed down within me. The words seemed to have been written for Owain. His *affliction* was the determining factor of his existence, but the emptiness, the anger and the hatred, had always been there, even before he joined the legions of the unliving. And as for *homelessness*...how many homes had he abandoned for one reason or another, fleeing either untenable circumstances or outright destruction?

But not even in Jeremiah's lament could Owain take comfort, not unless he could force himself to forget the next lines. *But this I call to mind, and therefore I have hope: The steadfast love of the Lord never ceases, his mercies never come to an end; they are new every morning; great is your faithfulness.*

Owain dug his nails into his palms until tiny beads of blood appeared. How could the scriptures mock him more directly? In life, *the Lord* had abandoned Owain. And then...*then*, He had denied

Owain the escape of death, had allowed him to be Embraced into this world of the undead so that he might stumble through the centuries, his thirst for vengeance never fully sated.

The love of the Lord...Owain laughed aloud. *His love of a cruel joke, perhaps.* The irony. The cruel, mocking irony. *Hope. Mercy.* Ultimately, they were words without meaning for Owain. And the only thing *every morning* brought was the necessity to slink away and hide from the sun.

Hope and mercy. Owain turned from the chess board long enough to spit the bitter taste from his mouth. He had no use for God. *Wormwood and gall. Fire and brimstone. Hell and damnation.*

"Sir?"

Owain did not turn to face Randal. "Yes?"

Randal was on edge. Owain could hear it in his voice. The ghoul-servant was familiar with Owain's black moods. "Sir, Señora Rodriguez has finished preparing the sitting room for the gentlemen's visit. They should be arriving within the quarter hour. Your menu choice for the evening?"

Owain smiled despite himself. Randal's utter professionalism in the face of a temperamental employer who, at a moment's whim, could end the butler's existence amused Owain. Randal was canny, and efficient, but not the friend that Gwilym had been.

In fact, Owain had forgotten about his engagement this evening, the gathering of the King Road Club, as they referred to themselves. "Prepare the trophy room. We'll meet there, I think." Randal did not flinch at the sudden change of venue. Owain didn't particularly care for the trophy room, but he was feeling contrary, and it was only right that Randal and Señora Rodriguez should pay the price. "Whatever hors d'oeuvres the señora has at hand should be sufficient, and…"

There was something that Owain wanted his guests to imbibe, but he couldn't quite put his finger on what it was. *Damn my memory.* He rose and went to the bookshelf behind his desk and laid his hand on the book he wanted without even looking. The leather cover, smooth and comfortable to Owain's touch, had replaced the original embroidered cover that, even well-maintained, had finally fallen apart under the weight of time. Eyes closed, Owain caressed the book for a moment before opening it.

There was no table of contents. This was a *commonplace book*, a handwritten collection of wisdom and information, normally handed down through generations like a family Bible. There were passages of scripture, legal contracts, bits of obscure prophetic nonsense—*A dragoun with a rede rose that is of grete fame / A bastard in wedloc boryn schall he be*—pithy sayings, recipes, pressed leaves, just about anything that might be saved for practical, sentimental, or forgotten reasons. The book was, perhaps, Owain's only solace, given to him by his one true love, hundreds of years ago.

It was difficult not to lose himself in reverie as Owain gently passed over the pages written in that graceful, curving script that he had gazed at for countless hours, memorizing every ascending stroke, every falling line. He read more closely, but less nostalgically, when he reached the section penned in his own scrawling handwriting. Even centuries of practice had produced only limited returns for his penmanship.

Shortly, he found the reminder for which he'd been searching: *"For a touch of the sweet amidst all too bitter life—absinthe."*

"Ah!" That was the connection. It all made sense now. "Absinthe, Randal. We do have some on hand, yes?"

Randal thought for a moment. This was not a normal request. "I believe so, sir."

"Good. That is what my guests will drink tonight. See to it."

"Certainly, sir." Randal retreated from the study to carry out Owain's orders.

Absinthe. That was what had been tugging at Owain's circumspect memory. The liqueur was made from wine and wormwood. Owain glanced at his notation again. *Sweet amidst bitter.* He'd certainly had his share of bitter. He didn't remember when he'd written the advice in the commonplace book; some time after his Embrace, of course, as the advice was not meant for the mortal palate but for Owain's more refined tastes.

As Owain felt the smooth leather in his hands and smelled the musty, yellowed parchment, he was amazed at how the mere physical presence of the book soothed him. Though relieved slightly of his rage at the chess game and at the world, he worried that the book might be too much of an emotional crutch. Better not to depend on anything—or anyone—external. This continual lack of recall also was beginning to concern Owain. It happened sometimes to immortals—so many days and nights, so many acquaintances, friends, and loved ones returned to dust, so much loss. Easier to block it all out, or to let it fade away.

Owain wasn't sure if that was what was happening to him, but he did know that his lack of passion, the spiritual lethargy that had been mounting over the past decades, was causing him to make careless mistakes, mistakes that could lead to his destruction.

Two nights ago at the exhibit, for instance, he had blatantly threatened Benjamin. Not even in his reckless days of youth had Owain operated in such a clumsy, heavy-handed manner. The zoning dispute was not so important that he should have acted so rashly, further magnifying the distrust between Benjamin and himself. Yes, Owain did have some financial interest in Mercator Manufacturing, and he had, through various third parties, bought up property around the acreage in question, property that would increase substantially in value with the construction of the distribution center, but there was no reason he couldn't have had incriminating evidence of some sort tied to Justice Chamberlain, or couldn't have discredited the citizens group, or couldn't have intervened at some other point in the appeals process. There were countless, more subtle alternatives to bullying and alienating an influential rival. Of course, the subtle alternatives wouldn't have been nearly as satisfying as seeing the shock and fear on Benjamin's face....

Ah, well, Owain sighed. *Water under the bridge.* He returned the commonplace book to its spot on the shelf, tracing his finger lightly along the spine of the gift given him by a woman long dead. "Am I a sentimental fool, Randal?"

Randal, standing in the doorway, was no longer surprised by his master's uncanny ability to detect his approach despite not seeming to pay the least attention. "Your guests are beginning to arrive, sir. And there is another visitor. Mr. Giovanni."

Owain's eyebrows raised at this. "Really? I can't remember the last time we had so many unannounced guests in one week. First the Gangrel, now

Giovanni." Randal, the keeper of Owain's calendar, was looking concerned. "It's all right, Randal," Owain reassured him. "I know what this is about. Show Mr. Giovanni in and see that the other guests are cared for while I speak with him. It shouldn't take long."

"Yes, sir."

"Oh, and see to it that the gentlemen have cigars while they wait…some of the Cubans."

Owain sat back. He had expected to see Lorenzo Giovanni a week or two ago. Like others of his family and clan—one and the same for the Giovanni—Lorenzo was extremely businesslike and efficient in most ways. He made a practice, however, of not sticking to hard and fast schedules—too easy for assassins or, worse yet, financial spies to zero in on him. That problem was exacerbated, Owain supposed, by the fact that Atlanta was not the friendliest of territories for the Giovanni. Though the clan had maintained significant business interests in the city for over twenty years now, Prince Benison did not often allow direct representatives of the family to remain in town.

Owain heard Randal draw back his hand but waited for the actual knock before responding. No need to flaunt one's capabilities before a rival, and though Lorenzo Giovanni was not an enemy, *everyone* was a rival.

Randal ushered in Lorenzo. His angular face was

dominated by a prominent nose, while his bushy eyebrows and pencil-thin mustache, both dark black and waxed to points, accentuated the sharpness of his features. Accompanying him was his bodyguard, a balding hulk of a man named Alfonzo, also dark-complected and of Italian descent. Both wore immaculately tailored suits.

"Lorenzo, how good to see you." Owain did not stand to greet his guests. Ironically enough, even though Lorenzo was the only individual in Atlanta that Owain knew of whose age rivaled his own, the representative of the Giovanni clan was not a vampire. He was a ghoul, fed on the cursed blood of his family but still human, more or less. It was an audition of sorts—serve *la familia* faithfully enough and Lorenzo might be Embraced into true immortality. According to Owain's sources, Lorenzo had already been a ghoul for over eight hundred years. Such patience. But, then again, the ghoul probably had little choice in the matter. If he were to become a vampire, it would not be until his elders decided the time was right.

"I trust all is well with you, Owain." Lorenzo's smile was surprisingly warm, genuine.

All part of the job, Owain reminded himself. As a ghoul, Lorenzo was expert at ingratiating himself to vampires—to his masters, and to those whom he dealt with on his masters' behalf. "Do sit down."

Lorenzo, flanked as always by Alfonzo, approached Owain's desk but did not sit. "I'm afraid I've come at a bad time. There were other cars in the drive."

"Nothing that can't wait," Owain assured him.

Lorenzo nodded his appreciation. His dark black hair shone as he sat and Alfonzo took up position close behind. "You're too kind." Lorenzo smiled like a man who could not be surprised; he exuded a quiet confidence, a professionalism, that most of the Kindred in Atlanta lacked.

As much as Owain knew about Lorenzo Giovanni, he expected that Lorenzo knew just as much about him. Most of Owain's past was not a deep dark secret, but it was obscured by the mists of time. He knew though, as Lorenzo surely did, that a small amount of determination combined with a large amount of money could uncover almost any secret. It was a lesson that Owain doubted other Atlanta Kindred had learned. They were either too young and inexperienced in the machinations of real power, like Benjamin, or they were simply too arrogant to go to the trouble, like Eleanor and Benison. Perhaps it was this complacency born of overconfidence, Owain pondered, to which he had fallen victim. What was it about the Kindred in this sleepy southern city?

"Owain?"

Owain realized that Lorenzo had asked him a question. Probably some inconsequential pleasantry, but still Owain cursed himself for again letting his mind wander, and this time in the presence of a potential ally, but one that could just as easily turn on Owain like a ravenous beast if weakness were apparent.

Lorenzo looked on inquisitively but politely, not making an issue of Owain's lapse. Again Owain appreciated the ghoul's professionalism; a working business relationship was obviously more important to him than pettily exploiting a potential embarrassment. This was a man with whom, in different circumstances, Owain could have been a friend—if Owain were still capable of friendship after years of atrophying emotions, and if Lorenzo could be trusted to serve anything other than a ruthless loyalty to his clan veiled by a thin veneer of amicability.

As if there had not been a gaping chasm in the conversation, as if he had not been caught in a blatant lapse of concentration, Owain opened his desk drawer and removed an envelope. He placed it casually before Lorenzo. "I could have sent Randal with this…"

Lorenzo opened the envelope but did not remove the check written for a considerable sum, drafted against the account of a large company which Owain controlled. "Nonsense. My family prefers to maintain personal, yet discreet, relationships with our supporters."

The money, though a substantial amount, was inconsequential to Owain. He was not purchasing anything in particular; the check was a gift, a guarantee of cordial relations. While Owain was a de facto advisor to the prince, and Benison was tolerant at best of the Giovanni, it didn't hurt to have a foot in more than one camp. And as long as the Giovanni made no overt moves against Benison, then Owain really faced no dangerous conflict of interests, although Prince Benison might not see it that way if he were to become aware of Owain's friendly terms with the Giovanni. It was a chance Owain was willing to take. He had tried his hand at ruling directly centuries ago. Now he preferred to remain farther back in the shadows, prepared to react to any eventuality. As the Nosferatu maxim stated: *Knowledge is power*.

"Your gesture of goodwill is greatly appreciated," Lorenzo continued, "and I would like to extend my family's sincerest regards…." With this, he slowly slid the envelope back across the desk to Owain. The two men observed one another for a moment. Alfonzo stood motionless, stone-like since the beginning of the conversation, behind his master. Owain knew what was coming next before Lorenzo spoke the words. "I accept the honor you proffer upon myself and upon my family, but this," Lorenzo indicated the envelope, "I return to you." He paused for a moment, as if to allow the solemnity of the moment its full effect, not that he needed to. Owain was quite aware that the Giovanni clan did not, on a regular basis, return monetary offerings. "There is no need for such gifts between friends."

Friends. Owain, recognizing the euphemism for what it was, restrained a grim smile. *You mean allies, Lorenzo. Allies, perhaps. Friends, never.*

"Indeed," said Owain, neither giving voice to assumptions nor insulting Lorenzo's intelligence by feigning ignorance of what the ghoul was about to suggest. Both men were treading carefully, aware that an unavoidable aspect of forging alliances was the gradual exposure of vulnerabilities to one's ally. Neither was willing to move too quickly, to risk a misstep, for betrayal could bring the wrath of the prince down upon them. Again they regarded one another.

Finally, Lorenzo spoke. His tone was casual, but he chose his words carefully. "You are certainly closer to the prince's ear than am I," Lorenzo stated. "Eleanor is *officially* Ventrue primogen, but the prince often seeks you out for counsel."

Owain nodded, allowing Lorenzo small steps along the slippery slope.

Not even the ghoul's off-hand manner could belittle the weightiness of his words. "Ofttimes issues that involve the Giovanni, for better or for ill, might arise…." Lorenzo let the thought dangle for a brief moment. "Issues that one friend might mention to another friend."

Owain nodded thoughtfully. Lorenzo certainly was proceeding with all due caution—not making a move against Benison, not overtly asking Owain to spy or even to betray a confidence, merely to *mention to another friend* anything of interest. "What friend would do less?" Owain asked.

Another brief silence hung between vampire and ghoul. Then Lorenzo smiled, a reserved display of relief. Owain waited for the polite excuse to leave he knew would come next.

"Well," Lorenzo sat back, more relaxed now, "I've kept you from your guests long enough." Quickly but gracefully, he was at the door, Alfonzo ever-present at his side. "As always, Owain, it has been a pleasure."

"Indeed."

The Giovanni ghoul and his bodyguard departed.

That matter resolved for the time being, Owain was tempted to return to his study of the chess board, but his responsibilities as a host prevailed. The mere thought of the game, however, served to raise his ire. This, when nothing else these days seemed to evoke any significant emotional response in him—not politics, certainly not socializing, not even feeding. All of his hungers, his desires, had ebbed away over the years.

Owain met his guests, five men all in their sixties or seventies from oldmoney Atlanta families established in the city since at least the Civil War, in the trophy room. As he entered, he felt their thoughts turn toward him. With the tiniest flex of his mental powers, Owain shifted those thoughts just enough so his guests would take no notice that he appeared at least forty years younger than they. He had been associating with these particular mortals for so long now that they were conditioned to such cognitive proddings from him.

His youthful features were one reason Owain only mingled with mortals in very small groups. A Brujah rousing rabble or a Toreador dancing with the goths could afford to look young, but among the financial *crème de la crème* of Atlanta, youth was a fairly inexplicable disadvantage. So Owain helped his mortal friends simply overlook anything about his appearance that might set him apart.

"*There* you are, Owain. We were starting to wonder," said Manny Gormann, sounding anything but concerned. Like the others, he was savoring a Cuban cigar. "How do you get these through customs?"

Owain shrugged. "Just knowing the right people."

"And this," Price Haynes, a retired investment banker, chimed in, indicating his glass of absinthe. "Franklin was saying that this isn't legal in the U.S. either?"

"Another case of knowing the right people," Owain explained modestly.

"Why in the world is it illegal, Franklin?" Manny asked.

Franklin, approaching eighty and the oldest of the mortals present, leisurely exhaled a long plume of fragrant cigar smoke. "Not sure exactly. Something to do with how they make it."

"Wormwood," Owain explained. "It's flavored with wormwood, like vermouth, except more heavily. Acts as a narcotic."

"Hm."

Aside from Owain, Manny, Price, and Franklin West, the King Road Club was comprised of Parker Goodwin and James Kirkwood. Owain, Manny and Franklin lived on King Road, and thus their semi-regular gathering had taken on its sobriquet. The governor, a nearby neighbor, attended on occasion.

"How many of these beasts did you kill yourself, Owain?" asked James, looking around at the various trophies mounted on the walls: grizzly, polar bear, lion, rhino, caribou, among others.

"I must confess," said Owain, "they came with the house, and I haven't gotten around to redecorating." This ellicited a general guffaw from the assemblage.

Owain's attention wavered as the conversation carried on from the decor to city and state politics to the golden days of presidents Eisenhower and Kennedy, all yesterday's headlines but hardly ancient history to Owain. The whole affair was tired old ritual. Owain listened disinterestedly to the talk, concentrating on the aroma of the cigars, a smell which over the years he had come to associate with feeding. Certainly there was financial information being discussed that could be useful to him, but how much money did one individual need? Owain could never hope to rival the worldwide monetary influence possessed by the Giovanni, and he had long ago amassed more wealth than he, in his role of waiting and watching, could ever imagine spending even on the most outlandish of bribes.

So Owain sat, and he watched, and he listened. He wondered why these men, every one of them, each wore a necktie to such a casual gathering? He knew the answer: that no gathering was devoid of social significance. Even an informal gettogether fulfilled the twin needs to see and to be seen. And by being here, these men were setting themselves above everyone else, in the great pecking order, who was not.

All this, Owain knew. And he knew that once he had been just as enslaved by the petty power games as were these kine. In his day, he had gloated over being seated at the high table, had lusted after his brother's position of prominence. But knowing this did not answer the fundamental question: why?

Owain's concentration was broken as he noticed

James Kirkwood, the overweight banker, lifting a sword from its place mounted on the wall where he had been examining it.

No one noticed, but suddenly Owain was at James' side. "I would appreciate your leaving that on the wall."

"Jesus!" James jumped, bobbling and almost dropping the sword, surprised as he was by Owain's voice, out of nowhere, at his shoulder. James carefully placed the sword on its mounting as he caught his breath. He chuckled at his own discomfort. "Buy this with the house too?"

"No," said Owain humorlessly. "That sword has been in my family for just over nine hundred and fifty years."

"Oh. I see."

Owain did not mention that the sword had been *his* for just over nine hundred and fifty years. He wasn't afraid that any harm would come to the sword—the steel was as flexible and strong as the day it was made—but, even today, he could not tolerate a guest in his home to go armed if he was not. Too many Welsh uncles had been struck down by ruthless nephews. Not that Owain had anything against being ruthless. He had killed numerous relatives. Nor did he fear James Kirkwood. The bloated pencil-pusher probably couldn't swing the sword, much less mount a credible threat. But survival instincts, even those from the dark ages, needed to be obeyed. It was one way, Owain mused, that he could be certain his mind had not completely atrophied. Long after emotion had wasted away, instinct survived.

Having stomached as much sociability as he could, Owain caught Franklin's eye. "Can I speak with you for a moment?" He led the old man to the study and closed the door behind them. "Do you play chess, Franklin?"

"Yes, I do."

"Take a look at this." Owain took Franklin over to the board. "What would you say about this game?" Owain knew there was no use, but he couldn't help entertaining the fanciful idea that a mere mortal might see something that he had not.

Franklin studied the board for a minute. "What would I say?" He looked a little longer. "I'd say White's game."

Owain smiled a tight, grim smile. "Indeed." He tried, unsuccessfully, to put the game out of his mind as he pulled a chair over for Franklin. *"Take off your jacket and sit,"* he intoned in a voice that a mortal could not resist.

Franklin sat, his eyes glazing as volition and independent thought were displaced by Owain's will.

"Roll up your sleeve." Owain watched woodenly as Franklin did as he was told. Owain felt no sense of anticipation, no hunger. He fed because he knew he must. When did this begin? he wondered. He remembered his early years as a vampire, the al-

most drunken euphoria that accompanied feeding, back before the idea of sex had completely lost its allure for him and draining a noble's beautiful daughter had been an erotic escapade. Somewhere along the line, he had lost all of that.

Franklin sat staring straight ahead with his right sleeve rolled up above his elbow. Veins bulged prominently on his gaunt, elderly arm. Slowly Owain knelt beside the chair and took Franklin's arm in his hand. The vampire felt no remorse for what he did. He was what he was. *The devil's spawn.* Owain was of two minds concerning feeding on mortals, but neither rationale placed undue guilt upon him for his dietary needs. First, as Darwin might have put it, vampires had reached the apex of the food chain. Mortals, lower on the chain, were like cattle to be harvested. Owain tried to adhere to this rationalistic approach, but he did not truly believe it.

Second, the view that he had spent most of his years subscribing to: that he had inherited the curse of Caine and was therefore cursed himself. God had turned his back on Owain, so now Owain was an instrument of vengeance. What had he done to be tortured so? And what mortal was free from sin that he or she should not suffer? Owain raised Franklin's arm to his mouth. Had this old man led a guiltless life? Had he never transgressed against God? *Doubtful,* was Owain's verdict.

A pained yet ecstatic moan escaped Franklin's lips as Owain bit into flesh and drank deeply. God had had his agent on earth. Certainly Satan deserved no less. It was this spirit of anger and vengeance that satisfied Owain more than the actual blood, but never fully. Though he did not truly hunger for blood—he couldn't remember the last time he'd been driven by such pains—his spiritual emptiness never completely receded.

Blood from the elderly tended to lose some of its richness. Owain thought of it as watered down. Some of the absinthe, however, had made its way into Franklin's blood stream, and the mix of sweet and bitter augmented the taste quite pleasantly.

Franklin's aged heart raced, urged on by adrenaline and the need to make up for less blood. Owain could feel the pounding. He made sure not to take too much blood from these older men lest he bring on a heart attack. Then he would have to deal with medical treatment or perhaps disposing of the body and covering his tracks. The number of people who knew where Franklin and the others were this evening was most likely more than Owain could reasonably expect to help forget. Unlife had been so much simpler before the Camarilla, before the Masquerade.

Done, and not wanting to push Franklin's heart beyond its limit, Owain licked the wound on the old man's forearm. The leathery skin closed back over, leaving no trace of the feeding, no scar. Owain stood and slowly passed a hand before Franklin's vacant eyes. "Franklin."

The mortal blinked for several seconds, then, slightly disoriented, looked up at Owain. "No, I'm all right. Just a little dizzy for a moment," he answered the nonexistent question.

"Let me help you back to the others," Owain generously offered. As they made their way back to the trophy room, Franklin, shaky on his feet, leaned heavily on Owain. Franklin was in good shape for his age—tennis twice a week, appropriate medication for his high blood pressure—but, still, Owain knew he wouldn't last too much longer. Ten, maybe fifteen years, then he would pass like the rest of the mortals over the years. Franklin was one of the few whose company Owain had come close to enjoying, unlike boorish James and overbearing Manny. Franklin would have to be replaced soon.

Back in the trophy room, Owain helped Franklin into one of the over-stuffed leather arm-chairs. To the others, Franklin pleaded a bit too much absinthe, and perhaps the strong cigar hadn't helped either.

"Gentlemen," Owain said, attracting their attention. "*Sit.*"

The other four men, without question, took seats around the room, their eyes taking on the same glassy look that Franklin's had again assumed.

"Randal," Owain called. The servant glided into the room pushing a cart with tidy compartments for plastic tubes, bags, needles, and with refrigerated compartments beneath. "I'll be in the study. Call me when you're done."

Storing the blood was so much easier than frequent hunting. Because Owain could only tolerate blood from certain individuals—patricians, nobles, gentry, the elite, whatever the title of the era—and since class distinctions were so blurred in modern society, he preferred feeding from an established herd rather than risking a mistake and striking upon sickeningly unpalatable blood.

In an hour or so, Owain would lick their needle marks and send them home full of memories of a pleasant evening and stimulating conversation. For now, Owain returned to his chess board.

Listen and learn.

Smile and nod.

Emigesh's sire Marla had been full of pithy soundbite homilies. But if she were so smart, why was Emigesh still walking around while she had crossed the wrong people and met her last sunrise?

Knowing is half the battle.

Which battle would that be? Emigesh wondered. But if she had known that, she might still be alive.

Emigesh had thought he was rid of her, but the

last few nights she had been haunting him from beyond final death. Not that her spirit was visiting him exactly. It was more like Emigesh was visiting her, revisiting events from her life, seeing them through her eyes. At times Emigesh felt that he had become her, experiencing a warped version of his reality from Marla's perspective, bringing her complete arsenal of wisdom fully to bear on his unlife.

An ounce of prevention…

Tonight, though, as Emigesh wandered through the streets with Aaron, Liza, and Jolanda, the haunting was different. Marla was gone. She mercifully had passed back to her final rest. But Emigesh's mind was still not his own. Marla's sire Antony was making his presence known; Antony the silent, who had paused from his brooding long enough to Embrace Marla and her littermate Paula and then given into despair and greeted the sun.

Emigesh walked the streets seeing the city as he never had before, through cold and cynical eyes. At times he was hard pressed to remember whether the two women sniping at one another were Liza and Jolanda bitching and taking jabs, or Marla and Paula with their incessant bickering that made greeting the sun seem more and more an attractive alternative. He was tempted to snap them both in two, to undo the error of his progeny…but no, they were not his childer.

As the night dragged on, Emigesh watched and he listened, always understanding more than they gave him credit for, smiling for their benefit. And beneath it all the hunger was growing.

Always growing.

The two hoodlums were perfect gentlemen. They didn't open the car door for Francesca or say "please," but neither did they threaten her, leer or curse at her, and for the likes of these, that was as refined as it got. Francesca sneered at them. Amazing how ever since that one gang banger had grabbed her ass and she had strangled him with his own intestines, they had *all* been perfect gentlemen.

Rico and Johnny picked her up at Los Angeles International Airport. They didn't speak to her, just nodded and led her back to the car. They got in the front, she in the back, and drove in silence. Even the vulgarities of the rap station on the radio were toned down to an unusually reasonable level.

At this early hour of the morning, traffic was not a problem. In only a short while the trio was driving into the heart of Watts. Stripped cars and burned-out shells of buildings decorated most every block, and even at four-thirty in the morning, numerous young men dotted every corner—protecting turf, selling drugs, pimping. There was as much activity as other parts of the city would see at midday.

They came to a stop in front of a small, nondescript stucco house in front of which, in the yard and on the porch, lounged at least a dozen young men and boys wearing ripped jeans, T-shirts with or without sleeves, boots or high-tops, and all with blue bandanas tied around a leg, arm, or neck. As Nico and Johnny got out of the car, their friends began to hoot and catcall…until they realized who the passenger stepping out was. No one spoke a word as Francesca walked down the sidewalk and in the front door.

Mohammed al-Muthlim was conferring with two bandana-bearing kine lieutenants. He looked up briefly at Francesca's entrance. "Be right with you." The two mortals made sure not to look at Francesca for too long. After a few minutes, Mohammed finished giving instructions about a certain house in Inglewood that needed to be "cleaned out" and sent the mortals on their way. He turned his full attention to Francesca. "Welcome, sister. Any problems?"

"None."

Mohammed's wide, African-American face was as handsome as any Francesca had seen. Seeing him again, she wanted to feel him against her; she wanted his blood. Aside from the natural attraction she felt for her sire, she had been constantly hungry the past few nights despite several feedings. Francesca sidled up to Mohammed.

"Good," he was saying. "I'm glad that went well. Our friend in Spain owes me a favor." Some day Mohammed would rule Los Angeles, as soon as the Sabbat finished with the idealistic Kindred experiment known as the Anarch Free States. But for now, while he played the role of powerful ganglord, Francesca was his link to the outside world. Her skills as an assassin were held in high regard across North America and Europe, and every assignment produced another favor owed to Mohammed by Sabbat who were potential allies or rivals. "Did the boys treat you well?" Mohammed smiled at Francesca, who was now pressing her leg against his thigh.

Francesca thought of Nico and Johnny and laughed. "They always do." She leaned into Mohammed, her taut breasts behind thin silk against his arm. The smell of his blood was maddening. A ravenous hunger, intense even for a woman of her insatiable appetites, tore at her from within. She wrapped her arms around his waist and bit down, through his grimy shirt, into his left shoulder. She sucked greedily, wishing she could drain every drop of his blood. An ecstatic spasm shook his body.

Mohammed ripped the silk from her left shoulder. Buttons popped and bounced to the floor. Francesca groaned at the pleasurable pain that shot through her body and sucked harder at the blood flowing from her sire.

The next thing she knew, they were lying on the floor amidst the remnants of her shirt, Mohammed cradling her head against his chest. Even lying down, her head was swimming, just as it had with every feeding the past few nights.

"*To freedom,*" Mohammed whispered.

"*To loyalty,*" she responded.

And then the blood on their tongues was mixing again as Mohammed pulled her to him.

Usually in the late fall and winter Liza wore at least a heavy shirt or a light jacket so she wouldn't stand out too much in a crowd. If the mortals' teeth were chattering from the cold, a vampire walking down the street at night in short sleeves attracted unnecessary attention. Tonight, though, she was bundled up for a different reason. Every few minutes, she could feel bloody sweat dribbling across her ribs or down her back. Her black T-shirt was already saturated, and now her black jacket was soaking up the moisture. Liza hadn't really sweated since she was a mortal, and now that it had been going on several nights nearly nonstop, she was pissed off. At first, she'd been puzzled, then worried, but her concern had long since given way to irritation and ever-present anger. She wasn't fit company for human or Cainite, which was bad news for her friends.

Aaron and Emigesh were in the back seat of the car, not saying or doing much of anything. They didn't seem to mind an occasional slow evening. Jolanda, on the other hand, was bored out of her skull. She sat in the front passenger seat with the door open, legs splayed wide, quite unladylike in her short skirt, and time after time took the red-hot cigarette lighter and pressed it into the BMW dashboard, filling the car with smoke and the putrid odor of melting plastic.

The downtown parking garage was empty except for a handful of cars, including the white BMW which someone had unwisely left parked overnight and which Liza and company had comandeered. No one seemed very motivated toward any particular end tonight, so after wandering aimlessly through various neighborhoods for a couple of hours, the four had drifted just as purposelessly into the echoing confines of the garage, and there they were still.

Just like she had been for over a week, Liza was starving. She had fed last night on a corner drug dealer who was a frequent meal for her, but Liza's hunger had taken hold, and she had been unable to pull herself away. Instead of licking the wound and saving her mortal for another night, she had drunk long and desperately until there was no more blood to be had. In her unsatiated hunger and frustration, Liza had left the body on the street and run off into the darkness. She didn't have a problem with killing mortals. They were a dime a dozen. But just like having been faced down by Prince Benison last week, the memory of losing control didn't sit well. There were many times, for sure, that Liza gave into her primal urges. That was what was so fulfilling about her introduction into the Sabbat—the power of the unrestrained Beast and its mastery over mere mortals. Recently, however, as she'd struggled to ease the burning hunger that constantly gripped her, she had not given in to her predatory instincts. She had been overwhelmed by them, helpless in the face of her need.

All these thoughts were swirling around in Liza's mind, sometimes asserting themselves, more often sublimated by the unrelenting hunger which still gnawed at her. The only distraction tugging at her attention was the tang of burning plastic as Jolanda again held the cigarette lighter to the dash. Liza hated that smell. She hated it with a passion. And together with the unceasing ache that was her hunger, it was making her queasy, another unpleasant throwback to mortality that had been plaguing her in recent days, especially after she fed. Last night after killing the drug dealer and fleeing, Liza had grown so dizzy that she had fallen to the sidewalk and heaved back up some of the blood. It was all so strange, and unpleasant, and infuriating.

Jolanda, always stifled by a lack of creativity, was making a large smiley face out of burn marks on the dashboard. She disinterestedly placed the last dot of the mouth. The smoke and the stink drifted to Liza. She was forcing herself not to slap Jolanda when a thump from the rear of the car distracted them both. All four vampires looked back over their shoulders.

In the back seat, Aaron let out a bored sigh. Emigesh just smiled. "Your turn, Aaron," Liza grumbled.

Aaron sighed again, then opened his door and hauled himself up out of the seat. His ponytail swayed back and forth as he ambled around to the trunk and opened it from where the locking mechanism was torn away. Staring up terrified was the bound and gagged security guard for the parking deck.

Aaron lifted him by his collar. "What?" Aaron asked.

The guard's eyes were wide open. After a moment, he swallowed hard and then tried to speak through the gag without success. Aaron impatiently slid the gag down so the man's mouth was clear.

The guard took frantic shallow breaths. Aaron looked on expectantly, still waiting for his question to be answered. Finally, the guard managed to speak. "I…I can't breathe…in there."

"Fine," said Aaron. "Now you've breathed." He slid the gag back down and roughly shoved the guard back into the trunk, slamming it down even though it no longer latched. Aaron leaned down close to the car. "So shut the hell up, or you won't *need* to breathe any more!" He retook his seat and slammed the door. "Some people."

That seemed to be the excitement for the evening, until Jolanda resumed her lighter art. She pressed the lighter for the right eyeball of the smiley face. Without warning, Liza smacked Jolanda's hand hard. The lighter popped out and landed on Jolanda's leg. She screamed and jumped, knocking the heating element out the open door. Lack of creativity aside, Jolanda let out a long, descriptive string of expletives directed at Liza and various members of her family.

Liza pointed a long claw at Jolanda's face. "I don't want to hear it, bitch! One more word, and your ass is mine!"

This was enough to stymie Jolanda's outflow of adjectives as she pondered the danger of mouthing off one more time. Neither woman moved. Their faces were less than a foot apart. Liza, wanting badly to take out her frustrations on someone more durable than a mortal, hoped Jolanda would say something else.

Each woman's attention was riveted on the other when Emigesh lunged forward from the back seat with a mad cackle. Before anyone could react, he grabbed Jolanda by the head and wrenched with a sudden fury. Liza was knocked back against the steering wheel. The horn blast didn't quite cover the loud crack inside the car.

Emigesh was scrambling for Liza. She caught a glimpse of his bulging bloodshot eyes vivid against his tan skin. His fangs were bared, and he was still cackling madly, desperately.

Liza pushed him away, and in doing so forced herself back against the door. Her knee was caught under the steering wheel. She couldn't get any leverage against Emigesh as he pulled himself on top of her, scraping at her eyes. Emigesh's laughter turned to frantic maniacal grunts. Whatever had possessed him, he wanted nothing more than to rip her throat out.

Finally, Liza was able to smash her elbow into Emigesh's nose. It made a satisfying crunch and blood spurted readily. As her attacker wailed, Liza used the brief respite to open the door and tumble out of the car. Back on her feet, her rage took over. She reached into the car, ignoring Emigesh's renewed swipes, and dragged him out by the hair. He lunged at her again, but Liza blocked him. She let loose her fury and gouged at his eyes, one claw striking true down through an eyelid. The violence of the blow wrenched the eyeball out of the socket with an audible *pop*.

Emigesh screamed and stumbled backward, bumping into the car. He cupped his hands over his face, cradling the dangling eye.

Liza stood ready to pounce, to finish the job. Aaron, dumbfounded, was climbing out of the back seat. Liza eyed him warily. She flexed her claws in anticipation, her reflexive instincts primed.

The brief distraction gave Emigesh the room he needed, but he had no more stomach for the fight. He slipped around the front end of the car and was off across the parking garage.

Liza wanted to take after him, to drag him down and finish shredding his face until there was nothing left but bone and strips of flesh, but she wasn't about to turn her back on Aaron. Where did he stand?

As Emigesh's echoing footsteps vanished into the night, Aaron looked back wide-eyed at Liza. He held his hands up in the air. "Don't look at me!" he cried in alarm.

They stood there for maybe a full minute facing one another, Liza slowly growing calmer. Aaron lowered his hands. "What the hell was that?" he wondered.

Liza didn't answer. She was still controlling her temper, forcing herself not to rip Aaron apart, whether he had anything to do with Emigesh's attack or not. Then, at the same instant, they both remembered Jolanda.

She was leaning against the door, her head hanging limply out the open window. Her eyes were open, and though her neck was obviously broken, she was conscious. This was hell for a vampire. She made a thick gurgling sound as she tried to swallow the blood in her mouth, and her left arm twitched spasmodically.

She would heal. But it would take time and blood. Lots of blood. And this, Liza realized glancing around the garage after the noise of the fight, was not the place. As Sabbat, she revelled in a good gory fight, and the anarchs didn't mind pushing the Masquerade to the edge, but there was no point attracting too much mortal attention, and if the police got involved, it could get ugly.

She got in the car. They had already ripped off the cover of the steering column and it would only take a minute to hotwire the beamer. "You comin'?" she asked Aaron as she worked. For an answer, he hopped into the back seat.

For the moment, thankfully, Liza's hunger was forgotten. The car roared to life, but she was too busy planning her next move to be gratified. She would take Jolanda to a safe place. They had several abandoned houses they holed up in at different times. And there was blood in the trunk—the security guard, who was again banging around, alarmed that the car was running.

As they pulled away and Jolanda's head bobbed up and down on the door frame, the face burned into the dash smiled happily at her. Liza hoped to catch sight of Emigesh. Her head was full of the unpleasant things she would do to him. Aaron sat hunched in the back, wondering what was going on, trying to stay out of the way.

SIX

Nothing changed.

No matter how many hours, how many nights, Owain stared at the chess board, no messianic flash of inspiration came to him. There was no spectacular move to resurrect the game. There was no hope.

He awoke in the evening cursing Harold Godwin and his queen. At least, Owain mused, after all these years there was someone new to curse. He thought of how his opponent must be gloating and tried to steel himself to go ahead and concede rather prolonging the humiliation. Owain could take decades for his next turn, of course, but what would be the point? He could end it all with a brief message and start fresh. But the thought of conceding galled him almost as much as the idea of being beaten. He'd been beaten too many times over the centuries—in love, in politics—yet he survived, a claim most of those who had bested him could not make. *Is survival worth losing?* Owain wondered, not sure of the answer, considering what his nightly existence had become.

He felt trapped in his own home but could not muster the energy to leave, to hunt, to plot. *What is a Kindred worth who does not hunt or scheme?* Owain should have exacted some sense of satisfaction from the news that Justice Chamberlain had approved the zoning ordinance that Owain had spoken to Benjamin about, but he felt nothing. He thought of defeated Benjamin and then asked himself the question from the vantage point as victor. *Is survival worth losing?* What would Benjamin say to this? How would he respond to such injury and insult, to the threat Owain had carelessly thrown at him? Would the younger vampire nurse his hatred or come after Owain? The young often acted rashly—witness the anarch's display at the exhibit last week. *That*, Owain thought, *is why they do not survive to be old.* Again, it was pride versus survival.

The sound of a car entering the half-mile driveway caught Owain's attention. No need to tell Randal; Arden would have alerted him by now. Owain's gaze wandered back to the chess board. He was sick of the sight of it. Not bored—he knew he might relive this ritual night after night for the next several years—but filled with a masochistic fascination, like prodding an open sore over and over that would long ago have scabbed over left to itself.

As Owain brooded, the minutes ran together until Randal was knocking at the study door.

"Sir, Mr. Bowman to see you."

Mr. Bowman. Owain sighed. Albert Bowman. Acquaintance of many years. Madman. What could have possessed the Malkavian, Owain wondered, to have climbed atop the prince's sculpture, naked, no less? Might as well ask birds why they sing, or lovers why they care. Yet Albert lived from one catastrophic stunt to the next. That, Owain noted, was a display of power and influence in its own right. There was at least one fool the prince would suffer.

Randal opened the door and ushered in Albert. An improbable number of chains dangled from his leather jacket and clinked together—an interesting contrast to the red, white, and blue plaid slacks he wore. His bushy beard, just long enough to tuck into his pants when he wanted to, was tangled in the chains, but Albert didn't seem to mind. He was more concerned with the bundle he held under his arm as he stood bow-legged just inside the room, watching Randal suspiciously until the servant closed the door.

"Good evening, Albert."

Slowly and carefully, Albert began a circuit of the room, checking behind each piece of furniture, behind the drapes, all the while clutching his roughly basketballsized package wrapped in brown grocery bag and masking tape. Without a word, he made his way around the study, looking for…whatever it was that he was looking for. Owain watched patiently until Albert was satisfied. Finally, the Malkavian nodded greeting. "Owain."

Albert was the Kindred in Atlanta whom Owain had known longer than any other. They had met in the eighteenth century in Spain and spent varying amounts of time together since then, a fact that, at Owain's suggestion, they had decided to keep secret when Albert came to the States in the forties. In that three hundred or so year period, Owain had grown somewhat accustomed to the Malkavian's antics, but still the specifics, like "Albert's Ride" at the exhibit, and the fact that Albert managed to survive his own mischief, never ceased to amaze.

Albert continued to warily survey the room, as if he expected some undiscovered danger to leap out at him at any moment. "And how are you tonight?" Owain asked.

Albert ignored the question and, craning his neck to see all about, quickly shuffled over to Owain. *"I can't stay long,"* he whispered urgently.

"Do you have some place safe that you can keep…" he paused and looked around again, *"this?"* He patted the bundle under his arm.

The size of the package and its rather hasty wrapping gave very little clue as to what it might be, and Owain knew from experience that, with Albert involved, the possibilities stretched well beyond the likely or the rational. "What is that, Albert?" Owain asked, as a master might ask a pet that had offered a small creature, gnawed upon and unidentifiable, as a gift.

The question caught Albert off guard somehow. *"It's…it's…"* he struggled for the right word, *"secret."* Obviously he couldn't tell Owain, or it would cease to be secret.

"Ah. Indeed." Owain held his chin in his hand. "Is it…dangerous?"

Again Albert ignored Owain's question. *"Can you keep it? Can you keep it safe?"* he hissed.

Owain wished he knew what was in the bundle, what exactly was so important to Albert. Probably it was completely innocent. But then again, Albert had a way of perpetrating acts, the consequences of which tended to pass him by but then enveloped whomever was unlucky enough to be left in his wake. Owain remembered one time in Spain when Albert had become infatuated with a young shepherd, and to gain the young man's attention had disguised himself as…

"*Owain, will you keep it?*" Albert stood there, all solemnity, like a small child who desperately needed to be excused to the bathroom.

Owain covered his eyes. "Yes, Albert." He couldn't believe he was saying it. "I will keep it."

Owain could only tell that Albert was smiling under that massive beard by noticing that the deep wrinkles on the Malkavian's forehead had changed directions. For the first time since arriving, Albert spoke in a normal tone of voice. "Well, that's certainly a load off my mind." He was quite cheerful and unconcerned now as he winked at Owain and then thrust the package forward at him. Owain hastily accepted the bundle, almost in self-defense. He felt there was something else he should ask Albert, but the Malkavian was already halfway out the door and calling back over his shoulder, "I must go. I must go. Places to see; people to be." He stopped for just a second, cocked his head and scratched his beard, realizing that something he'd said wasn't quite right, but then he shrugged and continued on.

Though the room was in perfect order, Owain, standing by his desk holding a sloppily wrapped mysterious package, couldn't help feeling a bit as if a whirlwind had just blown through. He looked down at the whatever it was he held in his hands. Sometimes he wondered if it was worth it, dealing with Albert. The Malkavian kept company with the prince's childe Roger, and Benison himself seemed to exercise a strange tolerance for Albert, his clansman. Perhaps having another Malkavian around, and one that was obviously insane, lent an extra air of stability to the prince. It was only an air of stability, Owain knew. The prince's temper was ever cocked with a hair trigger, and that didn't even begin to address his frequent conversations with nonexistent partners, conversations that other Atlanta Kindred wisely never seemed to notice.

At any rate, with his regular proximity to Roger and Benison, Albert was a good source of information, facts that the prince would not otherwise have revealed, even to a trusted advisor.

Owain looked down at the package again. Albert hadn't said anything about not unwrapping it, so there was no way opening it could be construed as a violation of their agreement. Owain had said only that he would "keep it," with the implied qualification that he would keep it safe. And knowing what was in the bundle could very well enable him to more effectively keep it safe. *Hell*, Owain thought, *it might need to go in the refrigerator.* He tested its weight. *Not too heavy for its size. Hmm. Too large to be a human head*, he thought, *unless there's a lot of padding around it.*

Owain began to pick carefully at the masking tape and brown grocery bag wrapping. He thought briefly about summoning Randal and having him open the package, but why risk an efficient ghoul? *So much bother to break in another.*

As Owain peeled the paper away, he found a second layer of wrapping, this one of torn rags, old T-shirts, and what seemed to be at least three rolls of tape. Neither Owain, nor anyone else, could ever take this all apart and put it back together the same way. Perhaps there was a method to Albert's madness. Perhaps, but Owain was doubtful.

Finally, the last rags fell away and the mystery object sat exposed on Owain's desk. Owain took a step back, not sure at first if maybe his eyes were playing tricks on him. It was nothing he would have guessed or even remotely considered. Against his better judgment, Owain slowly reached out and touched the white ceramic armadillo. It was probably about actual size and, as far as Owain knew, seemed to be a reasonable likeness—pointed snout, small ears, ridged shell. Owain shook his head. He tapped the armadillo. Only a hollow clink. He shook it. Nothing.

Owain stepped back again and massaged the bridge of his nose. "Randal," he called.

The dutiful servant appeared in less than a minute. "Sir?"

"Will that," Owain lifted a finger to point at the armadillo, "fit in the safe?"

Randal looked at the armadillo, then back at Owain. "That, sir?"

"Yes. That."

Randal looked at the armadillo again and at Owain again. "In the safe?"

"Yes. In the safe."

Randal looked at the armadillo for a long moment. "I...believe so."

"Good." Owain returned to his chess board. "See to it."

For another long moment, Randal stood in the doorway staring at the armadillo. Eventually he resigned himself to following the instructions. "Yes, sir. In the safe." He picked up the armadillo and, keeping it at arm's length, inspected it all over. Then, still keeping it at arm's length, he took it away.

☥

"Do you have to slam the door?" Roger asked irritably. Albert never closed any door without slamming it. But Roger's Pacer couldn't take too much rough treatment if he wanted it to last. Then again, he could always steal another car. Albert had not yet slammed the car door, but there was no question in Roger's mind that his friend would slam it, as soon as he came out of Evans' house. *His freaking mansion.* Roger was practicing. He wanted to convey the proper degree of indignation without sounding pissy. Albert needed to know that Roger didn't appreciate having his car door slammed.

Albert needed to learn some respect for other people's property. Just because he was a vampire didn't mean he could go around tearing up other people's stuff and slamming people's car doors whenever he wanted.

But, Roger worried, how much anger was too much? What if Albert got angry right back and told Roger to piss off? What if Albert flew into a violent rage and slammed the door even harder, and broke off the antenna, and kicked out the headlights? What if Albert never spoke to him again? It could happen.

Roger felt another panic attack coming on. His heart started beating. It wasn't supposed to do that. He'd never heard of another vampire's heart beating, but then again, he'd never had the nerve to ask anyone about it. He'd been too afraid that whomever he asked would think something was wrong with him. Maybe something was wrong with him. It wasn't like he could go see a vampire doctor and ask why his heart was beating. Roger took a deep breath, concentrated on stopping his heart from beating. An alarming thought shot through his mind. *What if I'm not really a vampire? What if I'm still mortal and just think I'm a vampire?* Of course, it would be difficult to account for the fact that the majority of the time his heart was *not* beating, and that for the past twenty-five years he'd had no nourishment except for human blood.

Caught unaware, Roger jumped and shrieked as Albert jerked open the passenger door. Somehow, Roger managed to smash his finger between his knee and the steering column of the little Pacer and yelled again. Albert dropped into the seat so hard that the entire car bounced up and down. Then he reached over and pulled the door shut forcefully enough to rattle the windows. The rear-view mirror crashed to the dashboard.

Roger's heart started beating more quickly. His hand was trembling with rage as he picked up the cracked mirror.

Albert looked at the mirror. "Damn. Another seven years in the shit."

Roger wanted to scream, wanted to rattle off everything he'd been practicing mere moments before. But he couldn't. What if he offended Albert?

Albert stuffed both hands into his bush of a beard and began scratching his chin. "One down, one to go. Let's hit the road!"

Roger turned the key and cringed at the horrible screeching sound. In his agitation, he'd forgotten the car was already idling. He only stalled once starting down the driveway. "Damned clutch needs work."

As the car jerked and shuddered along, Albert was struggling to get a map that was jammed into his pocket. The map was a wadded-up collection of wrinkles and tears. "Turn left!" Albert yelled suddenly as they reached the street. Roger was so startled that he obeyed immediately, cutting across the oncoming line of early evening traffic. Horns blared. Tires screeched. Unheard curses were uttered. "Left again!" Albert shouted. Again, another ill-advised turn across traffic.

"Stop that, you crazy bastard!" Roger shouted back, so rattled that he almost swerved over the center line and created a head-on collision without any extra help from Albert.

Albert looked saddened all of a sudden. "You called me...crazy."

Roger was speechless. He *had* called Albert crazy, and though it was true, some Malkavians were sensitive about that kind of thing. "I...I..."

Albert buried his face in the map and sobbed, loud, spastic moans that wracked his body.

Roger was mortified. He had finally done it. His temper had caused him to step over that fine line, and he had alienated his only true friend. Albert was the one comfort in Roger's unlife as the prince's childe. But all that would end now. Roger kept worriedly glancing over at his distraught, possibly emotionally scarred, passenger. *Such a fragile soul under that rugged beard*, Roger thought. "Albert...Albert, I don't know what to say."

Albert, red-eyed, looked up from his increasingly rumpled map, snot running from his nose into his beard. "Say? Say!" he bellowed. Then, instantly, his expression transformed and became completely neutral. "Say," he asked mildly, "did you know that three out of four dentists surveyed think that that fourth dentist is a stupid son of a bitch?"

Roger stared dumbfounded, his guilt and his anger mingling in a jumbled hodge-podge of emotion.

Albert nonchalantly reached over and jerked the steering wheel, averting another potential collision. "Are you sure you've driven one of these before?" he asked.

Roger felt numb. He had exhausted his capacity for being upset over the past half hour, and merely stared ahead and drove. He couldn't deal with Albert any more at the moment. Other things were more important. "Are we about there?"

"Oh, yes," Albert assured him, rustling through the remains of his tattered map. He found the spot he needed. "Only about forty-five minutes to go."

"What? Forty-five minutes?" Roger thought he must have heard wrong. "We were only fifteen minutes away when we were at Evans' house. How can it be forty-five minutes?"

"Short cut." Albert grinned. "Forty-five minutes and we'll be in Salisbury."

"*What?*" Roger snatched the map out of Albert's hands and tried to make some kind of sense of it without straying into the other lane yet again. "This is a map of England!"

"Nobody else could get you to Salisbury in forty-five minutes. Betcha."

Roger took a deep calming breath. "Albert?"

"Uh-huh?"

"Do you ever feel like your heart starts beating?"

Albert, head cocked, glanced over at Roger.

"Never mind." Roger turned the car around and retraced their route, all the while berating himself for thinking that Albert might know where he was going. They passed the driveway to Owain Evans' estate and continued back toward downtown. Roger tried to ignore Albert, who was playing with the radio, changing stations and trying to knit the snippets of songs into one cohesive tune. Shortly, the skyline loomed ahead. Atlanta was not the huge conglomerate of construction and infinite high-rises that some cities were, but it seemed eerily large to Roger. Most of the skyscrapers had popped up in the past ten to fifteen years, but he still knew his way around, as long as he didn't listen to Albert.

There were plenty of parking spaces across the street from Peachtree Gardens. Most visitors to the nursing home came a good deal earlier in the day. Roger turned to Albert. "Okay. Give me an hour." He almost added, *And don't get in trouble*, but there was no point.

Roger placed his card key on the metal plate and the front doors of Peachtree Gardens slid open. Mostly, being the childe of the prince was a headache, but it did have a way of smoothing over some difficulties. Visitors were not allowed at this late hour, but Benison had his influence in the mortal world and had arranged certain accomodations for Roger.

Roger strode past the night attendant who had standing orders never to mention these late-night visits. Roger had no idea what the explanation given to the attendant was—perhaps that the resident was part of the federal witness relocation program—but undoubtedly it was a fabrication. Roger made a point of staying out of sight of the other employees. No sense in making more people curious. He reached room 256 and paused outside the door. This could be the night. Roger eased the door open.

Tabatha Greene was resting quietly. She was always resting quietly. Every night Roger came to her bedside hoping that she might have regained full consciousness, and every night she was resting quietly. Her skin hung loosely on her body, the only movement the rise and fall of her steady breathing. Roger pulled a chair to the bed and took her small gaunt hand in his.

"Hello, Mama." He should have gotten used to seeing her like this by now, Roger always told himself. After nearly twenty-five years, he shouldn't have felt that lump in his throat, shouldn't have had to force the words out. "I hope you're doing well tonight. There's not too much going on with me. Prince Benison is still angry at my friend Albert, so we're trying to stay out of trouble. At least *I'm* trying to stay out of trouble." Roger sat for some time stroking her hand, telling himself that she could open her eyes any second, that she had heard every word he'd spoken to her over the years, that she would be proud of him.

That last was the most difficult to believe. Roger had never been able to hide anything from his mother. He'd come home from Vietnam a hero, at least as much of a hero as anyone could be from that conflict, and it had been that combat prowess that had attracted Benison to him. After Roger had been Embraced and become a vampire, it had been another secret that he couldn't keep from her. And it had been too much for her. Though she was only forty years old, his mother's stroke had been brought on by the realization of what her son had become. Roger was determined to make it up to her. The determination that had made him a hero was now directed toward seeing that his mother recovered, that she regained the life he had caused her to miss.

It's only a matter of time, Roger told himself, lowering his head to the sheets, trying to hold back the tears of blood. "I *will* make it up to you, Mama." Roger couldn't imagine existence without her. If she regained consciousness...*when* she regained consciousness, even for a second, he would take her frail body in his arms and Embrace her, and then she would be with him forever. Nothing would stand in the way of that plan—not the Third Tradition prohibiting creation of progeny without permission of one's elder, not the blood bond which held Roger to Benison's will. This, Roger knew, was too powerful a need. Certainly Benison of all Kindred, with his notorious doting on Aunt Bedelia, would understand and acquiesce. Roger was willing to take that chance. He was willing to take any chance for his mother.

But for now, she was not conscious. The situation of twenty-five years had not changed, so Roger must ensure, at the least, that it did not change for the worse. As he had so many other nights, Roger dug into his right index finger with his thumbnail until a bead of blood welled up. Slowly, carefully, so as not to stain her bed clothes with a drop of crimson, he raised his finger to his mother's lips. The vampiric blood dribbled in between dry, cracked lips and she swallowed.

"I will make it up to you, Mama," Roger whispered. He gently caressed her face, then washed the bloody tears from his own face before rejoining Albert.

The bouncer at the door waved Liza through. She was a regular face at Nine Tails. No need for her to show ID or pay the cover. The bouncer was so used to seeing her that he didn't notice how ashen her complexion was, or the bloody rag she carried and frequently used to wipe sweat from her face. Liza stumbled through the front door, unable to avoid jostling several people and spilling their drinks. She usually liked it here at Nine Tails with the techno music blaring and the smell of blood in the air. The mortal S&M crowd was laughable—their chains and piercings and tough looks. Over the past couple of years, Liza had shown several of them what real sadism was, and in the end, none of them had been able to take it. None of them really lived for it like she did. Poseurs, every one, they had begged for mercy. Begged and received none.

There were also the beautiful people—the grungy frat boys and shiny daddy's girls who came to watch their twisted counterparts and, if they were really daring, to pay five dollars to be whipped by one of the dominatrices on the Nine Tails payroll.

They were all background for Liza, background and meat. She came because Nine Tails was a major anarch hangout, stomping ground for the vampires who took orders from no one, who acknowledged the influence but not the authority of the Camarilla. The Camarilla, Prince Benison and all his ilk, ignored the insolence of the anarchs because centuries ago there had been a war with the anarchs, and now the Camarilla had no other choice. A population of young rebellious vampires full of animosity toward the Camarilla was a breeding ground for the Sabbat, and Liza had enlisted a couple of recruits over the past year.

Tonight, however, Liza had come to Nine Tails because she needed help. She had nowhere else to turn. The crowd parted before her as more and more people realized that she was having trouble standing. She stumbled past the bar and out onto the dance floor, squinting, blinking, trying to clear her blurred vision. All around her, young drunken mortals danced. The swirling bodies and the pounding music closed in. Liza could smell blood as it coursed through each of the vibrant mortals, and the hunger was tearing away at her from within. She latched onto a muscled young man who'd taken off his shirt, gave up trying to hold herself up as her face drooped toward the veins that bulged in his forearm. The Beast was rising, the hunger overpowering. It was all she could do to summon the strength to open her mouth. Her fangs slid down into place....

Someone was pulling Liza away from the luscious veins, denying her the nourishment she so desperately required. She couldn't lift her head, couldn't summon the energy to curse at whomever had hold of her.

A door opened and closed. Fresh air. The music was farther away now, though Liza could still feel the pounding of the bass through the wall. The wall. She was leaning against it. She was outside the club, her vision clearing somewhat, enough that she could see Aaron standing before her, helping hold her upright.

"Liza, are you okay?" Aaron, shorter than Liza, was looking up at her, his long ponytail tucked over his right shoulder. "Liza?"

Her head was clearing. They were in the alley beside the club. The smell of so much mortal blood was distant, but Liza could not put it out of her mind. She focused her gaze on Aaron. Vampiric vitæ was more potent, more satisfying than mortal blood. Surely he could spare a little. If he only knew how hungry she was.

"Did you hear about Emigesh?" Aaron asked, not aware of the growing danger he was in. "He showed up Wednesday night down at Little Five Points. He attacked a group of mortals!" Aaron paused to allow the immensity of what he was saying to sink in, but Liza was only half listening. She was too busy fighting the hunger, trying to keep the Beast at bay. "Of course, the prince was furious," Aaron continued. "He called in Xavier Kline. Last night, Emigesh was staked out and left for the sun."

Slowly, the words began to sink in. Emigesh was destroyed. Liza didn't have the energy to feel satisfied or angry or sad or anything. She would've killed him if she'd caught him, but the prince's one-man brute squad had taken care of that. And then there was Jolanda. Normally, vampires could recover from most injuries. For some reason, though, even fed the blood of five mortals over the course of three nights, Jolanda had wasted away. Her neck had not healed, and she had moaned horribly from hunger, which had made Liza even hungrier, if that was possible. Finally, the moaning had stopped.

Liza hadn't done anything with the body. In the five intervening nights and days it had probably deteriorated beyond recognition. Liza didn't know. She'd had to get away. Her hunger had grown so acute that she'd had to leave or else fall upon the stagnant blood seeping from Jolanda's broken body. That same hunger had grown more intense and more painful until now Liza felt as if her insides were on fire.

"Can you believe it?" Aaron asked. "Emigesh just snapped."

From growing desperation and all-consuming hunger, Liza found the strength that had been draining away for the past few weeks. In one sudden motion, she pulled Aaron to her and wrenched his head back to the side. He called out in surprise and pain, but Liza was already tearing into his exposed neck.

Muscles and tendons ripped. Blood flowed into

Liza's mouth. She swallowed greedily, sucked harder, needed more. In her need, she was overpowering. Aaron could not free his arms from where she had them pinned at his sides. Gradually, he let go of the shock and the pain as he became lost in the rapture of the kiss. His rhythmic moans kept time with each mouthful of blood that Liza drew.

She could not stop. As the blood flowed and she felt it course into her body, Liza wanted more. And more. She let go of his neck and tore into his shoulder. Blood splattered down her front. She gulped down chunks of flesh in her frenzy.

Aaron's moans died away. He was wracked by muscular spasms, but then these too ceased. His body was hanging limply in Liza's iron girp. Still she could not help herself. She bit into other parts of his body—arms, legs, chest—searching for any pocket of blood that might have eluded her. Frantically, she tore at his clothes, sinking her fangs in again and again.

There was no more blood, but still Liza hungered! Kneeling by his corpse, driven by frustration, she raised her face to the sky and screamed. Never had the hunger affected her this way. She was aware again of the music pounding on the other side of the wall behind her. Nine Tails. She could feed more inside. Damn the Masquerade! The Masquerade didn't account for pain like this.

But as suddenly as it had come, the strength of frenzy was gone. Liza was powerless to rise to her feet. Frantic but too weak to do otherwise, she slumped atop the mangled body.

Liza whimpered. She struggled to raise a hand to her face. Her nose was bleeding. And so were her eyes. She could see only red darkness. As she felt blood seeping from all parts of her body, the last sensation Liza knew was hunger.

Eleanor was always frustrated trying to lay a proper spread for the weekly bridge nights. There were only so many blood jams, blood pralines, and blood teas that one could prepare. But, ever the dutiful hostess, she persevered. And regardless of the lack of creativity of the refreshments, Rhodes Hall itself was always immaculate. Never a single cobweb in any corner, not a speck of dust on the lace draperies or any window sill. Not that Bedelia, Marlene, or Hannah had ever complained—or offered to provide refreshments, for that matter. Not once.

"I bid four spades," crowed Aunt Bedelia.

Eleanor smiled to hide a sigh. To make the evening a complete waste, it was her turn to be Bedelia's partner. The old prune of a woman was such an erratic player, and so often asleep, that the game was pointless as often as not. Hannah at least knew her cards, even if she was totally asocial and tight-mouthed to the point of catatonia. But even that was preferable to Marlene. The idiot. She prattled on about God only knew what and God only cared. And she was a better conversationalist than bridge partner.

Even so, it only took Marlene and Hannah a few minutes to run away with that hand. Bedelia hadn't even played spades. Eleanor despaired of what Kindred high society had become. She would have preferred to spend the evening with Benison and debate politics. Anything would have been more engaging than this. But appearances needed to be maintained, and as the prince's wife, she unfortunately was the one to maintain them.

Marlene paused from her mindless chatter long enough to bid. "Two diamonds. Bedelia, dear, are you with us?" The prince's decrepit sire was quietly snoring. Again. Eleanor disguised another sigh. It would be rude to go out of their way to wake Bedelia, so there was little recourse except to listen to Marlene's drivel. "And you know," Marlene continued, "even after the prince went to all that trouble to exhibit my art at the museum, there were a few folks who didn't bother to show up. Can you believe it?"

Eleanor almost envied Bedelia her age and eccentricity which allowed her to drift off whenever she pleased and completely ignore Marlene.

"I don't recall," Marlene ticked off on her fingers, "seeing Xavier Kline or Owain Evans."

"Evans was there," Hannah stated curtly.

"Yes. Hannah is right," Eleanor agreed. "I'm not surprised that Xavier doesn't have time to appreciate...art." She managed to smile sweetly at Marlene while calling those metal monstrosities *art*. "He probably had some children to frighten or kittens to dismember." Marlene tittered approvingly at Eleanor's sarcasm. "But Hannah is right that Evans was there." Eleanor was all too aware that Owain Evans was there. He was always skulking around in the background, watching everything like a vulture over a battlefield. And Benjamin had told Eleanor about the threat. Her face reddened at the very thought. Surely Owain realized that such a threat would anger her. Perhaps the upstart Ventrue needed to be put back in his place, advisor to Benison or not. Eleanor was the prince's *wife*. "He was there."

"Oh?" Marlene looked puzzled. Not an uncommon achievement, Eleanor noted.

"Probably," Hannah added in her same matter-of-fact tone, "you were distracted by Bowman's romp on your sculpture."

At the mention of the incident, Marlene's cheeks flushed visibly, even beneath the over-done makeup she habitually wore. She tried to speak but was so flustered she couldn't achieve more than a stutter.

Aunt Bedelia chose this moment to return to lucidity and piped in as well. "Albert Bowman? Little Albert with the big beard? What a nice boy, and dear Roger's friend."

Marlene was dumbfounded at this. Already embarrassed that the entire affair was a topic of discussion, Marlene was now unable even to criticize Albert who had brought her such grief. All of these ladies, the harpies of Kindred society in Atlanta, knew that although Bedelia was something of the free spirit, to put it delicately, she was the prince's sire and the voice he listened to most closely. No one directly contradicted her. So if she said Albert Bowman was a nice boy, Albert was, at least within the confines of the bridge game, the nicest of boys.

Not wishing to weep in front of the other ladies, Marlene quickly excused herself. As suddenly as Bedelia had tuned in, she seemed to have nodded off once again. Eleanor looked across the table at stodgy Hannah, the Tremere chantry leader who seldom spoke. When she did, however, the words struck to the heart like a poisoned dagger, and for the first time that evening, Eleanor's smile was genuine.

"I have heard," offered Hannah, unusually conversational, "that Xavier Kline has been busy in recent days as well." Eleanor raised her eyebrows inquisitively, although she knew exactly what the

Tremere regent was talking about. "There has been a noticeable increase in the…" Hannah paused as if searching for the correct word, but Eleanor was certain this conversation had been scripted well in advance. "…in the *lawlessness* of Kindred in the city these past few weeks."

Eleanor shrugged noncommittally and sipped her tea. "Anarchs and neonates," she tsked. "They do cause so much trouble."

Hannah smiled politely. This was a night for rarities, Eleanor noted. "We have even had trouble within the chantry," Hannah added. "Several neonates were…disciplined." Now it was Eleanor's turn to smile sympathetically. Hannah fidgeted somewhat, not comfortable with such extended social interaction. "Perhaps I should check on Marlene." The tall, slender Tremere excused herself, terminating the conversation as gracefully as she was able.

Eleanor, left only with the dozing Bedelia, laughed to herself. That was as much talk in one evening as she had heard from Hannah in a whole month previously. What led the regent to such gregariousness? And to volunteer information about problems within the chantry to an outsider—that was not typical of *any* Tremere, not even the most talkative, among whom Hannah did not number.

There had been an increase in more than just *lawlessness*, as Hannah put it, among the Cainites in the past few weeks. There were vampires going insane, attacking mortals in public, attacking one another without provocation, breaking the Masquerade in ways that left Benison little choice in how to deal with them. That's why he'd sent Xavier Kline after that maniac anarch. Neonates had been *disciplined*, Hannah had said. *Destroyed*, more likely, Eleanor was sure. It was too bizarre for coincidence. There was some connecting thread running through it all. Sabbat plot? Was an invasion imminent?

Or did these goings on smell more of Tremere treachery, Eleanor wondered. But then that must be why Hannah had broached the subject. She knew that Eleanor, and by extension Benison eventually, would suspect the Tremere and so she hinted that the Tremere too were suffering from…whatever affliction was causing Kindred to heedlessly violate the most sacred of the Traditions. Of course there was an ulterior motive behind Hannah's seemingly off-hand comments. She was Tremere, after all.

Eleanor sat back and sipped her tea. Bension had been strangely distant since this trouble had started. It wasn't like him. She decided, as Bedelia snored daintily, to speak to her husband the prince about this matter.

SEVEN

Owain could see the castle ahead through the branches. The whitewashed walls sparkled in the moonlight. The prince would be pleased that Owain had responded so promptly to the summons. How long had it been, Owain tried to remember, since he had seen Prince…Prince Benison.

The wind shifted slightly. Owain stopped and took a hard look around. *What's going on?* he wondered. He was in Atlanta, in Grant Park, not in the hills of France. And the rounded white structure ahead was the Cyclorama, not a medieval castle. Owain shook his head trying to clear his thoughts. What had come over him? It had been at least seventy-five years since he'd even set foot in Europe. But why was he in the park?

The summons—that much was real. The passenger pigeon had arrived at his house only hours ago. Most of the world believed passenger pigeons extinct, which was true of the variety mortals were aware of, but the prince had kept and bred his own since the American Civil War, or the "War Between the States," as he called it in his generous moods. If he was brooding or angry, it was the "War of Northern Aggression," or the "Second American Revolution." At any rate, he fed his pigeons on his own vampiric vitæ, creating a reliable breed of ghoul messengers. Benison often bragged that they never failed to deliver his correspondences. It was true tonight, at least. The bird had delivered the prince's summons, so Owain had roused himself from his miasma of apathy, and after hasty preparations, he was here.

His head clear, Owain scanned the surrounding area as he climbed the sweeping staircase to the entrance. No signs of anyone else in the park. He was met at the door by Vermeil, one of the prince's ghouls. Like Benison, Owain favored ghoul servants rather than creating a brood of lesser vampires to serve him. While an Embraced childe would eventually grow in power and rival his sire, a ghoul remained forever dependent, forever subservient. Owain looked around for Byron, Vermeil's partner, but saw no sign of him, and Vermeil offered no explanation. Seeing one ghoul without the other was like a puppet show of Punch with no Judy.

"The prince is waiting inside," Vermeil informed Owain in his rumbling baritone. Owain nodded. Apparently, just as he had secure access to the High Museum, the prince had arranged a means of entrance at the Cyclorama as well. Not surprising. Owain's own network of contacts and spies was perhaps more subtly placed than Benison's, but certainly the prince's was more extensive.

Owain strode through the main gallery and into the Cyclorama proper. He stepped up onto the seating platform, which was making its slow rotation around the circular chamber. The exhibit's sound was off, but the shifting illumination of the scene was functioning. The ceiling-high painted canvas was displayed in conjucntion with plaster figures of soldiers, wagons, bodies, scenery, and the like in the foreground. The various media were combined so skillfully that it was difficult at first glance, and sometimes at second or third, to discern where the painting began and the actual three-dimensional props ended. The auditorium seats, mounted on a large hydraulic-powered platform, rotated, showing the various scenes on the canvas in sequence, recreating the Battle of Atlanta, the direct precursor to the city's fall and subsequent burning in 1864.

Seated in the center of the rows of seats was Prince Benison, elbows propped on the seat in front of him, chin and auburn beard resting on his clasped hands. He did not avert his attention from the canvas. Seeing no sign of the prince's ghoul assistant Horndiller, Owain approached carefully, slowly enough to show proper respect, yet not so silently that he might startle the prince if he were completely engrossed in the replicated carnage before him. Benison was probably the most physically intimidating vampire in the city, with the possible exception of Xavier Kline; and though Owain was older and not powerless, he had no desire to surprise the prince or test his reflexes.

Owain approached to within four seats of the prince and stopped. Benison, still staring straight ahead, spoke: "Do you ever think back to battles long past, Owain? Not the victories, not the glory, but the defeats. Wondering if you did everything you could have? Wondering how many men died because of your mistakes?"

Owain nodded, confident the prince could sense his response.

Finally Benison turned toward him. There was a heaviness about him, defeat weighing upon him like Owain had never seen before. "Do you hear the voices, Owain? Do they cry and scream at you through the day as you slumber, accusing you, calling you to account for every failure?"

Again, Owain nodded. "Sometimes." The prince had never allowed Owain to see this side of him, the self-doubt, the second-guessing. Owain was not so naive as to interpret this as weakness the way many Kindred would. He knew such doubt himself, but had managed to survive for hundreds of years. Perhaps the prince respected Owain enough to know that he would not make such a mistake.

"John Hood was a good man," said Benison, indicating the painting. "He was missing an arm and a leg by '64, but he never shirked his duty, never backed down in the face of adversity. There wasn't a man alive, not even Bobby Lee, could have saved the city, not after Joe Johnston gave up the line all the way from Chattanooga." Owain listened patiently. Since the prince had not bade him sit, he remained standing. "At least Hood knew what he was up against."

In the prince's emerald eyes, Owain could see the earlier despair washing away, replaced by smoldering rage. This was more how Owain was used to seeing Benison, charging headlong over any obstacle, trampling danger underfoot. Only this time it wasn't so simple.

"There's something eating away at my city," the prince almost snarled the words. "At first I thought it was just unrest. I have to deal with that every decade or two. Kindred forget which side their bread is buttered on. Need to be shown who's in charge. Especially the younger ones, mostly the anarchs. If it weren't for the Justicar and the Council I'd clean out all the riff-raff. To some extent my hands are tied, but I do what I'm able." Wildness was flowering in Benison's eyes. Owain inched backward imperceptibly. He had seen the prince fly unpredictably into deadly rages. "I'm not sure what I'm fighting, Owain. You've heard about what's going on, I'm sure."

"Somewhat." Owain had heard about some of the trouble—outbursts of Kindred violence reported by the media as gang warfare or freakish violent crime. Gangs had never been a severe problem in relatively peaceful Atlanta, and from anything short of a bombing, the populace was slow to panic. But still, such behavior was unacceptable under the strictures of the Masquerade. Owain remembered days before the Masquerade, before the Camarilla or the Sabbat, back when in many places vampire lords held sway over the countryside and peasants huddled in their huts after sunset. Owain had been one of those vampire lords.

"Seemed like just the anarchs at first," Benison continued, "so I looked the other way. There were some fights, but nothing outside the areas I allow them—southside, Little Five Points, Reynoldstown. Then there were blatant attacks on mortals," the account was stoking his anger, "and violence against kine and Kindred alike beyond the anarch territories!" The prince slammed his fist on the seat he had been leaning on earlier. The hard plastic split from top to bottom.

Owain inched back a a bit farther.

"So I sent Xavier after the worst of the offenders. But it's *not* just the anarchs. My respectable subjects have snapped as well!" Benison ripped the damaged chair from its base and began crushing it in his powerful hands.

Owain was growing increasingly anxious over where this outburst might lead. When agitated, the prince was not known to deal with matters in the most…rational of manners.

"Ebenezer's childe Langley killed a mortal *police officer!*" Benison crumpled the seat until it cracked into jagged plastic fragments. He threw the remainder to the floor with disgust and then tossed his hands up in exasperation. "Ripped his arm off and then smashed him beneath his own cruiser. *That* is difficult to explain away. Luckily the media took it for some bizarre hit and run, thought he lost his arm in the accident." Mauling the chair seemed to provide release for at least some of the prince's fury, but Owain remained watchful. "Four other Kindred have turned up dead, shrivelled up like they'd starved, even though the bodies were full of blood; at least the bodies *had* been full of blood before it all drained out—eyes, ears, mouth, nose, anus. Blood everywhere. Even my ghouls, Horndiller and

Byron went delirious. Byron even tried to attack *me*, for God's sake!"

Owain hated to think what must have happened to Byron. The prince was not a cruel man, but in defending himself he would have dispatched Byron in no uncertain terms. *And besides*, Owain noted, *like a dog that turns on its master, a ghoul that bites the hand that feeds it must be put down.*

The prince seemed to have regained his composure to the point that Owain felt comfortable addressing him. "Those are more than I had heard. Do you have any suspicions?"

Benison guffawed. "Suspicions I have aplenty. What I need are answers." He brushed the remaining bits of plastic from his hands. "Sabbat? Some diabolical plan?"

Owain considered this for a moment. His sources hadn't revealed anything on that front, but all things considered, they might not necessarily. "Always a possibility, but with trouble still brewing in Miami, it seems odd that the Sabbat would divide its attention."

"True," the prince agreed grimly. The Sabbat, at least, was something he could root out. It was composed of individuals he could discover, confront directly, and rend limb from limb.

Owain tried to make connections. How could such a madness have taken hold of vampires within every strata of Kindred society? "Tremere magic?"

Benison shook his head and began gnawing on his lower lip. "Hannah mentioned to Eleanor just the other evening that she'd had problems with some neonates as well. She wasn't very specific, so I checked into it a bit, and two of the lesser chantry members have gone missing. I'm certain Hannah had them put down."

Put down. The same words that had run through Owain's mind moments before. Kindred were, for some mysterious reason, going wild, like dogs. The Beast was taking control, and in the Camarilla world of the Masquerade, where vampires prided themselves on retaining a certain amount of their humanity—whether that was actually the case or not—such dominance of the primal Beast could not be tolerated. *Perhaps,* Owain thought, *there is something of the smell of the Sabbat clinging to this after all.* Then a strange incongruity struck Owain.

"How did Eleanor learn this?"

"A passing comment from Hannah at their bridge game, but Eleanor suspects it was more than a passing comment," Benison elaborated. "She thinks Hannah wanted word passed along to me that the Tremere were having their own problems, so I'd know they're not responsible for whatever it is that's happening."

Owain nodded agreement. "She's most likely right in that."

The prince, seeming to notice that Owain was

still standing, and several feet away at that, motioned to the seat next to him. "Please, sit."

Owain did so, leaving a seat between the prince and himself and hoping Benison wouldn't notice. "Hannah is not one for small talk." As Owain pondered Eleanor's news, something bothered him about his fellow Ventrue's assumption. "She certainly didn't let that comment slip accidentally. Hannah, that is. She wanted you to know the Tremere were having problems as well." Owain gathered his thoughts. "And that may be all there is to it. She may be trying to clear herself of suspicion, as Eleanor suggested, because Hannah knows other Kindred are naturally suspicious of the Tremere."

"And with good reason," Benison added.

"And with good reason. Yes." It had been so long since Owain had taken an active interest in local politics, since anything other than his own boredom and sense of loss had occupied his thoughts. This was not chess. He was sluggish in connecting his converging trains of thought. "And that might be all there was to it." Benison waited for Owain's point. "But why wouldn't Hannah, as regent of the Tremere chantry, tell you that herself formally, so there was no room for misunderstanding? Why risk Eleanor not coming to that conclusion and you not getting the message?"

Benison pondered this briefly. "I suspect she had

no doubt that Eleanor was astute enough to register the comment and report it to me."

"But why wouldn't Hannah tell you directly?"

"It would be a public admission that the Tremere had no more an idea than the rest of us of what is going on," said the prince. "It would be an embarrassment."

"Yes," Owain agreed, "and if the Tremere did know what was going on, they would keep quiet and use that information against everyone else." The prince nodded. "Officially," Owain added.

The light of realization began to shine in the prince's eyes. "So publicly the Tremere have made no statement regarding the crisis…"

"While privately they have allayed your suspicions," Owain completed the statement.

"But what of the disciplined neonates?"

"Hidden, or destroyed," Owain shrugged, "or some lesser punishment. It hardly matters. Probably Hannah was vague intentionally, so that you might jump to the wrong conclusion. As did Eleanor."

The prince shot Owain a hard glance at that comment. One could only go so far in criticizing the prince's wife. Probably one reason that Benison did seek out Owain's opinion was that he was, to some extent, a rival of Eleanor's, though she, the former archon, held the Ventrue seat on the primogen and took the fore in political matters.

Owain was more a neutral voice, or so the prince undoubtedly thought. At any rate, Owain knew better than to push too far on that front.

"So," the prince concluded, "the Tremere are most likely behind my problems." The familiar light of vengeance shone in his eyes.

"Possibly, but not necessarily likely," Owain cautioned.

Benison's gaze turned questioning.

"Hannah may, like you suggested, only have been assuaging your concerns," Owain pointed out.

The prince's brow furrowed and he clenched his fists. With a roar of rage, he ripped another chair from its base and hurled it across the room. Even in his fury, however, the prince was careful not to hit the painting or the models and possibly mar the tribute to the defining days of his mortal existence. "Damnation!" he bellowed, language he never would have used had ladies been present. "I want to take action, and you give me 'maybes' and 'possibilities.'"

Owain remained respectfully silent as Benison gradually calmed once again. "One thing is certain," Owain eventually continued. "Hannah would not have revealed the internal goings on of the chantry without direction from higher up. Either her comment was a decoy to falsely ease your suspicions, or she was instructed by her superiors, possibly her lord or pontifex, to divulge that information."

The prince, his passions in check for the moment, still fumed. "Then we have nothing to go on."

"No answers, but much to go on," Owain politely contested. "Watch the Tremere closely. Perhaps inquire discreetly with other princes as to whether they are experiencing similar difficulties. This madness seems too imprecise a weapon only to be levelled at Atlanta."

"There are even whispers," the prince growled, "of the Dark Times, of the approach of Gehenna, and of a curse upon us Cainites."

"Every age has its religious fanatics," Owain assured the prince. "The approach of the millenium, and any catastrophe, makes them more active, but no more accurate."

"And there is still the Sabbat," Benison reminded Owain. "I believe it is time to call in several younger Kindred whom I have heard rumored to have Sabbat sympathies, and question them rather vigorously." The prince seemed to derive satisfaction from the idea. "That should also serve to keep the anarchs in check."

Owain waited deferentially. Even if they didn't know what they were dealing with, they had decided whom to check up on. That much, having established at least a vague plan of action, seemed to comfort the prince.

"Come." Benison rose and Owain followed him

from the auditorium. Vermeil, absent Byron, waited at the door. "Clean up inside, lock up, and meet me at the car," Benison instructed.

"Yes, sir."

Owain's Rolls was in the lot beside the prince's limousine. It was odd, Owain thought, that he had become so disoriented, just an hour earlier, between the car and the Cyclorama. Could it be related to his other maladies, to the absentmindedness and ennui that had so plagued him of late? Then another thought struck him. Poor deceased Byron had become delirious. All over the city vampires were going insane. Was there a curse? Was he under its sway?

Owain shook his head and chastised himself for even thinking such nonsense. But at the same time, a familiar wave of exhaustion swept over him. Did he really care, he wondered, what the problem was, with him or with the city? It would be so much easier to return home and study his chess board, to leave the problems to the prince, and Eleanor, and Hannah. Even descending the stairs at the prince's side, such ideas sounded ever so attractive.

These thoughts were interrupted by the sound of gunfire.

The first shots strayed high, the bullets zinging over Owain's and the prince's heads. Automatic weapons of some type. Owain knew that much from the sound of the shots, though he'd never bothered to learn much about modern weapons. As

Owain crouched to make a smaller target, he realized that Benison was charging off to their left—the direction the shots were coming *from!* Instinctively, Owain glanced to his right. Two figures were charging in ambush from that side, raising guns to fire.

More quickly than he could even think, Owain whipped off his overcoat and tossed it billowing into the air. With the merest of psychic prods from Owain, the two attackers opened fire on the garment as it fell to the ground. In that brief instant of mental contact, Owain knew that the attackers were vampires as well, but younger, and not trained in the older arts.

The two men, both armed with semi-automatic machine guns, stopped to examine the lifeless overcoat. Perplexed, they kicked at it in the dirt. From behind them, Owain advanced from the shadows where he had so easily blended. Again instinctively, he reached for his sword—the sword he had not worn into battle in centuries and even now was hanging on the wall of his trophy room. He realized his error instantly, and snapped down the stiletto from the forearm sheath he had strapped on earlier that evening, but the delay cost him.

The two vampires turned just as Owain attacked. The first stumbled backward firing into the air, his throat slit by Owain's lightning swipe. The second, however, fired a burst that caught Owain in the left shoulder.

He was knocked backward by the force of the blast and hit the ground rolling. The next burst of bullets chewed up the ground where Owain would have been, but already he was around and on his assailant. A jab through the eye into the brain, and the contest was decided.

Owain quickly checked his first victim. The slit throat was severe enough that not even a vampire could recover quickly enough to aid his compatriots. Owain, slowed but not incapacitated by the slugs in his shoulder, rushed on to help the prince.

Benison was in the midst of a scene of pure carnage. Three bodies, vampires, Owain assumed, lay broken and bleeding on the ground. Benison, bleeding from dozens of bullet wounds, wrestled on the ground with two more attackers. Two additional enemies stood nearby with weapons levelled, waiting only for a clear shot at the prince.

Owain, with centuries of practice to his credit, let fly his knife, catching one of the bystanders square in the throat. He staggered and fell.

The second man turned and fired.

At the same instant, a cannon went off by Owain's ear. It sounded like a cannon to Owain, at any rate. Actually it was a .45 magnum fired right behind him, and fortunately for Owain, it was wielded by his driver Kendall Jackson. Her shot slammed through her target's forehead and continued on its way with most of the back of his head.

An echoing, spine-shattering crack from Benison's direction indicated the fight had concluded. He tossed aside the final of the two more recent corpses and staggered toward Owain. The prince's surcoat was shredded and bloody. He must have taken countless rounds at close range and was bleeding profusely from wounds in his chest, arms, belly, and head.

"Jackson," Owain instructed tersely, "stake one, then bring a fire axe from inside and decapitate the rest." She relayed the information to Vermeil who, alerted by the gunfire, had rushed out of the building. He turned back and went for the axe.

"A fine show, Owain," the prince bellowed. "They didn't have cavalry. Infantry with no support. What were they thinking?"

Owain ignored the prince's anachronistic tactical analysis. Benison was still functioning somehow. How could he sustain so much damage and walk? Owain was feeling slightly weak at the knees from loss of blood, and he'd taken significantly fewer hits than the prince. "Jackson, let Vermeil handle the axe. Help the prince to the Rolls and take him back to Rhodes Hall." Owain noticed that Jackson had been hit in the leg by that last burst of machine gun fire, but she did not hesitate to carry out his orders. Surprisingly, the prince leaned on her shoulder and allowed himself to be aided.

"After them, Owain! We'll take the attack to

them!" Benison called back over his shoulder. A moment later, Jackson roared away.

The prince taken care of, Owain retrieved his stiletto and staked the vampire in whose neck it had been embedded. Then he took the axe from Vermeil, who had just returned, and with a single stroke apiece, beheaded the defeated aggressors while Vermeil dragged the staked vampire to the prince's car.

There was no time to dispose of the bodies properly. The police would be arriving any second, as much gunplay as had gone on. Surely someone in the houses ringing Grant Park had called 911. The prince would have to rely upon his pawns within the police force and the coroner's office to safeguard the Masquerade.

These gun-wielding vampires were no mad or cursed Kindred, and they were no regular inhabitants of the city. They were Sabbat. And this was no coincidence.

As Owain joined Vermeil at the limousine, the wounded Ventrue heard something above the wail of approaching police sirens. It was a soft tune floating on the evening breeze, but somehow it made itself known to Owain over the blaring sirens. The music caught hold of Owain's attention and would not let go, not even when Vermeil urged him into the car so they could escape. The chaos swirling around Owain was immaterial. Suddenly the song was all that mattered, all that was real, more than the carnage on the lawn, more than the throbbing in his shoulder.

"Go without me," he told Vermeil, and the ghoul didn't wait to be told twice. His tires screeched as he whipped out of the parking lot, not anxious to be stopped with a staked vampire in the back seat.

The song continued. It was familiar somehow, similar to a tune Owain couldn't quite recall.

The police lights were visible now, coming south on Boulevard at high speed. And another squad car from the other direction, lights flashing. They converged at the Cyclorama parking lot. Spotlights scanned the area, and officers with flashlights and revolvers drawn moved among the lifeless bodies on the lawn.

But Owain was long gone.

Terror gripped Gisela by the shoulder. Death stared at her from inches away. Smiling. Laughing at her. Mocking her with its skeletal grin. She wanted to pummel its bony visage, to reach out and crush its infernal skull in her vise-like fingers. She wanted to make it *pay!*

But the hunger would not let her. It kept her arms wrapped around her body trying to keep the pain at bay. It kept her doubled over in agony. Somehow she would crush it. She would grind the bones to dust and spit upon the remains. Her wrathful scream tore through the night. She would not die like Dietrich, whimpering, crying like a little baby. She would rule Berlin one day! Herr Himmler had as much as promised. She would not die like a pitiful mewing kitten. She mustn't!

"AAAARRR!"

"Gisela? Gisela! What is the matter? Where is Dietrich?"

Death was speaking to her. So a tongue did waggle behind his white teeth. Well then, she would just have to rip it out after she kicked through those teeth.

"Gisela, calm down!"

How dare Death try to console her, to ease her toward him. She would not be comforted. She would not go quietly.

Then Death's mask fell away and Frank was looking down at her. They were in her basement lair, the place that stunk of rot, the place where Dietrich, *the leprous scheisskopf*, had wasted away in his insanity until finally he'd virtually exploded, his very skin rupturing and spraying blood all over like the pipes from the factories used to spew their chemicals into the river in the good old days.

The blood. Gisela could still smell the liters that foul demented Dietrich had bled. And him claiming hunger. He knew nothing of the hunger that tore at Gisela.

"Gisela, calm down." Death's voice was gentler now, closer.

Yes, come closer. Who else was there? Gisela tried to recall, but another wave of hunger swept over her, consumed her, ravaged her. Death. Death only. Ever so slowly she reached up, her hands inching upward, trembling with rage. Rage and hunger. She could feel his face—his mouth, his nose, his ears.

"Gisela, I am here."

Yes. You are come for me. But I will not go! "AAAARRR!"

"No! Let go!"

You are so soft, Death. I will crush you!

"Ah! No! Gisela!"

But Death was slippery as well as soft and managed to pull away. Gisela was slipping beneath the waves of her hunger. She held in her hand…an ear? *But Death's head is a skull,* she thought, perplexed. Then she smelled more blood. Death's blood. As Death ran screaming away. Gisela licked the ear. Sweet blood. Death's gift. But it did not ease her pain.

The Beast rose within in her, and she chewed at gristly flesh. First the ear, but that was no comfort. Then a finger. And another. Palm. Muscles. Tendon. Knuckle bones crunching. She tore at her own flesh and wept pained tears of blood.

In the end, another wave of hunger rose above her and carried her away.

EIGHT

"Why?" It was a question Roger should have known better than to ask Albert by now. As usual, Albert's pleas were impassioned, if not rational.

"Can't you hear it? Listen." Albert turned his face to the sky and closed his eyes. A blissful expression came over him.

"I hear traffic."

Albert frowned, looked over at Roger. "That's why I'm taking you. Once you hear..." His words were interrupted by what might have been gunfire in the distance.

"I can't leave my car here," Roger protested, but Albert pulled him along.

"Nobody's going to mess with your car."

Roger was doubtful. He hadn't grown up in Reynoldstown, but he'd grown up in a neighborhood not too different from it. Albert was insistent, though, and against his better judgment, Roger acquiesced.

Albert led him through the run-down low-income residential area. When they saw other people, mostly young African-American men, they re-routed so as not to attract undue attention. Albert was in a hurry and, for once, didn't want to be slowed by distractions.

They came shortly to an old Baptist church, long since abandoned and left to the depravities of urban squalor. The little remaining paint peeled from bowed planks. Windows were broken, the steeple partially collapsed.

"Why are you bringing me here?" Roger whispered, then wondered why he was whispering. Albert shushed him nonetheless.

They waited in the shadows as a young black man entered the building. Roger noticed for the first time that a dim light flickered from within the building. Again, Albert was lost in his blissful reverie, eyes closed, face upturned. Until Roger smacked him on the arm. *"What?"* Roger pestered him.

Albert sighed. "You still don't hear?"

What? The voices in your head? Roger wanted to ask, but he knew that might hurt his friend's feelings. "*Hear what?*" Roger whispered instead.

Albert sighed again and threw his hands up into the air. "Fine. Have it your way." With this, he took Roger by the sleeve and pulled him toward the front door of the church.

Roger held back. "But there's somebody in there."

"Exactly." Albert's sudden grin unnerved Roger, but he followed.

As the door creaked open and they crossed the threshold, Roger did hear, and he felt foolish for having questioned his friend. Without meaning to, Roger stopped and stood in the open doorway. The sweetest sound he had ever heard wafted over him. It was a song, a song he almost recognized, and as it passed through him and over him, it carried away his worries, all the nightly concerns that weighed so heavily upon him.

In his mind's eye, Roger could see the prince smiling proudly at his childe, not ashamed of the timidity that had taken hold of Roger since his Embrace. For in this vision, Roger was not timid. He was the tall powerful hero that he had been during the war, an African-American fighting for a country that despised him, but fighting valiantly regardless, because it was the right thing to do.

And he saw his mother. Her eyes were open, and she was rising from her sickbed of so many years. She smiled at Roger. She loved him. She didn't hate him for what he'd become. She put her arms around him. Tugged at his shirt.

No. That was Albert. Pulling him forward. Toward the front of the dilapidated sanctuary. Toward the slim, pale woman who sang, whose song took Roger where he had wanted to go every night of his unlife. Roger let himself be led.

There were mortals already present—African-American, Korean, young, old, male, female—and with Albert, Roger knelt down beside them. He'd been hungry earlier in the evening, but now thoughts of mortal blood were far from his mind as he closed his eyes and willingly let the song take him.

His mother smiled....

Owain easily eluded the police. There was no mortal born who could see him if he wished otherwise. As squad car after squad car rushed to the Cyclorama and then shortly began combing the surrounding areas, Owain quickly wove his way among the houses of the neighborhoods bordering Grant Park. To his keen senses, some of the buildings still smelled of fresh paint, the fruits of gentrification. Many of the other structures had seen better days. Everywhere shadows obligingly reached out to envelop Owain, hiding him from unfriendly eyes as he followed the music that had caught his interest so suddenly and so intensely.

In the back of his mind, he still worried about the bodies left behind. A few would no doubt crumble to dust before the police knew what was happening. Sabbat vampires, however, because of the incredible attrition rate within the sect, tended to be relatively young, and so several of the decapitated corpses would most likely be recovered by the authorities. *Ah, well*, Owain thought. *Nothing to be done about it now.* The prince would have to deal with that little difficulty. He would know the necessary strings to pull.

Such thoughts vanished instantly as Owain was once again captivated by the lilting tune that called to him through the night. There were only a few bare notes, but their simplicity and elegance reminded him of…and then the melody shifted again, blurring the association, pushing it just beyond Owain's grasp. The song was maddeningly familiar and deceptively vague. The powerful infatuation it induced overpowered all other concerns—his painful shoulder, the bodies, the prince's health.

Where was it coming from? Owain wondered. Following the music, he travelled north, crossing the downtown interstate connector. The large houses of the Grant Park area gave way to slightly smaller frame buildings in dire need of upkeep. Scrawny trees full of kudzu shared cramped yardspace with waist-high weeds and junked cars. Small brick stores were dark, windows and doors barred against the night.

More mortals loitered about here plying their goods, whether drugs or their own bodies. *They don't hear it*, Owain realized. Otherwise, they would be streaming in the same direction he was. *There is magic about this song.* Owain, in his days and nights, had experienced powers that modern men would scoff at rather than believe existed. Even some Cainites, never mind the proof provided by their own existence, refused to believe in other supernatural powers. Owain knew better.

As he continued on, he revealed his presence to none of the mortals who were so unsuspecting—unsuspecting of the magic in their midst, unsuspecting of the predator passing so closely, to whom it would be a mere trifle to reach out and snuff their lives like a candle flame between his fingers.

Vermeil did not hear it either, Owain remembered. Were ghouls as imcapable of perceiving the song as mortals seemed to be? *No way to know.* And what of other vampires? Was Owain going to find all the Kindred of Atlanta converged at the source of the mysterious music?

Still the song drew him onward. Owain had covered several miles, leaping fences with ease, passing chained dogs before they'd even noticed his scent, proceeding swiftly and silently through the night. Even so, the music did not grow louder. The melody and the tune constantly shifted, frustrating Owain's efforts to place what he was sure he almost recognized, but the volume never increased or decreased. Owain could not tell if he was drawing closer, or if perhaps he had inadvertently turned away and was heading off in the wrong direction. The notes maintained their delicacy, as if they were being sung in a tender whisper for him alone from only feet away.

But just as that realization crossed Owain's mind, he turned the corner and knew that he was there.

He stopped. Litter blew down the street before him as the wind picked up to a steady gust. Large raindrops began to splatter loudly to the ground, speckling the broken sidewalk dark. Still, the music called, inviting Owain to the old church ahead, battered by time more harshly than it was now battered by the increasingly strong rain that slapped against weathered planks and crumbling ceiling. Owain wasn't sure how he knew the music was coming from the church, but there was no doubt in his mind.

Slowly, deliberately, his measured paces carried him down the center of the street toward the object of his quest. The mortal denizens of the night had all run for cover from the storm, but Owain was oblivious to the stinging rain and biting wind that whipped his hair and overcoat behind him.

The church was obviously abandoned, at least by the mortal worshippers of the God who had so cruelly taunted Owain over the centuries. Try as he had on occasion, Owain had never been able to achieve the rewarding detachment of atheism. He couldn't quite come to accept that some impersonal force or blind chance had visited such an abundance of injustices upon him, from watching his fool brother ascend the throne of beloved Rhufoniog nearly a thousand years before, to the most recent inexplicable collapse of Owain's battle strategy on the chess board. Owain was only too aware of God's existence, and of his mocking laughter at insults grand and small.

For that reason, it was with mixed feelings that Owain approached the dilapidated church, and it was this cynicism born of centuries of experience that allowed Owain to hear the song more clearly. It still beckoned, but Owain was no longer enraptured by its lure. Its beauty did not cease to tug at him, but now it did so gently, and Owain's will was his own.

Anger was kindled within him at the thought of having been entranced, of having traipsed across half the city like a lustful mortal drooling after a plunging neckline. Anger, and then not a little curiosity. Not since his days among the illfated Templars in France had Owain sensed preternatural power so keenly. Perhaps there were wonders hidden in Atlanta to rival the forgotten mystical practices of the Knights of the Temple.

The otherworldly spell of the music broken by very worldly yet potent cynicism, Owain found himself still standing in the middle of the street, water running down his face, hair plastered against his neck and shoulders by the rain which had moved well beyond spattering speckles and was rapidly progressing to torrential downpour. Blood, still trickling from his wounds, mixed with the water. He moved over the crumbling sidewalk and through the tall weeds into the shadows around the church.

The building had not been cared for in years, and Owain suspected that normally kine and Kindred alike would pass it by without a second thought. He didn't believe he had been down this street before, but even walking past, he wouldn't have spared a glance for the sagging church were it not for the music. Owain was not the only one to have taken notice this night, however. He could hear heartbeats from within—seven, maybe eight mortals. So vampirically enhanced senses were not required to detect the song. But then why weren't more mortals streaming to the church? And why, Owain wondered, hadn't he heard the song before? Was this the first time it had been sung? Many questions puzzled him, and still there was the sweetly enticing music, though now he could listen to it with more detached appreciation rather than being drawn in completely as he had been before. There was much here to discover, and Owain felt strangely intrigued.

Stepping through overgrown shrubs, willing his fingers to claws, and fighting the increasing stiffness in his shoulder, he began to scale the side of the building. Silently, Owain made his way toward the half-collapsed steeple, testing each claw hold lest one of the rotting boards rip loose in his grasp. A fall would hurt nothing more than his pride, but until he answered at least a few of his questions, Owain did not want his presence discovered.

The footing became more treacherous near the top, but he found an opening easily enough and managed to squeeze through without dislodging any of the precariously attached boards. If the steeple had ever been more than ornamental, all traces of the bell or bells were long gone. Across from Owain, the ceiling had caved in and what remained sagged dangerously, so he had to squat to move even slightly into the small chamber in order to reach the trap door set in the center of the floor. With the patience of a diamond cutter, he opened the door.

The softly lilting voice, which had remained at much the same level all the way from Grant Park to this point, flooded in around Owain. It wasn't that the volume increased as much as that the very sound—and Owain could tell it was a woman's voice now—seemed almost to take on a tangible substance. The sound surrounded Owain, caressed him, gently called him onward. He began to lower himself through the trap door, then caught himself and stopped. He fought the impulse to climb down through the chamber below him and down further into the sanctuary with the others, an impulse which felt so natural, so reasonable.

Another moment of steeling his will, and Owain was fully in control of himself once again. The momentary struggle, an actual contest of wills, was something he had not experienced in decades. It was hardly an effort at all to shield his mind from the Kindred of Atlanta, but whoever was singing below…this was something different. The internal conflict was made more difficult by Owain's injuries as well. Not only was the pain distracting from his concentration, much of his energy had been diverted over the past hour to the healing process which his vampiric vitæ had already begun.

The room Owain was staring down into was little more than a closet, the one door blocked by rubble consisting in part of what were probably pieces of the old ladder once used to reach the belfry. Closer to Owain was a portion of collapsed floor through which he could see a corner of the sanctuary and flickering light from an unseen flame. The delicate vibrato of the alluring song wafted through the hole to him, but he could find no angle that afforded a view of anyone in the sanctuary beneath.

With graceful ease, Owain lowered himself through the trap door into the belfry antechamber. He had no way to be sure the floor below would support his weight. Staying back from the edge of the hole, squatting low, and keeping his weight spread as much as possible, he maneuvered to a better vantage point and hoped the slight creaking of the boards would be masked by the rain and wind outside.

The mortals knelt in a small cluster near the front of the sanctuary, their heads bowed as if in worship. Behind them, broken pews were shoved in disarray against the walls. Owain strained his neck to see a bit farther back and was quite surprised by what he saw. Kneeling a few feet behind the mortals were two figures he recognized and knew rather well—Albert and the prince's son Roger. Roger blended in well enough; aside from two women, one Korean, one caucasian, the other five mortals were African-American. Albert, however, stood out almost anywhere he went. Something about his wiry figure and unruly beard, even when he was quietly kneeling like now, seemed to separate him from whatever crowd of which he might be a part.

So I'm not the only Kindred to hear the song, Owain

realized. *But why these two and no one else? Are others on the way?* Owain supposed he was hidden well enough if any one else arrived. He preferred to remain out of sight and learn more about what others were doing than what they learned about him.

Since he had opened the trap door and briefly been overcome by the attraction of the song, Owain had been blocking out the music, refusing to allow it a foothold by which it could take control of him. The longer he held it at bay, the less concentration was required to do so. Owain suspected that Albert was capable of the same control, but Roger, from the looks of him a much younger vampire, maybe fifty years undead, seemed to be as entranced by the music as the mortals. Whatever magic was at work, it was potent enough to snare the unwary vampire no matter how old. Owain had not forgotten the sensation that had brought him across town before he'd been able to regain his senses.

The most significant question remained: who was singing? Owain could not see the very front of the sanctuary, the direction the mortals and Kindred alike faced and seemed to direct their reverence toward. Carefully, quietly, he began to edge around the hole for a better view. Outside, the storm was increasing in its intensity. Rain and wind lashed against the old church. Trying to see the front of the sanctuary and at the same time not to crash through the crumbling floor, Owain was half stretched out on his belly, as much as he could be in the cramped space without getting so close to the edge as to be visible.

It may just have been his imagination or perhaps a trick of the acoustics, but as Owain inched to where he could see the figure before the toppled pulpit, her song, incredible already, became even more crisp, her voice more clear and sharp. A shiver ran down Owain's spine, and he dug his fingernails into his palms, forcing himself not to give in to the beautiful sound, not to let himself be carried away by the soothing tones as he wanted to be. Luckily, Owain had never allowed himself, in life or unlife, the luxury of solace, whether from sources human or divine, and this case was no exception.

Owain maintained his hardened will as he looked upon the vision of pale beauty who stood before the assembled congregation. Narrow face tilted upward, eyes closed, her barely parted lips moved with a grace and ease that betrayed none of the consequence of her song. He listened more carefully, trying to determine wherein lay the power of the music, so that he could more effectively defend himself against it, and realized that, even though the song was not composed of words, certain images were conveyed. The melody was a living and breathing thing unto itself, rising and swelling, then gently flowing away, leaving only serenity and peace in its wake. Owain watched the hem of her lace gown as it rippled in the draft, and he was reminded of the salty foam on the cold Irish Sea. He could hear the waves rolling in to the rocky shore and squinted against the windborne spray. Amidst the chill, the melodious and comforting warmth tenderly wrapped itself around him. The cold was held at bay, the rumbling of thunder far away. There were ships at sea that would shatter against the rocks in the coming storm, sailors who would be dragged to the bottom like so many before, but Owain was safe and warm upon the shore. The flickering fire beckoned....

Owain shook his head, returning himself to the church. Thunder did rumble in the distance, but the wind was blowing through holes in the belfry, not in from a coastal sea, and the fire that beckoned was from some fisherman's shack but rather from the candles in the sanctuary. The power of the song was more potent than Owain had suspected. Perhaps it would be better, for now at least, not to concentrated too intently on the music itself, he decided.

Just as Owain thought this, the tempo of the music began to shift subtly. The beautiful pale siren was still the picture of serenity, but her song slowly grew in intensity. At the edge of his consciousness, Owain could just feel the pull that he continued to block, the desire to join the others, to become one with the group below. As the song evolved, an urgency was added to that desire, and slowly as Owain listened, that urgency took root and continued to grow, entwining itself around every strand of the music.

Owain was well in control of himself now, but as he watched the mortals and even Albert and Roger, their expressions changed from content to yearning. Probably, Owain imagined, the music did not evoke images of the Welsh coast and the Irish Sea for them. Whatever opiate they were experiencing, though, was no longer enough as the song took hold of their needs and made them dominant over all else. Just as years before Owain had seen the reassurance others found in God or in family but had been had been unable to derive such comfort himself, now he could feel where the music was taking this group but refused to be taken himself.

As his thoughts began to wander, movement below caught Owain's eye. The siren and her congregation still held their same places, but new players had entered the stage. First one, then a second, and then a third woman drifted into the sanctuary from where Owain could not see. They seemed almost to float on the notes of the song, their bare feet hardly touching the worn and moldy carpet. Two of the three were pale, like the siren, the third a rich, dark brown. All were beautiful and young, girls really, maybe seventeen. Owain had not noticed the youth of the siren before, caught up as he was by the ancient texture of her song.

Unlike the siren's short and simple hair, the newcomers possessed wild manes with bits of ivy and honeysuckle braided throughout the tangles. They danced to the rising song, and their movements bespoke barely harnessed savagery. They reminded Owain of the wild maenads of Greek mythology. While the siren sang, the sound issuing from an unfathomable well of loss and pain and need, and the gathered mortals and Kindred swayed and shivered, the newest three arrivals circled. As the song gathered intensity, so did their dance. They too were riding an escalating wave of primal desire.

Owain clenched his fists against the song, and the power of his blood, the potency of his curse, enabled him to hold his own, to watch and listen but not be carried away.

Slowly, the siren raised her hands above her, and her song gathered force. The maenads twirled and spun, the energy of their desire whipped to a frenzy. The mortals, too, moaned and twitched. Some whipped their heads from side to side, eyes held tightly shut, need and ecstasy hopelessly entwined. Roger whimpered. Tears of blood dribbled down his cheeks. Of all those congregated, only Albert knelt and listened placidly.

The dance of the maenads grew more ragged and

furious. Their white chiffon gowns alternately billowed and clung to the slender forms as the women whirled. For brief instants, the sheer fabric revealed the curve of hip and thigh and breast. One after another, the dancers threw back their heads, lashing about their ivy-laced hair like cruel whips. Fangs glimmered in the candle light.

The draw of the hunger was overwhelming. Even Owain felt it.

The maenads tore at their gowns, rending bloody gashes down taut, quivering chests. As one, they howled madly at the vaulted ceiling and then fell upon the mortals.

The Korean woman's body jerked with the recoil of the blow as one maenad bit into her with the force of a rattlesnake lunging at a victim. Some of the mortals were knocked over sideways as the dancers pounced and drank deeply but briefly. Even Roger and Albert were fed upon, but no one, mortal or vampire, was roused from the trance. Each attack seemed to be the culmination of the victim's vision of ecstasy. Pain and rapture mingled and were one.

Owain could feel the power of the song, but he had no way of knowing what each individual below was experiencing. He was too busy maintaining his own self control. Otherwise, he might have leapt down into the sanctuary and fed as well.

The climax of the song and the feeding lasted

less than a minute. With an abrupt shift in cadence, the music dropped away to a calmer level. The strain of desire and urgency that a moment before had seemed its entirety began to fade. The soothing undertones began to reassert themselves.

The maenads reacted as if they had been struck a physical blow. They reluctantly withdrew from their final victims, obviously wanting desperately to continue feeding. But they obeyed the song. Their bodies shuddered momentarily as the frenzy gave way to the increasingly soothing melody.

For the first time, the siren spoke, weaving one word into her retreating song: "*Adref.*"

Owain's mouth fell open. His heart almost broke at the sound of the word.

The maenads responded also. Slowly, they backed away from the kneeling and sprawled congregation and withdrew beyond Owain's line of sight.

As they recessed, the siren, stately in her beauty, slowly moved forward. Her song died away to a faint whisper but carried just as clearly to every hidden corner of the church. She approached a young black man who was unconscious, bent down to him, and gently licked the wounds the maenads had inflicted on him. Not even then, with her tongue upon his neck, did her song cease. It continued as if a living being of its own.

One after another, she licked the wounds of her

flock, and as she did so, the torn flesh was healed, and each person smiled in their slumber.

Owain edged back from the hole and leaned against the wall, a profound exhaustion sweeping over him. The flickering melody still carried to him, but it was the one word the siren had uttered that echoed in his ears.

Adref.

Spoken in his native Welsh that he had not heard for so long.

Adref. Homeward.

For an instant, he thought he smelled the sea air again, and it was more than he could stand. Battling the stiffness of his momentarily forgotten wounds, Owain slipped out through the trap door and down the outer wall of the church.

Adref. Homeward.

He left the church, rushing through the night more swifly and silently than a shadow. More so than miles, time and his own actions separated Owain from his true home, and since there was no way to run there, he ran away into the accepting darkness of the night.

It was not often that Prince Benison called upon Hannah at the chantry. Luckily, her neonates always maintained the facilities properly, so no additional preparations were required before receiving him. Though with only two apprentices on hand instead of four, they were hard pressed to molify Hannah's fastidiousness and perform their other duties. But the nights of an apprentice were not meant to be filled with leisure.

Hannah personally greeted the prince at the door of her sprawling mansion, most of which was given over to the chantry's needs.

"Good evening, Hannah." The prince was gracious, as he always was unless particularly riled. He seemed to have healed with no ill effects from the injuries Hannah gathered he had sustained two nights before. "What news do you have?"

Hannah frowned. She had less to report than she would have liked, and though Benison was physically well, the tension coiled within his massive form and burning intensely in his eyes was unmistakable. There had been so little time, and all her regular studies placed on hold...but the prince would not care for excuses. "The prisoner that Eleanor had Vermeil deliver..."

"Yes?" The prince was hungry for any information.

"He is definitely Sabbat. Or *was* Sabbat, at any rate."

Benison slammed his fist into his palm. "Just as I suspected. And...?"

Again Hannah frowned. She fidgeted slightly where she stood, realizing suddenly that she had neither shown the prince in beyond the foyer or offered him a seat. She did not have a mind for niceties, and the prince had more urgent matters on his mind. Therein lay the problem. "The Sabbat conditioning is so complete, and the bestial nature of his mind…"

"What did you find out?" Benison interrupted her.

Hannah choked off the elaborate explanation she had been rehearsing in her mind. "Only that his pack was instructed to wait outside the Cyclorama and attack whomever left. I did not discover the identity of his superior who issued the order, if he even knew. And my impression was that he was not aware that you were the target of the attack."

Now it was Benison's turn to scowl. "Your *'impression?'*" This was obviously not the news the prince had hoped to hear. "Eleanor entrusts you with this interrogation on my behalf while I'm convalescing, and that is all you can tell me?" The prince's severe tone betrayed the pressures under which he labored. "I expect I can do better myself. Take me to him."

"He was questioned quite…thoroughly, I assure you."

"Still," the prince insisted, "I will try my hand…" A sudden realization swept over him. "Questioned 'quite thoroughly,' you say? He did not survive the interrogation?"

"The magics required to bypass Sabbat conditioning are not gentle," Hannah pointed out.

For an instant, Benison clenched his teeth and tensed every muscle in his body. But then, remarkably, he closed his eyes and sighed deeply out of frustration. "I see."

They stood in silence for a moment, but Hannah could not stomach the disdain she imagined radiating from the prince. Somewhat awkwardly she began to ask, "May I show you in…to a seat, or get…?"

"I'm afraid I don't have time to dawdle," said Benison, implying perhaps, Hannah wondered, that she could have used her time more efficiently? "What can you tell me of this…" he fumbled for the right word, "…this *affliction* that is destroying my city?" He nearly spit the words out, his bitterness and frustration getting the best of him momentarily.

"There has been so little time, Prince Benison." She could see him bristle, and so hurried on. "My experiments are under way. I *have* determined that magics of some sort are at work, though of a type with which I am not familiar. I have begun consultation with my superiors both in this country and in Vienna, for as you know, this 'affliction' is not a localized matter." Though she glossed over certain technical details, Hannah held nothing back from the prince. She could sense that he would brook no duplicity in this matter, and she was not willing to risk his wrath.

"The affliction," she explained, slightly more comfortable engaged in professional discourse, "does seem to be blood related. The magic is triggering a transformation of some sort within the vitæ itself, but as I said, I am not familiar with the particular forces involved."

Benison had listened silently, never shifting his gaze from the chantry regent until she was finished. "A curse," he muttered, almost to himself. "It has been called down upon us, and now we are doubly cursed—once for the sins of Caine, once for our own." The prince seemed to have forgotten Hannah for a moment, but now he returned his focus to her. "Time is what we may not have," he reminded her. "I suggest you *become* familiar with whatever forces are at work."

Without another word, the prince turned and stalked out of the chantry. Hannah watched him go. Having enjoyed his stated and implied reproach not at all, she resolved that she would just have to work harder…if that were possible. It would have to be.

It was all Benison could do to keep himself from smashing his fist through the window of the limousine. He wanted—*needed*—to throttle someone.

As Vermeil drove him along Ponce De Leon Avenue away from the Tremere chantry, he fumed at the thought that there was nothing he could do. *There must be something!* But what? If Hannah and her sorcerous ilk were helpless against the curse, how could he save his city?

And there were other complications. The Sabbat attack might signal that those hellspawn thought he was weak enough to overwhelm. He would have to watch for signs of a gathering assault. He would almost welcome such an opoprtunity to release his pent up fury in battle.

But he must not allow himself to be distracted—the curse. That had to be his main focus. If the Cainites of his city and the world had brought divine retribution down upon themselves, then he would have to counteract that somehow.

His city would not be destroyed. He would not allow it.

♀

Mohammed's pacing was interrupted by the knock at the door. It was not a welcome intrusion. "What?" he barked.

"Hey, man," came Marvin's voice from the other side of the door. "Pancho headin' to the store. You want anything?"

Mohammed couldn't believe his ears. He yanked the door open. "You're bothering me to see if I want something from the store?" he snarled.

Marvin took a step back but said nothing.

"What'd I tell you before?"

Marvin still didn't say anything.

"What'd I tell you?" Mohammed asked again, his voice full of venom.

Marvin cringed. He was staring at the tops of his shoes and not about to look up. "Said not to bother you less it was damn important," Marvin mumbled.

"Is going to the store damn important?"

"Guess not." Marvin glanced up for a second then decided to check out his shoes some more. "Sorry, man."

"You're gonna be a lot more than sorry, you don't get your head out your ass." Mohammed slammed the door. He couldn't believe he'd ever seen anything in Marvin. The vampire leader of Crypt's Sons, arguably the most powerful gang in L.A., resumed his pacing. Still thinking about Marvin, Mohammed had to admit that even if the mortal wasn't too bright—*not too bright? hell, he's 'bout stupid as they get*—he was awfully good in a fight, and that went a long way.

And unlike most of Mohammed's undead lieutenants, Marvin was here.

The past two weeks had been pure hell. It was always a tight line between Mohammed's public persona as L.A. baron and anarch on the one hand, and his covert identity as Sabbat leader on the other. He controlled dozens of vampires and hundreds of kine through the gang, and a sometimes overlapping smaller group of vampires through his Sabbat coven. The last thing expected, or needed, was for his vampire underlings to start randomly freaking out and attacking one another for no discernable reason.

One or two cases had been weird, but then most everybody had gotten in on the act. His top undead gang leaders had attacked each other, but not out of jealousy or anger or something Mohammed could have settled. It had seemed more like hunger. The guys had just flipped out. He would have suspected crack if it had been the mortals.

And as if all that weren't bad enough, after the bastards started freaking out, then they just keeled over. *First they go all maniac and freak out and feed, then they fall over dead, blood oozing out all over the place like they couldn't hold it.*

Despite Mohammed's best efforts, the violence and chaos had spread all the way down both organizations. The Crypt's Sons' top guys were fried—dead or freaked out or hiding. So some of the small fries, mostly mortals, had decided it was time to move up and started taking care of some personal grudges within the gang. Mohammed had put a stop to that quickly enough, but still all of his right hand men were missing or down for the count. Mohammed could only do so much by himself. Without proper guidance, the Crypt's Sons were like hundreds of lone piranha swimming off in different directions.

It was worse within the Sabbat coven. Of the ten members, not including Mohammed, six were shrivelled up and dead, one had gotten his head ripped off, and two were missing for several nights now. That only left one.

Mohammed heard moaning from the back room. He turned his pacing in that direction and stuck his head in to check on Francesca.

It had taken the chains and the straps together to hold her down. Twice before, she had ripped her way loose and carved up a total of three of Mohammed's gang mortals. Both times, Mohammed had subdued her. For some reason, no matter the desperation of her frenzy and the severity of her delusions, she had been unwilling or unable to turn the full force of her fury against her sire. Now the chains and straps seemed to be doing the job.

The bed where she lay was soaked red. Bloody sweat dribbled from all over her body. Mohammed had removed her saturated clothes and covered her with a sheet, but now it too was drenched. Mohammed moved closer and knelt beside his whimpering childe.

"So hungry...so hungry..." she kept muttering when she could manage speech. At times she licked around her lips, ingesting again the blood that periodically ran from her nose. No matter how much she had fed the past few days, it had not helped. In fact, the pain and delusions seemed to worsen after she'd fed.

Mohammed dabbed her forehead with a blood-stained towel that had once been white. Unlike with the others, he felt more than the regret of a general deprived of the services of a fierce warrior when he looked at Francesca like this. She had been much more than a top-notch assassin and a sultry diversion. Otherwise, he wouldn't have cared so much. A killer or a great piece of ass were not difficult to come by. Francesca had started out as merely the spoils of war, snatched out from beneath Salvador's nose, but she had come to mean much more to Mohammed.

Salvador.

He was something else Mohammed had to think about.

Before all hell had broken loose, Mohammed had been about ready to make his move against El Hermandad. Now the Crypt's Sons were decimated, and there were even rumors that Salvador was back in town from Central America or Africa or wherever he'd been stroking his ego by spreading revolution of the underprivileged. If Salvador was in fact back, then the attack would have to wait. Of course, it was delayed indefinitely at this point anyway.

Francesca arched her back, moaning and convulsing violently, her face contorted in agony. Mohammed looked on helplessly as her life's blood dripped from every pore of her body.

There had to be someone behind all this, he just knew. Someone out to get him. The madness and slow, painful death was too subtle for Salvador, he of propaganda and grenade. But the Camarilla elders—they were devious enough to set loose something like this, whatever it was. They wouldn't care how many Cainites were dragged under by this infernal curse, and with the Tremere on their side, they might very well have the means. If so, the Sabbat and the anarchs could soon be seeing their final days. Or perhaps something this drastic might finally push the anarchs into the Sabbat camp. Otherwise, it would take Mohammed years to rebuild his coterie.

Yes, the Camarilla elders were godless killers, and Mohammed hated them with every ounce of his being. Of course, he knew, if he could have unleashed a merciless curse of death upon his enemies, he would have done the exact same thing.

NINE

"*Quel fromage?*" Pierre could not believe the stupidity. "This is the only cheese I have, idiot."

"That is fine," René stammered apologetically.

"If you do not like it, I will eat it all," threatened Pierre. He'd had the foresight to bring extra cheese on the patrol, and he did not have to be so gracious as to share with the imbecile René.

The year was 1758. The patrol had been sent out in response to sightings of Iroquois, allies to the English *cochon*. One farmhouse had been burned, the farmer and his family mutilated. So now Pierre and the others were banished from Montreal for days at least, spending their nights in the rain and the cold, on the hard ground, instead of Pierre with warm and soft Danielle. All because some farmer had been stupid enough to get himself killed.

"No, no," René pleaded, "I said it was fine."

"Fine." Pierre cut a hunk of cheese and handed it to René the half-wit.

"*Merci.*"

The two chewed their cheese and hard bread in silence. The pile of sticks and leaves sputtered and smoked, but there was very little in the way of fire to warm or illuminate the night. Everything was too wet—the wood, the ground, the dripping trees, the soldiers' clothes and bedrolls, the powder....

Probably the muskets would not fire even if we did see Iroquois, Pierre mused. "How is your cheese?" he asked with an edge to his voice.

"*Trés bien.*"

A very good answer, Pierre thought. He snorted at René. *And for this I left Paris.*

Shuffling by in the rain came François, on his way to relieve Yves on watch.

"Iroquois in the woods," Pierre teased him, "*n'est-ce pas?*"

"*Je crois que non.*"

The dour soldier continued on his way, and Pierre and René crunched their bread and cheese. Pierre was contemplating crawling into his soggy bedroll and trying to go to sleep. *The sooner I sleep*, he thought, *the sooner this miserable excuse of a day is over.* That brought only a momentary smile to his face. *Ah, but the sooner today is over, the sooner the miserable excuse for tomorrow begins*. There was no winning.

Pierre's quandary was interrupted a moment later by a musket shot in the distance and a panicked scream from the same direction.

Pierre and René jumped to their feet, as did the other soldiers at their various smoldering faux-campfires.

"Yves!" René cried.

Pierre grabbed his musket and rushed ahead, but had to stop and wait until Arnaud managed to light a torch and caught up. "Hurry, idiot!" Pierre shouted. "Yves will be scalped because of you!"

They ran, stumbling, through the forest. The cloud-covered sky lent no light. The woods were dark as pitch. Men were calling all around, yelling for Yves and François. They pounded through the underbrush, spraying standing water and mud in every direction. When at last they reached the sentry post, Pierre wished he had not.

In the flickering torchlight, they saw Yves lying in the mud, his throat ripped wide open. Next to him lay François, and a foot or two away, much of his face.

Suddenly out of the trees above, something large dropped onto Arnaud. He screamed in Pierre's ear. The torch, knocked from Arnaud's grasp, fizzled in the mud and was out.

More screams echoed through the forest. Pierre was caught in a jumble of limbs and fell to the ground, landing hard atop his musket. He frantically tried to get loose from the other bodies. Who was it? René? Jean-Paul? Everyone had been rushing this way after the first screams.

Finally Pierre was free. He rolled through the muck, scrambling away from the blind melee. He couldn't be sure that his bearings were correct in the dark, but Pierre ran the direction he hoped the camp lay. They would regroup there. They couldn't fight Iroquois in the complete dark of the forest…if these were Iroquois.

The mud and darkness and Pierre's rising terror made for rough going. He had the sick feeling that whatever had attacked and done that to Yves and François, it wasn't a native war party. Finally, he reached the camp and tried to calm himself enough to load his musket.

The others will be here in a moment, and we will stand ready for the attack.

As he finished loading and rammed the shot home, however, Pierre noticed that none of his compatriots had joined him. Of the twelve, he stood alone in the camp. He noticed, also, that there were no longer sounds of combat emanating from the forest—no shouts or gun shots or tromp of musket-laden men crashing through the underbrush.

Only silence.

And then a snarl. Or…was it perhaps laughter?

From the deepest shadows strode a golden form, wolf-like with bared fangs but walking upright like a man, a very large man.

Without hesitation, Pierre raised his musket. He pulled back the hammer, quickly aimed, and pulled the trigger. The hammer clanked down…and nothing. The powder did not ignite. The musket did not roar defiance and send the creature back to hell.

The beast was on Pierre, pressing him on his back into the muck. Claws ripped at his face. The fangs came closer….

☥

Nicholas was awake all at once. He reached for his throat, but nothing was attacking him. The darkness around him was broken by passing lights in the distance. Before he could place the strange sights and smells all about, another spell of dizziness took hold of him. He braced his arms against metal walls and tried to resist the nausea that assaulted him as well.

Mercifully, it passed. Nicholas forced himself to swallow the blood that had risen in his throat and instantly was reminded of the hunger that tore at him, the burning emptiness that had grown steadily worse for…how long had it been? More weeks than he cared to remember. Two full moons had come and gone since he had entered this accursed city.

He lay back, giving in to the weakness that gripped him after the spells, and tried to overcome the disorientation that the visions brought. He was lying in the shell of a burned-out car under an interstate. The Canadian wilderness, the gunfire, the screaming—they weren't real, at least not in this time and place. Though the vision was far from random.

Nicholas knew the story well, how Pierre Beauvais and his unit had gone out on Indian patrol near Montreal and were slaughtered to a man. That's what the French Canadians had thought, at any rate, since Pierre's body had never been recovered. The soldiers had not met any Iroquois that night. They had been decimated by a Gangrel elder, the Golden, and Pierre had not joined his comrades in final death. That night in the stink of cold mud, he had been Embraced as Kindred, some fifty years later to Embrace another in turn, Jebediah Romey, Nicholas' sire.

These were the stories that Gangrel passed from generation to generation, from clanmate to clanmate as they travelled the broad expanses of the world and came across one another. Only now Nicholas was living the stories through the eyes of his ancestors, as if he were they, as if the pain and the terror were his that very first time. Sometimes when the spells came, Nicholas was thrown back into these memories of blood. First Jebediah, now Pierre. When would it end? When would the hunger and the visions leave him?

The entire city was gripped by this madness. For weeks it had been growing worse—anarchs going berserk in the streets, attacking large groups of mortals, or one another; seemingly respectable Camarilla Kindred suddenly pouncing on their sires, trying to drain the rest of the vitæ that had given them unlife. Nicholas had watched it all from a distance, not wanting to involve himself in these strange city ways, not realizing until later that it was all part and parcel of this deadly sickness of body and soul, this curse which had been brought down upon them all.

The mortals, too, were confounded by the sudden surge of violence and chaos, but the kine were so short-sighted. They never did see the lurkers in the shadows.

And now the city had grown deathly quiet. Those Kindred still unscathed hid like cubs in their havens. Only the brave and the foolish still roamed the streets. The brave, the foolish, and Nicholas. Several times he had set out to leave the city, to escape the foul air, the ever-pressing swell of kine, but each time he had been brought down by the curse, to regain his senses later knowing neither where he had gone or what he had done. Certainly he had violated others' hunting grounds, for the hunger always took him powerfully at those times, but none had challenged him. Dead or in hiding were the timid city Kindred.

How had it started? Nicholas gripped his head, extended claws digging into scalp. He tried to hold at bay the hunger twisting his innards, the pounding that wracked his skull. *That first night*, he thought back. *That first night in the city.* The hunger had started then. The pain. The visions. What had he done that night? It was difficult to think clearly through the rising tide of dizziness, the nausea that only made the hunger worse when he fed. *Evans. Evans' house. The package.* Did the package Nicholas had carried from Germany have something to do with it? Or was Owain Evans some black sorcerer cursing all those around him, bringing the city to ruin?

Nicholas crawled out of the blackened car. He would find out, and he would make the hunger stop.

"Going out again, sir? So soon? And on Christmas Eve?"

Owain stopped by the front door. He methodically pulled on his overcoat, adjusted his scarf, even tucked his new sunglasses into his breast pocket. Only then did he turn and acknowledge Randal's comment. Owain patted the ghoul on his cheek. "Do you know, Randal, why Señor and Señora Rodriguez have been with me for so long?"

"Why is that, sir?" Randal looked puzzled by the seeming non sequitur.

"Because they keep to themselves."

Randal heard the ominous tone in Owain's voice and, wisely, did not reply. Owain closed the door behind him and got into the waiting Rolls. "Oakland Cemetery, Ms. Jackson."

"Yes, sir."

Kendall Jackson possessed the ideal demeanor for a ghoul servant—she listened attentively, asked only necessary questions, and carried out orders impeccably. She often reminded Owain of Gwilym. How many years had it been since…since that unfortunate business that had deprived Owain of Gwilym's services? Five hundred? Six hundred? That had been near Christmas as well. And in all that time Owain had gone through ghouls like so many pairs of shoes. Some had shown promise, but none had combined that rare blend of savvy, prudence, and competence that had made Gwilym so invaluable.

None, except perhaps for Ms. Jackson. Maybe, Owain reflected, he was being too harsh on his servants. The fact that Gwilym was his first ghoul and had served the longest might have skewed Owain's objectivity. Jackson was a better driver than

Gwilym had been a horseman, and although the short Welshman had been good in a fight, Jackson was absolutely deadly, as she had proven again in helping save the prince at the Cyclorama several weeks before.

That fight had been a miscalculation on Owain's part. He was lucky that both he and the prince had walked away. Ms. Jackson had stepped in and performed admirably, and with a few extra feedings, her wounded leg had healed quite nicely. Time and blood had served to effect Owain's recovery as well.

His thoughts from one ghoul to the other. Randal served various administrative duties quite capably, but he retained a certain smugness that, in earlier centuries, Owain would have squelched in an instant. For the past few decades, though, he just hadn't had the energy or the interest. Perhaps it was time for a change in personnel, should a suitable replacement come to Owain's attention.

Owain's attention recently had been occupied by something other than chess, though this new diversion was just as maddening in some ways. With chess, Owain stared at the board for hours upon hours, night after night, torturing himself to find what he could have done differently, what he might still do to salvage a patently hopeless situation.

His new passion was the siren. Now that he had heard her song, he realized that he would always hear it, no matter how far across the city he was.

His estate was at least a half hour away from the broken-down church, but still the night breeze carried the sweet notes to his ear. It seemed to happen every week or two; Owain had discerned no set pattern as of yet. Did the rites commence whenever the siren and her brood grew hungry, perhaps?

Owain had hunted through his library for references he vaguely remembered to rare vampires with voices capable of driving mad kine and Kindred alike. *Daughters of Cacophony*, they were called by some, but that exquisite song was the farthest thing from cacophony that Owain had ever heard.

Twice again in the intervening month since the first visit, he had secreted himself in the tiny room beneath the belfry and observed the proceedings, which had always followed the same pattern. The congregation gathered as the siren stood alone at the head of the sanctuary. A few of the mortals seemed to be there every time. Others missed once but were back the next time. Roger had been present each time, while Albert had only been that first night.

How could Albert stay away, Owain wondered, if he heard the music? And what of the other Kindred in the city? Did the siren choose, somehow, who heard her song? But she couldn't know that Owain was spying on the proceedings.

There were five more questions for each that Owain thought he might have answered. That was the real reason he traipsed across town each time he heard the song drifting through the night air, Owain reminded himself. Not because he was compelled to do so; not because, even holding himself apart from the full experience of those congregated, he found visions of his faraway home in the music; not because each time she spoke that one word, *adref*, for him and him alone.

None of those things were the reason.

"Oakland Cemetery, sir."

Owain looked out the window and saw that they had, in fact, reached their destination. The old cemetery, full of stone crosses and mausoleums, loomed behind the boundary wall. Several years ago, Prince Benison had issued an edict that no Kindred, upon pain of final death, should enter Oakland Cemetery. He offered no explanation, and those few rash enough to inquire were punished harshly as a sign of the prince's seriousness on the matter. Owain had always assumed facetiously that the edict was handed down by the little voices with whom the prince had a habbit of conversing. Unlike some Kindred, Owain held no macabre interest in the trappings of the dead. He had no problem staying out of the cemetery.

Across the street stood the gloomy Fulton Bag Factory, the brick shell of an abandoned plant that supposedly was to be renovated and turned into luxury apartments. Owain doubted the project would ever be completed. The building was too close to the cemetery which, for whatever reason, Benison felt so strongly should not be disturbed. Surely the prince would pull strings in city hall to prevent such an intrusion.

Owain didn't need to tell Jackson to wait there. That was what she had done the last two times the mood had struck Owain to go for a drive. If she wondered where he went after he left the car, or if she minded spending her Christmas Eve in such a manner, she kept her feelings to herself, as it should be.

Ostensibly, Owain left her near the cemetery because a Rolls Royce closer to downtown attracted less attention than one parked in low-income Reynoldstown. As he made his way east following the siren's lilting song toward the church this night, however, he realized to his surprise his ulterior motive: he wanted the siren to himself. The truth staring him in the face, Owain laughed. In addition to his curiosity, his petty jealousy had been reawakened by this otherworldly performer.

But were these human emotions that had deserted him for countless years so petty after all?

Owain's philosophizing was interrupted by a clatter off to his left. More quickly than a mortal could have comprehended, he whirled, at the same time assuming a defensive crouch and drawing a dagger from its sheath behind him on his belt.

The dog rummaging through trashcans took no notice of Owain. It was more interested in its Christmas Eve dinner. Christmas Eve. Owain had even forgotten the holiday was at hand until Randal, in his impetuousness, had mentioned it. Normally, Owain would not have had the luxury of forgetting. The prince and all his bloody Bible readings would have made sure of that. But this year, with the "curse," as some were calling it, loose in the city, most Kindred were too frightened to gather, and Benison in his frustration had stopped trying to make them.

Owain relaxed and resheathed the dagger. He had taken to wearing it again after many years—in addition to the stiletto in his forearm sheath—almost out of nostalgia. Another ripple caused by the siren. The dagger's pommel and hilt were embossed with gold gilding, and it had once been a gift to Owain's nephew in honor of his kingship, a kingship Owain had ruthlessly guided the boy toward.

Owain hurried on his way. The siren's mesmerizing song seemed to follow a pattern. First was the lingering prelude as the congregation gathered. Perhaps this first part of the song was more accurately described as an introit, or better yet, the call to worship. For that was what happened. Those gathered came to fulfill their inner longings. They came out of desperation. How better, Owain wondered, could worship be defined? And what greater irony—and sacrilege?—than to transform a house of worship into a place of fulfillment, that which had always been denied Owain.

During none of his visits had the bloody rites progressed beyond this point before Owain had arrived. Was his timing that good, or could the siren be waiting for him? *Nonsense*. Owain rejected the possibility. There was no way she could be aware of his presence.

Eventually, without fail, the music would grow and build, the serene melody taking on more primal life. The maenads would join the ritual, the song and their dance growing fierce and tribal. And then a frenzied crescendo of feeding as the wild women gave into their bestial impulses. The mortals, as well, achieved some sort of spiritual or physical release at this point. Perhaps through their victimization, they achieved fulfillment, need perpetuating need, and insuring that the siren and her brood would never hunger.

Owain would liked to have revealed his presence to Albert, or maybe to Roger, to have discussed with them what exactly they experienced by letting themselves be dragged along on that emotional journey, letting themselves be fed upon. Or did they even remember it afterward? The mortals didn't seem to remember what had happened after the fact. They weren't ghouls returning to serve a master, rather they were cattle ambling toward the butcher. Owain suspected whatever happened in their minds, however the music manipulated them, that it was similar to the King Road Club where he fed on his social equals and then sent them away with the memory of thoroughly pleasant evening. With what memories were these mortals leaving?

Arriving at the church, Owain clung to the shadows, scaling the wall and taking his now familiar position. He felt a momentary lapse of dignity. Here he was, a Ventrue elder, hiding like an embarrassed voyuer. But there were questions to be answered, he hastily reminded himself. This was an exercise in intellectual curiosity for him, unlike the others for whom it was a matter of emotional weakness.

Most of those kneeling in the church were familiar faces—the two young African-Americans who might be a couple, the ever-present Korean woman with her thick glasses, an older black man, a middle-aged white woman, and two or three other mortals. Albert and Roger were both present as well. And, of course, the siren stood motionless before them all, her physical beauty overshadowed by the perfection of her voice.

Owain couldn't help wondering if Albert or Roger had mentioned these excursions to anyone else. If not, the three of them might be the only Atlanta Kindred who knew of the siren's presence. Owain had not seen any other vampires present at any of the rites, and surely if others had heard the song, they would have come. Owain cared because this was not the type of affair that Prince Benison would condone. The Ventrue doubted that Benison knew of the siren's presence in the city. Normally, the prince made a formal show of allocating hunting grounds. The more public the pronouncement among the Kindred, the less chance of confusion and territorial struggles down the road. Order and, perhaps even more so, observation of the proper forms were high priorities with Benison. With the curse, order was rapidly breaking down. The prince would not tolerate the insult upon injury of an interloper in his city, especially not at this point. So it seemed unlikely, aside from the fact that Albert was still keeping away from Benison and that the prince could barely stand the sight of his childe Roger, that they or anyone else had revealed the existence of these rites to the prince.

As the song began to rise, the tempo gradually increasing in intensity and emphasis, Owain settled back against the wall. This time he thought he would listen more than watch. After the past rituals, he felt he had mastered himself to the point that he could more completely immerse himself in the song without risking joining the group involuntarily as had nearly happened the first evening. Owain fished around in his breast pocket and then put on his sunglasses, the first pair of shaded spectacles he'd ever owned. By the time they had come into vogue, Owain had been long past worrying about the sun. Or rather, if the sun were an issue, it was much more of a worry than sunglasses could have helped. In this case, however, they blocked a bit of the flickering candlelight from below and helped Owain keep to his own thoughts.

From the beginning, the siren's song had prodded a buried memory in Owain, something just beyond his reach. It was a feeling he'd nearly grown used to, almost but not quite remembering something, as he'd grown less and less connected to the milestones of life over the years. His mind had played tricks on him fairly often, obscuring that which should have been readily apparent to him.

One strain of the music in particular, variations of which she revisited throughout the ritual, had caught Owain's notice. It had taken the second and third nights for him to be able to pick it out. The strength of his blood allowed Owain to maintain more mental control than the other listeners, but now, as he tried to pull apart the music to find that familiar motif, he realized that it was that very control he was going to have to relinquish, at least in part, if he were to delve beneath the surface of the music. And so he clung to the familiar strain of the song and, against his better judgment, let it take him where it would....

The tune was that of the ocean breeze, the cold

Irish Sea again. Gazing out over the sea from the western coast of Wales, Owain realized something else about the word, *adref*, which the siren had spoken: though she pronounced the word in nearly flawless Welsh from Owain's youth, her tongue imparted the slightest of accents to the sound, the most musical of imperfections which he recognized even from mortal days as Irish.

The telltale accent, the lapping waves of the Irish Sea—she had come from, or at least passed through, the Emerald Isle. With this thought, countless nuances of the magical song unfolded before Owain like a rich tapestry unfurled to the light. He could see now that each listener would hear that word, *homeward*, in the tongue of his or her homeland. In that way, the siren's song was made whole to each lost soul it reached. It became truly that person's, yet never lost the siren's story. With the realization, the other strands of the song crowded in upon Owain, flooded in upon him, a warmer, calmer version of that harsh sea.

But Owain held steady. He did not relinquish that strand which was the siren, the impetus of the song that had initially attracted him. Her song was a lament, an outpouring of sorrow for love lost, for a homeland stolen from her. She beseeched the ancient gods who had walked her land in the earliest of days. *Take me back*, she pleaded. *Take me back to meaning and to love. Take from me these mean-*

ingless years, the burden of time, the burden of failure.

The notes struck true with Owain. He could find not the first seed of pride or hatred in them. Only loss and suffering. He could not imagine such pain without bitterness, such tragedy without recrimination. It was that elusive touch of purity that so mystified him, that was so close to what he knew, yet far, far beyond him.

The true emotion of her song took hold of Owain. Such catharsis he'd never felt—not through vengeance or victory or hatred. Even in loss, Owain had always found only bitterness, never nobility.

Swept away by the searing truth of her song, Owain could not hold at bay the other swelling strands of the music. Again they poured over him, like the sea, not to be denied. They carried him away from the shore, each wanting to pull him a different direction, every strand wanting to impart its vision of loss and need, of discovered comfort and warmth.

One strand in particular beguiled Owain, drawing him after it. Somehow these notes seemed most similar to the siren's own song. The tune, first light and playful, then restful and soothing, carried Owain with it, away from the coast, away from the siren's sorrow, over Snowdonia, on to the the far fringes of the mountains. Rhufoniog, Owain's ancestral lands, lay before him, and not marred by modern roads and bridges. This was the land of his childhood. Filling his vision were the wood and stone walls of Dinas Mynyddig, his birthplace, the earthen defensive works of his family's seat of power. He'd known the scene as a boy, and later as a lord of the night.

The song carried Owain's awareness over the walls to one open window. *Adref. Homeward.* For this was home for this part of the song. Through the window, he could see a woman with child, rocking, and singing. The words were faint, for she sang quietly for her unborn, but the tune was that of a lullaby, its notes caressing the babe in her womb. Her face was familiar to Owain. Often he had seen portraits of her, but never did he remember her face in life, for his mother had died shortly after his birth.

She was more lovely than he'd ever imagined. He wanted to reach out and stroke her cheek, but this vision was not a thing of substance, only of sight and sound. Anything more, the feel of sea spray on his face, was merely a trick of the mind. But still...

Like holding sea water in his hand, Owain could not keep the vision. The scene grew blurry, shifted, and the collection of notes gained strength, grew richer. Still a lone woman rocked and sang, the same window but a different woman, busy with knitting and no child, an absence that would shape her life. She sang the same song, wistfully, to none other than the night. It was the song Owain, as a young man, had stood in the chill night to hear. She was his one love. His one brother's wife.

"*Angharad.*"

Her name spoken, the vision disappeared, a tide pulled back to sea, and Owain knew then that the strand of the song he had followed was his own. The siren's sorrow had dipped into his soul and joined his story to the song, and only now did he truly hear it—his loss devoid of bitterness, his sorrow untainted by anger.

Owain opened his eyes. His spectacles were smeared with tears of blood.

Dear God! When did I last cry? He muffled his sobs, more from embarrassment than from fear of discovery. But that too was a concern. Had he alerted those below to his presence? Had he actually spoken aloud, or was the name part of the song, now forever entwined with the siren's sorrow?

Owain leaned forward from his perch to see through the hole into the sanctuary. The maenads had just finished feeding. They were backing away from the sprawled mortals. Already, the siren was moving among the prone bodies, gently licking their blood-stained wounds, healing their injuries. She approached Albert, who was still kneeling despite having been fed upon, and as she licked the torn flesh of his neck, his eyes fluttered open. He had an odd smile on his face; odd for Albert because normally, even when he smiled, maybe especially when he smiled, he had a rather crazed gleam in his eyes. This time, though, he was the picture of perfect contentment, head lolled back in the siren's arms, eyes staring lazily up at...*at Owain*.

Owain jerked back from the edge of the hole. He'd grown careless after the strange trauma of the visions. Had Albert seen him in the shadows? There was no way to be sure. Not all Kindred had vision as acute as Owain's, but he couldn't assume that was the case with Albert. Surely Albert wouldn't go to the prince. He and Roger were violating Benison's wishes just as surely as was Owain. Of course, Roger was the prince's childe, if not his favorite person, and Albert was a fellow Malkavian, even if not in the best of graces currently. One thing Owain had learned long ago: he couldn't outguess a Malkavian. Benison had proven surprising on occasion, and Albert had never been anything but, as long as Owain had known him.

There were too many possibilities, too much to think about, and Owain was feeling somewhat shaky after his experience. He tried to wipe clean his glasses, but his hands were trembling—*damnation!*—so he stuffed the spectacles into his pocket.

The other nights he had sat here, Owain had

rushed away before those gathered below had recovered from the rites, but tonight Owain, too, felt
the need to recuperate. He didn't trust his body to
get him silently away from the church, so Owain
took a deep calming breath, and he waited. There
was much to think about, but for now he was trying to think of absolutely nothing.

The night he had found himself in the burned-
out car, Nicholas had paid a visit to Owain Evans'
estate. He had leapt the outer wall and, knowing
better what to watch for this time, had avoided
detection. He'd alerted neither human nor dog nor
ghoul. He had perched in the branches outside the
mansion and waited. As the sun peeked over the
eastern horizon, Evans had neither left nor entered,
so Nicholas had sunk into the ground to wait out
the day.

The next evening, he had risen from the earth
prepared to exercise patience honed over generations and generations of hunting. He had not had
to wait that long. Evans had left in his car, and
Nicholas had followed.

Pursuing an automobile through the city was not
a task at which Nicholas had much practice. Keeping out of sight as much as possible, he had run
like a Kindred possessed of demons, or one attempting to outrun the sunrise. Several surprised mortals

had doubtless seen him, but to their poor eyes he would have been less than a blur in the night.

The greatest challenge had come when Evans' car had turned onto the interstate and taken that barren road through the heart of the city. A partially wolven form streaking down such a highway would have stretched the Masquerade beyond its breaking point, but still Nicholas had not been daunted. He had kept pace on other roads and through neighborhoods lining the highway, rushing ahead at some points and waiting to make sure he had not lost his prey. He had leapt from roof to tree, over cars and fences, constantly shifting forms to gain the surest footing and quickest route.

Thankfully, the car had pulled off the interstate and come to a halt near a large graveyard. When Evans had continued on foot, Nicholas had been forced to fight his instinct to pounce. The Ventrue had to know something about this curse. From within his fever, Nicholas had grown sure of this, but ripping Evans' throat out, the Gangrel had decided, might not be the most productive way to find out what. So he had followed farther.

Evans had led him to a falling-down church, into the steeple of which the Ventrue had climbed, strange since there were people in the sanctuary. So Nicholas had waited longer.

And while he'd waited, the sound of soft music had made him prick up his ears. It had been a lone voice, as clear and crisp as the breeze over the open prairie. No songbird had ever sung so sweetly. The very sound eased Nicholas' hunger, for he had again grown weak and pained after his long run.

Suddenly, the very buildings around him seemed to be closing in on Nicholas. Why had he tarried so long in this city? Nicholas longed for the wide open spaces that the music suggested to him. Not even the outdoors was enough room in this madly thronged place of humanity. He longed for the howl of the coyote, the snarl of the mountain lion.

Nicholas turned and fled the city. Forgetting his hunger, he ran and ran until the buildings gave way to hills, and the hills to mountains, and not until the Christmas morning sun was searing his flesh did he give into exhaustion and once again sink beneath the earth.

☥

When Roger awoke in the church, the others were gone—the mortals, the beautiful pale singer, Albert—all gone. There were still two or three hours of darkness, so he had no worry on that account. Slowly, he rose to his feet. His footsteps echoed as he left the empty building.

Roger didn't know how to thank Albert enough for leading him to this miracle, this soothing balm in an unlife of misery. Each night that they came and Roger gave himself to the music, he was visited by the loveliest of visions. He could see himself strong and stalwart. He saw the prince greeting him with pride, sometimes bowing down before him. But more electrifying than any of that, Roger saw his mother rise from her bed. She hugged and kissed him. He twirled her small body in his arms.

While the music lasted, the visions were real. Roger wanted nothing more than to stay there with his mother, embracing her. The beautiful pale singer was showing him heaven, the way it would always be after his mother awoke and he Embraced her into eternity. Knowing it could happen, knowing it *would* happen, Roger could face the challenges of mundane reality.

He arrived at the car to find it up on blocks, the tires, the battery, even the AM radio gone.

A surge of rage shot through Roger. How could people show so little respect for the property of others? He forgot his moralizing the next instant as pain ripped through his abdomen and he doubled over in agony. The cramps again, and he could feel the bloody sweat beading up all over his body. How he wanted to be back in the church listening to the music, spending time with his mother in that most perfect of worlds.

Roger stumbled over to another car, a beaten-down Escort, and ripped open the door. Despite his pain, he had the car hotwired within a minute. It was Christmas Eve. He needed to see his mother, and that was too far to walk.

Roger tried to dab all the blood from his face before going into the Peachtree Gardens. If the night attendant noticed anything out of the ordinary, he didn't let on. Twice more before Roger reached his mother's room, he was almost brought to his knees by the pain. His insides were seizing up. He wanted to feed, but even that had only made things worse the past few days.

Room 256. He was inside and at his mother's side.

She looked so small and weak here, not like he'd just seen her. Maybe, Roger wondered, he should take *her* to the church. The music might work its magic on her. But if he moved her and something went wrong, he would never forgive himself.

"Hello, Mama," Roger said softly. "I just came from the church again. The one I told you about that Albert and I have been going to." She would like that he'd been going to church. "I'm going to make you better, Mama. There's a faith healer at the church, and we're gonna make you better."

Tabatha Greene lay still, barely breathing, as Roger told her all about the beautiful music—she had always loved music, he knew—and about how it was going to make her better, and about everything he had seen.

Roger noticed that just talking about the music had made his pain and hunger lessen. He could feel the faith healing at work. Next time he heard the song, he would rush here and take his mother to the church. They had waited long enough, endured enough. The music could bring him heaven on earth. Roger told his mother all of his plans.

"So for now," he smiled at her, "we've just gotta keep you strong." As he did during every visit, Roger pricked his own finger and carefully let a drop or two of his vampiric vitæ trickle into her mouth. He waited for her to swallow as she always did. When she took longer than usual, Roger leaned over her and peered down at her face.

His mother coughed in his face. Roger was close enough to feel the spray, but when he wiped it off, his hand came away smeared red. Roger stared at her, uncomprehending.

She coughed again, this time more forcefully, and again blood sprayed over him. She began shaking all over, and gagging sounds filled her throat. Before Roger could lift her up to clear her airways, the sounds stopped, as did her shaking.

She released a prolonged sigh, air leaving her body not to be replaced. As Roger looked on, frozen by terror, blood ran from her nose and her ears and the corners of her eyes.

Finally, she was completely still. Roger stared in shock. He opened his mouth but was robbed of speech. All of his dreams, all of his plans for the future, for heaven on earth...

Roger buried his face in his mother's nightgown and sobbed.

TEN

Frank raised a hand to scratch his ear, which was still very tender. After four weeks, it had finally healed over and grown back, itching all the while. As it had grown, so had grown the hunger within him—nagging at first, never quite sated; then stronger, constantly pricking his body and mind. Now it tormented him without pause. Just last night he had fed upon an entire Pakistani family, and it helped not a bit. In fact, he had grown so ill afterward that he had vomited most of the blood into the sewer. *Pakis aren't even any good for food anymore!* he thought, disgusted, spitting at the memory.

His leaving the underground tunnels last night had been a rare thing. Since Gisela had died, he had laid low, waiting and watching from here in the sewers. Frank rubbed his ear again.

Gisela had tried to kill him, to rip his head off, and she would have if he hadn't gotten away. Two nights later when he'd warily ventured back, the basement floor had been a bog of sticky congealing blood with what was left of Gisela lying in the middle of it.

Frank had spit on her body. *Try tearing my head off, whore.*

But the whole city was that way—vampires falling upon one another to feed. *Crazy!* Diablerie was one thing, but mindless bestial frenzy...

There were many others beside Gisela who had fallen prey to the curse. The Endtimes, the darkness before the final light—Gehenna. The antediluvians would rise up to claim their childer. But Frank would be ready. He and his Sabbat brethren would stand their ground...those Sabbat brethren who hadn't already fallen victim to the curse.

It had to be a Camarilla plot to weaken the Sabbat before the coming and the final battle. It was so obvious!

That was why Frank was waiting here tonight. He had expressed his suspicions to Herr Himmler, and the Fuehrer had been rightfully impressed. "Find out what you can," he had charged Frank.

So Frank had asked around, put out subtle feelers, hinted at what he might know to see how others responded. *Ellison and those Camarilla Nosferatu aren't the only ones with contacts in this city!* Frank's probing had paid off far better than he could have hoped. And so he waited.

Footsteps. Distant. Deliberate.

Frank squeezed back into the shadows. This rendezvous was not without its risks.

The echoing footsteps grew closer slowly, methodically, confidently. There was no sound of hesitation in them, no pauses or missteps in the slime and filth of the sewer. Gradually, a figure became visible through the murky darkness.

Frank gasped in astonishment. *"Wilhelm."*

Approaching Frank was the prince of Berlin. The most accepted of two rival claimants to the title of prince, at any rate, but such trivialities seemed far less important when face to face with greatness.

Wilhem's bright blue eyes almost shone in the darkness. His slightly round Prussian face was relaxed. A warm smile came easily to his lips now that Frank was revealed. The prince offered a hand in friendship. "Frank?"

Frank stared dumbstruck for a moment before reaching out. The prince grasped his hand firmly and shook. Frank, again, was tardy to respond, and then did so a bit too vigorously. Wilhelm seemed not to notice Frank's thick blue hide. The Nosferatu antitribu had been unable to maintain his less…peculiar visage while the hunger gnawed at him and left him weak.

"You are Frank," the prince clarified.

"I…yes, yes…" How else, Frank wondered, could he muck this up? "Of course I am," he said a bit too abruptly.

The prince didn't seem to mind as he continued smiling warmly and nodded greetings. His finely tailored suit should have looked out of place in the sewers, but the man looked completely at ease.

Instead it was Frank, who lived in and nightly traversed these tunnels, who was uncomfortable. "I…I was expecting Kleist," he stammered, "or…someone else. Not…" Frank was growing flustered as well as muddled.

"…Not me?" Wilhelm suggested.

"Yes. I mean, no. Not you."

"I heard you had important news to discuss," the prince, all charm and grace, explained, "so I came myself. Times are bad, and I owe it to the Kindred of Berlin to do what I can."

Frank rubbed his scaly hands together. *Offer some tidbit of information, then find out what he knows*, he told himself. *Herr Himmler will reward me well for raising the curse!*

The prince was waiting patiently.

"I have heard," Frank proffered in hushed tones, "that there is a curse upon our city." He paused for a moment, waiting for the prince to present his view of events, but Wilhelm was still smiling and listening. "I have heard," Frank continued, "that it is only the first of great plagues sent to weaken us Kindred before…" He paused again, in case the prince wanted to contribute, but to no avail. "Before the Endtimes, the days of darkness when the eldest of the elders will rise to consume their young." Still the prince waited. "Before…" Frank looked around meaningfully, "Gehenna."

Wilhelm was still watching Frank. The prince began to nod gravely. "I have heard of this curse as well."

Frank expected more in the way of response, but that was all the prince said. So Frank expounded upon his views. "It is our own fault," he pointed out. "Mixing races, allowing foreigners free run of our lands. Certainly our forefathers are displeased in their resting places."

"Certainly." Wilhelm, almost imperceptibly, glanced at his watch as he shifted his weight from one foot to the other.

A dull ache stirred in Frank's belly. Hunger or anxiety, he wasn't sure which. "The curse—I know how it started."

Wilhelm's eyebrows rose at this.

Frank was gratified to see he had the prince's interest, except that Frank had no idea how the curse had started. "I spoke with a vampire…a woman…a Tremere, very high up, very high. I cannot tell you her name…"

"I understand," the prince graciously conceded.

"She said a Tremere elder cast the curse upon us," Frank went on. "On our city…to get at you, so the Tremere could take over."

"I see."

"This woman…my friend, she helped perform the ritual." Still the prince listened attentively. "I might be able to find out how to remove it."

Wilhelm was clearly impressed by this. "That would be a great service to all loyal Kindred. Obviously this woman…your friend, she does not take to such treachery."

"No. She does not. You are exactly right," Frank agreed. "That is why she told me."

"Of course," the prince nodded. "Then things are bad in the east of the city as well?"

"Oh, yes," Frank acceded. "Kindred grow sick. They go mad, attack one another." Frank absentmindedly rubbed his ear. "Some kine have been struck down by the curse. Some fear our curse may draw too much attention from the mortals if they are affected in large numbers."

"I see." The prince stared directly at Frank for a moment, then raised his arm to better see his watch beneath his sleeve. "I am afraid I must go, Frank." Again, the prince reached out and shook the Nosferatu's hand. "You have been quite helpful. If you discover more news, my man Kleist is not difficult to contact. Again, many thanks." With that,

Wilhelm turned and strode away into the darkness leaving Frank to decide what he had learned through his interrogation of the prince.

Idiot! Wilhelm could not believe that he had wasted his time on such a cretin. Kleist had been right. Another dead end. Another crazy speaking of curses and Tremere plots. *Did the fool think that I hadn't already conferred with Etrius in Vienna, the most highly placed of Tremere? Of course everyone had suspected the Tremere.* Which didn't mean that they weren't the cause of this madness. For that reason, Wilhelm had summoned Maxwell Ldescu, Tremere regent in Berlin. The prince had been surprised when Ldescu had arrived accompanied by Karl Schrekt, the Tremere Justicar.

The problem, this curse, was more widespread than just in Berlin. Similar outbreaks of madness and violence were being reported all over Europe and in the Americas as well. Ldescu and Schrekt had had little choice but to be quite frank concerning their ignorance in the matter.

Their Tremere underlings across the globe had had no luck in discerning the cause of the malady, or exactly how it spread. There was no consistent pattern of who was at risk. In tests on "volunteers" where identical subjects were exposed to the same degree to victims already afflicted, one subject was affected, the other was not. Possibly Kindred of elder generation were more resistant, but even this trend was not inviolate.

One fact, and one fact only, the Tremere had discovered for certain: this was no mere contagion or vampiric mutation of a mortal disease. Clinging to each victim, living and dead, was the aura of foul magic, a vile twisting of nature with which the Tremere were unfamiliar, a supernatureal tainting of the blood that ate away at both mind and body. Truly the entire race of vampires was cursed.

Ldescu and Schrekt hadn't said as much, but Wilhelm could tell they were worried—no, more than worried. Scared. That was why he believed them.

Wilhelm could see moonlight ahead and smell fresh air as he approached the ladder that had let him down into the sewers. Frank Litzpar had been an utter waste of time, but one couldn't pass up even unlikely possibilities in such a crisis as this.

When the strange attacks had started, Wilhelm had suspected some trickery from Gustav. The old bastard would stop at nothing to reclaim what he erroneously thought of as "his city." Kindred had inexplicably withered away, starving though their bodies were full of fresh blood. Wilhelm had reports that the curse had struck even more severely among the Sabbat. No, this was all too indirect for anything from Gustav. The goat was less subtle than the *blitzkrieg*. Too indirect, and too massive.

Vampires all over the world were falling victim. Already, almost one in five Kindred in Berlin had been stricken, and those were only the instances of which Wilhelm was aware. From the sounds of what the idiot Litzpar had said, the former East Berlin where Gustav still managed to hold sway was just as bad, if not worse. At least that would keep the elder Ventrue off Wilhelm's back—for the time being.

On Christmas Day as families across the city of Atlanta awoke to presents under trees, as they worshipped the holiday's patron deities Christ and St. Nick, as they seriously attempted to treat others as lovingly for one day as they might each day of the year, Owain tossed fitfully in his slumber.

In these days of electric interior lighting, now that windowless rooms were no longer an inconvenience, many Kindred chose to sleep in beds, just as they had in their mortal days. Others clung to the old ways, out of habit or out of the mistaken belief begotten from legend and feature film that they must.

Owain fell somewhere between these two extremes on the spectrum. His resting place was too small to be mistaken for a proper bed. Centuries ago there had been a certain security in utilizing a coffin during the daylight hours. The practicality of being relatively easy to hide, somewhat mobile if one employed trustworthy retainers, as well as the advantage of keeping away superstitious mortals who were loathe to disturb a corpse, especially if its demise had resulted from the plague or some infectious disease—these factors had all been more integral to Owain's thought than any tradition of the undead.

But neither did he while away his days in a pine box. His "bed," for lack of a better word, was enclosed to provide the sense of security to which he had become accustomed, but easily three times the width of even a luxurious coffin, with plentiful head room and padded satin interior. Owain occupied his daily berth with a satisfaction many mortals reserved for their automobiles. He knew that he had cheated death. That was the flip side of the coin that was the vampiric curse of Caine. Owain had no interest in affecting the trappings of death. Leave that to the children of the modern city, so desperately needing to manufacture tragedy to provide a veneer of meaning to their insular little lives.

Owain had no need to seek out tragedy. It had sought him out time and again over the years.

A vampire's daily rest was not completely analogous to true sleep. In some ways, the hours were spent restfully. Physically, the body might heal.

Otherwise there were no demands or functions using precious blood. For Owain, however, there was no spiritual rejuvenation, no feeling of daily renewal, no recouping of emotional energy. Over the centuries, the uncompensated outflow of vigor had left Owain drained and listless. Even so, he had come to find a certain nihilistic reassurance in the hours of slumber. If God wished to exasperate Owain every night of his existence, at least the daylight hours were free of aggravation, if not actively pleasant.

And then sometimes came the visions.

They were not dreams, for to dream would imply hopes and fears for the future. Nightmares perhaps, dreams never. Owain had long since abandoned active longing. He had grown used to the dull ache of having that which he cared for torn away. Even his successes—for he had certainly achieved wealth and influence and longevity, the last of which in particular for vampires equalled power—even these rang hollow.

Now even his hours of blissful negation were interrupted.

First there was only mist, a cold and forboding fog that lay stagnant, unmoving. It possessed a timeless quality, as might the mists of nothingness before creation, or the mists that hugged a barren rock long after man and his hidden masters had destroyed their only world.

Ever so slowly, movement, a parting of the mist revealing a hillside rising from the surrounding clouds. And on the hillside, a lone wooden staff, tall and straight, carved so that a human hand might grasp it and find support. A feeling of stability hung about the staff. It was embedded in the earth as firmly and as surely as had been the sword anchored in the stone.

Around the staff the mists began to swirl. Joining the primal dance, the staff slowly twisted and bent. At its crown, wooden strands pulled away from one another, stretching in different directions, and as the branches reached meanderingly toward the sky, parting the mist further, tender green buds sprang forth along the length of each bough. Sprang forth and opened into small rounded leaves.

Following the lines of the branches, the mists continued to separate until rays of glowing sunshine bathed the tree on the hillside. As the tiny leaves spread wide in the warm light, blossoms sprouted and luxuriously unfolded into delicate flowers, white with traces of pink, shining in the rays of the sun.

All this Owain saw as if he were standing on the hill, yet the sun did not dazzle his eyes nor burn his flesh.

But a shadow fell across the hillside. A tall mound rose out of the surrounding mists to blot out the light of the sun, its slopes grown green over ancient terraces, dark and foreboding. Darker and darker the shadow grew, until the tree was only memory.

Atop the mound stood a stone tower, a shrine circled by ravens. The clouds lay heavy and thick around the tower. Lightning slashed through the churning vapor. Thunder shook the ground.

Owain stood within the tower without ever having taken a step from the first hill. The stone cross on the altar rocked on its base. Dust rained down from the highest reaches of the tower. Pigeons took flight.

Again thunder shook the earth, and then the earth was moving of its own accord, rumbling and quaking. The cross crashed from the altar, smashing to pieces against the stone floor. Rock and mortar began to crack and tumble from above, but Owain stood immobile, unable to move, to flee.

From below, as well, the world closed in as the ground buckled and rose, knocking Owain from his feet. The cobblestones split and peeled away before the heaving earth. Above, the tower shuddered and came thundering down.

It had not been the most pleasant Christmas that Eleanor could remember. There had been absolutely no gathering of Kindred. She had mentioned the lack of festivities to Benison several times, but that had only sent him stomping off in a huff. It was not the best of timing, all this trouble during the Christmas season.

Eleanor had seen her share of troubles. Before she had married Benison, when she had served as archon to Justicar Baylor, her sire, she had settled clan disputes, quelled civil unrest among Kindred and kine, and even tracked down a renegade mage and the demon that had possessed him. But this, this curse was far worse than anything else she could remember.

She had received a message from Baylor. He was in Chicago trying to sort out the mess there. Just when some semblance of a balance of power had been achieved among the contenders to become prince, every faction was riddled with sudden vacancies as Kindred either succumbed to the curse or went into hiding. Stability crumbled to dust. Anarchy reigned. And still lupines and Sabbat loomed in the shadows.

The trouble, Baylor had confirmed, was not just in Atlanta, or in Chicago. Riots had broken out in the Sabbat northeast, in Miami. Gang warfare was escalating in Los Angeles as anarch barons jockeyed for position. Even in normally staid Europe, the casualties were appalling.

But that was no reason to cancel all the festivities.

Eleanor had argued that in times of crisis, the

observance of ritual and ceremonial gatherings was all the *more* important, but Benison had not been swayed.

Eleanor's train of thought was interrupted as the prince stalked through the living room. He took one look at the gilded magnolia and holly boughs on the mantlepiece, then snatched them up and crumpled them to bits. "I thought I said to remove this trash from my home!"

"Our home, dear," Eleanor said calmly. She could appreciate the fact that her dear Benison was worrying himself sick. He was watching the city that he'd built fall apart around him, and there seemed to be nothing he could do. A Sabbat attack or an anarch revolt he could crush. Lupines he could battle to the death. A usurper of his title he could tear limb from limb. But a mysterious curse that could strike anyone next...*that* drove the prince to distraction. *But*, Eleanor reminded herself, it was not her fault that Benison had not seen that holly bough before he had sat down, and she would not be robbed of the remainder of her holiday season, or whatever she could salvage of it. "I will remove the Christmas decorations on New Year's, just like every year, and not a day before."

The prince glared. He raised a finger, but then clenched it into a fist and stomped out of the room. Marriage had done him some good, Eleanor noted. No broken furniture, no smashed windows. She wondered sometimes how he had managed this city before she had come along.

A rather loud knock sounded at the front door of Rhodes Hall. A few moments passed before Eleanor remembered that all three household ghouls had wasted away quite dramatically, not to mention poor Alex Horndiller, and good help so hard to find. Certainly Benison wasn't fit to receive visitors this evening, so it seemed to be left to Eleanor.

As she turned the knob, the door came crashing open. Hopping lithely out of the way, she still barely missed being smashed by the large oaken door. Into the foyer stumbled Roger carrying in his arms—*Dear God!*—Eleanor realized, a body.

"Eleanor, you're here," Roger boomed in a deep baritone. "Good." His face was lined with the dried tracks of bloody tears. The side of his head was covered in blood as well, fresh, not dried. From his ear? Eleanor couldn't tell. Despite his distressing appearance, Roger spoke with a forcefulness and confidence that Eleanor had never seen in him before. "Lock the doors and bring me my rifle. The Yanks have broken through, and it won't be long before they're here." Eleanor had no chance to stop him before he had pushed past her with the limp burden in his arms into the living room. "This poor lad's taken a belly wound. Fetch some towels. And whiskey. Might as well make him comfortable."

Eleanor had no idea what Roger thought he was doing, but worse than that, he had just tracked mud and blood all over her foyer and living room, and now he was laying the body of his "poor lad" on the cream and mullberry couch.

Roger turned and saw Eleanor standing dumbfounded in the doorway. "Woman!" he bellowed. "Are you hard of hearing? Fetch my rifle, the towels and whiskey."

The violent gleam in Roger's eyes was quite foreign to him, Eleanor was sure.

"I'll teach those damn Yanks to charge into my city," Roger exclaimed. "I won't stand for it! Not one minute!" Still lacking towels, he tore a strip from the draperies and began dabbing the forehead of his wounded charge. "What good is a wife," Roger wondered aloud, "if she can't follow orders?"

A *wife*?

The words shocked Eleanor almost as much as seeing her French draperies tattered for bandages. Something was wrong with Roger. He wasn't raving exactly, but his manner, his attitude toward Eleanor, the righteous indignation burning in his eyes—it was almost like watching...

At that moment, Benison came stomping down the stairs, his footsteps rattling the chandelier in the hall. "What in the name of Matthew, Mark, Luke, and John is going on down here? Who makes such a ruckus in my home?" Roger's rather dramatic, and loud, entrance had done little to improve the prince's mood. "Roger? Have you taken leave of your senses?" The prince, most often, didn't care to see his childe under the most favorable of circumstances, which these were not. Benison had Embraced a mortal war hero, a fearless combatant, and had ended up with a spineless vampiric recreant.

After just having ordered Eleanor about, Roger paused, slightly puzzled, when he saw Benison. The prince did not pause.

Eleanor tried to restrain her husband. "Benison, I wouldn't…" but the prince had already brushed past her.

"What is the meaning of this?" Benison demanded, face to face with Roger.

Roger glanced at the body behind him on the couch, not a "lad" at all, but a small gray-haired woman as dark of skin as Roger. Again Roger seemed confused.

Benison seemed suddenly to notice the mess—the mud, the blood—and then he noticed the woman's body. Though the body itself was scrubbed clean, she was adorned in bedclothes encrusted with stale dried blood. The smell of death hung about her motionless form. The prince's meager patience was at its end.

He pushed Roger out of the way and reached for the corpse. "How dare you bring…"

The instant Benison set a hand on the body, pure rage twisted Roger's face. Eleanor saw the change and tried to warn her husband, but Roger struck too quickly. He landed a powerful fist against Benison's jaw, knocking the prince to one knee.

"How dare I?" Roger roared. "How dare *you*? Invading my home!"

Benison remained on one knee for a moment, more shocked than hurt. Slowly, he stood, drawing himself up to his full height.

"Benison," said Eleanor urgently, having moved into the room, "he thinks he's you."

The prince may or may not have heard his wife. With one lightning-quick motion, he backhanded Roger, propelling the younger Malkavian back over an end table. The ornate lamp that had been on the table shattered against the floor as Roger crashed against the far wall, tearing a large hole through the wallpaper, plaster and sheetrock. Two pictures fell from the walls, frames and glass exploding into hundreds of fractured bits.

Benison stepped toward his childe. The prince was spoiling for a fight and ready to finish this one.

Roger leaned, stunned and blinking, against the wall. After a dazed moment, he looked around the room, slowly, as if seeing it for the first time. "Prince Benison?" he asked in an unsure voice. "Sire?"

Eleanor advanced into the room to the prince. She placed a hand on his shoulder. "Benison…"

Her presence, her touch, had a soothing effect on the prince. He held his ground, but did not unclench his fists nor shift his glare from Roger.

Suddenly, Roger groaned and doubled over in pain. He dropped to his knees, then fell prone to the floor, crying out in distress.

Eleanor started forward but Benison held her back. "It may be a trick," he cautioned.

Eleanor looked on as Benison edged toward Roger, ready for an attack should Roger's collapse merely be a feint.

"Make it stop! Make it stop!" Roger cried, then, "Save her, sire. It's not too late. Save her."

Benison knelt down over his childe. The prince had seen too much of this in the past weeks not to recognize it for what it was. The agony might end any moment, or it might go on for days. Benison was visibly forcing himself to remain calm, a difficult task so soon after his temper was sparked. "Roger. Childe. Can you hear me?"

"Save her," Roger pleaded. His eyes, squeezed shut a moment before, were open now, full of urgency and pain. "Save her."

Benison looked back at the body which Eleanor was examining. He was no stranger to death. The old woman had been dead for several days already. No one was going to save her. "Who is she?" Benison asked, somewhat uncomfortable with a personal question.

"Mother," Roger muttered half under his breath. "Save her. Take her to the church. Listen for the music."

For the next half hour, Benison and Eleanor listened as Roger, between debilitating waves of pain, rambled on about his mother and faith healing, about a pale young woman and an old church in Reynoldstown, about the most beautiful song that would cure all ills.

Eleanor was touched by the emotional display. Even as Roger lapsed completely beyond lucidity, he was trying to ensure that his mother would be cared for. Even when he'd been in the grip of the curse-induced dementia, he'd been trying to save her. But it was far too late. Too late for her. Too late for Roger. There was nothing to be done.

Like so many of the others, Roger succumbed in the end. His head lolled back, and blood seeped from his body as if from a sieve. As he was taken in by final death and his body began to decompose, Eleanor saw Benison's face hardened in a scowl, his brow creased with deep furrows. Again, Eleanor placed her hand on her husband's shoulder. He turned to face her.

"He was weak," said Benison gravely. "He was weak, and his blood is reclaimed by the earth. God spare us from this curse." He rose, and without another word, walked out of the room.

ELEVEN

Mohammed was ready for trouble, almost looking forward to it, really. He'd gotten word less than an hour ago that a couple El Hermandad were messing with the museum, the California Afro-American Museum that he had worked long and hard to see built. That he did not tolerate. Bravo, the Crypt's Son who had called, said the rival gang members were harassing people around the museum and had gone as far as to engage in minor vandalism. They had seemed in no hurry to move on, and the police had not bothered to show up.

That was something Mohammed would have to check into. The cops in his barony had certain areas that, at his insistence, were high priorities—the museum, Exposition Park as a whole, the USC campus across the street. Mohammed was going to have an explanation, and someone was going to pay for this lapse.

Bravo, a mortal himself but educated in the ways of the Kindred and in line to become a ghoul, had also said that the two vandals were vampires. He was laying low and keeping an eye on things until help arrived.

And here was the help. Mohammed had decided it would do the Crypt's Sons' morale good amidst all the paranoia and hysteria for him to make a public appearance and deal with this little problem personally. El Hermandad needed to know that they couldn't take him for granted. So he, along with two other vampires, two ghouls, and eight mortal gang members, had jumped into four cars and torn along Harbor Freeway. Presently they were double-parked—*Just let the cops hassle us!*—and walking briskly through the park toward the museum. Mohammed might not have had his best men with him, but what he lacked in quality, he made up for in quantity.

Organization, Mohammed thought. *You can't keep order without organization.* And he couldn't maintain his organization with every other vampire and ghoul under his command dead or in hiding from this so-called curse.

Maybe it is a curse.

At first Mohammed had suspected some disease, the way it seemed to be spreading, the way so many underlings had shown a similar progression of symptoms. He hadn't yet been Embraced in the '50s when two mysterious plagues had swept through the Sabbat, wiping out over a third of their number.

Mohammed's organizations surpassed those losses. Among his clandestine Sabbat followers, casualties were roughly eighty percent, worse attrition than even many suicidal war parties. His ghoul and Kindred gang losses had been closer to half. Still devastating.

Mohammed had tried to take precautions. He had friends on staff at USC's medical school, and he'd had one of the desiccated victims examined. Battery after battery of tests had turned up nothing. And if it were a disease, the doctor had pointed out, mortals would surely be falling victim as well. Mohammed was still just as much in the dark.

After Francesca had lost her prolonged struggle against the curse, Mohammed had burned the house in Watts. Nobody would make much of a fuss about one more fire-bombed building in that riot-scarred neighborhood. *Whatever that curse was, let it die with Francesca.* Mohammed had moved back to his crypt in Inglewood Park Cemetery—the source of the Crypt's Sons' name, shortened among most mortals. To some extent he had been laying low too, trying to regroup, conferring with his newly promoted lieutenants, like Kenny and Marquis who were with him tonight. So that was another reason this little demonstration was called for, to let everyone know that Mohammed al-Muthlim was still master of his barony. These two interlopers were going to wish they'd never heard that name, and they on the far side of Mohammed's territory from their own turf.

As he and his crew descended into the huge expanse of sunken rose garden in Exposition Park, Mohammed pressed his hand against the breast of the light jacket he wore. It was more than warm enough in L.A. for just shirt sleeves, even three days before New Year's, but some things a T-shirt didn't quite conceal, like the two wooden stakes that Mohammed could feel against his chest. No mercy tonight. Salvador's boys were going down, and going down hard.

Even close to midnight, the rose gardens were far from deserted. Ahead, a handful of Hispanic businessmen in suits laughed loudly, probably taking a walk after the Clippers game. Nearby a young couple were out for a romantic stroll, and on a parallel path through the garden to the right a group of students with backpacks made their way…to class? Not this late at night. The hair on the back of Mohammed's neck pricked up.

"Down!" he yelled as he dropped to the ground.

Some of his entourage followed his lead unquestioningly. Those who did not were cut down as a hail of bullets ripped through them from the right side. The "students" had dropped their backpacks and opened up with formerly concealed automatic weapons.

For the moment, the rose bushes and shrubberies were providing a modicum of cover. They wouldn't, though, be any help against the business suits directly ahead on the path who, Mohammed now saw, were reaching into their jackets.

At least four of Mohammed's mortals had gone down in the initial blast. Those remaining were trying to return fire but were sorely pinned down.

Not waiting to be strafed by the suits, Mohammed leapt to his left to take care of the "young couple" who would undoubtedly be drawing a bead on the distracted Crypt's Sons. In midair he took a slug in the back, but still managed to land next to the couple ten yards away.

The two, college-aged, were cowering in terror from the gunfire. Mohammed doubted that they were El Hermandad after all, but there was no way to be sure. He struck the male an upward blow that must have separated his skull from the top of his spine. The boy landed in the bushes several feet away.

The girl he grabbed just as several bullets ripped into her torso. The force of the shots knocked her backward out of his grip. She might not be dead, but she wouldn't be causing any trouble.

The shots had come from the business types wielding semi-automatic pistols. Mohammed's other two vampires, Kenny and Marquis, were leading a charge against the students, some of whom were busy reloading. Mohammed decided he would take care of the suits.

Again, he launched himself into the air, daring the Hispanic mafiosos to gun him down. They took him up on his dare. Bullet after bullet tore into his airborne body. Worse yet was the sawed-off shotgun one of the suits had lumbered out from under his jacket at the same moment. The gun roared to life, but not with the usual explosion of lead.

The foot-long wooden stake fired from the shotgun at point-blank range slammed into his chest.

Mohammed's lunge carried him into the four gunmen, knocking the first two to the ground. He landed hard on top of them. For a split second he expected to be paralyzed by the stake embedded in his chest, but the aim had been rushed and the deadly stake had not struck true into his heart.

When he tried to jump to his feet, though, his left arm failed him, some vital muscle or tendon shredded by the stake slanting into his shoulder. Mohammed only clumsily managed to roll over. The two suits still standing hesitated, not able to get a clear shot. It was enough time for Mohammed to rip the pistol away from one of the attackers beneath him and spray deadly fire at the two standing over him. They staggered backward and collapsed to the ground.

One of the men Mohammed had knocked down grabbed the stake protruding from the vampire and jerked it to the side. Searing pain shot up and down Mohammed's entire left side. Colored spots danced before his eyes.

Losing an incredible amount of blood from his many wounds, he fired blindly until the pistol's clip was empty. The kaleidoscope spots grew brighter, swelling until their edges met....

Mohammed was staring at the bright stars in the sky. *Stars? This is* L.A. The only stars he or anyone was likely to see in this town were on Sunset Boulevard. He blinked hard and the bright stars began to shimmer and dance around. It took a moment for him to realize that he'd blacked out. *The ambush...*

He reached up to the stake in his chest, and it all came rushing back to him, a bit too vividly. How long had he been out? The firefight seemed to be over.

Then there was a single shot not far away. And another.

If El Hermandad had won, they would be looking for him, and they would find him any second. Mohammed tried to crawl quietly toward one of the pistols on the ground nearby. If he were lucky, it might still have a few rounds left in it.

Every inch flashed excruciating tremors along his left side. The brick sidewalk was slick with blood, his mixing with that of the mafiosos.

The spots began their dance again. He had to stop. And the gun seemed so far away.

"Mohammed!"

They had spotted him. Another gun shot nearby.

Through the pain, he made one last effort to reach the weapon. He collapsed just shy. Too much blood loss. He was too weak. Desperately he licked at the sidewalk. If he could just get enough blood…

Hands grabbed him roughly and turned him over on the sidewalk. "Mohammed!" Marvin, now a ghoul, thanks only to the manpower shortage, seemed very relieved and lifted his domitor to his feet. "There you are."

Each movement was pure agony. Mohammed nearly blacked out again. After steadying himself, he quickly surveyed the scene. Very few of his men were standing "The others?" he forced out through teeth clenched against the pain.

"Rodney's shot up pretty bad. So are Kenny and Marquis, but they're alive, like you. All the other boys but Johnny and Pancho are dead. Rico's dead. Tickler's dead. Hey, do you know why they called him Tickler?" Marvin laughed, but quickly fell silent under Mohammed's withering glare.

Marvin turned to look behind him and managed to bump the embedded stake. Mohammed winced and cursed. "Marvin," he said, too weak to fly into a rage, "do you see this stake?"

"Yeah. You want me to get that for you?" He reached toward it.

"*Touch* it again, and you die."

Marvin's hand stopped mid-motion. He decided to use it to rub his chin.

Mohammed pulled away from his oafish ghoul, a painful act of will, and managed to stand on his own. "Find Bravo," he instructed Marvin. "One way or another, bring him to the house on Comrie Road in Inglewood. You know the one?" Marvin nodded. "I want to know if he set me up or if he was tricked."

Marvin nodded again and left to carry out his orders. Mohammed hobbled over to the others. These wounds were going to heal slowly, he knew. He had lost a lot of blood.

Pancho and Johnny were trying to help away Rodney and Kenny and Marquis. The ground was littered with bodies and spent shell casings. The rose bushes and shrubs caught in the fight could not have been more devastated by a plague of locusts. Flowers and leaves were stuck to bloody corpses, the bushes themselves stripped bare, in some places shorn down to the ground.

"Look at this, *jefe*." Pancho pointed at one of the

bodies. Mohammed recognized it immediately. Jorge Ramirez, cousin and ghoul to Jesus Ramirez, Salvador's second-in-command and de facto leader of El Hermandad while Salvador was off around the globe. Just as Mohammed suspected, and now he had all the proof he needed.

Without further delay, the survivors proceeded back to the cars. As much gunplay as had gone down, bystanders would stay away a little longer, but Mohammed didn't want to linger too long. There were barely enough able bodies to get the vehicles back.

Mohammed, with Rodney moaning and semiconscious in the back seat, was furious. He had been led by the hand into a trap. Whether Bravo had been turned or tricked, Mohammed should have seen it coming. But the park wasn't even contested territory. It was firmly within the domain of the Crypt's Sons, even on the far side from El Hermandad hunting grounds. What better place to stage an ambush? It had proven almost totally effective. *Almost*, though Mohammed. *And now I pay them back.*

But why stage such a daring, elaborate attack with only ten or so mortals and ghouls, not a single Kindred?

Why...unless El Hermandad were that desperate? *This was not Salvador's work*, Mohammed decided. *He would never send others to confront his* rival directly. Not enough drama. No, Salvador is either still out of the country or...Mohammed perked up at the thought, *or dead!*

Either way, Ramirez was desperate. Probably his men were dropping left and right as well. Mohammed hadn't had time to count the bodies. If the cops were being paid off—and it would have to be an enormous amount of money to overcome their fear of Mohammed—he didn't want to confront them while seriously injured and with no real backup. But tonight would be a considerable drain of manpower on El Hermandad, probably more so than for Crypt's Sons, because Salvador's gang was smaller from the start.

They took a desperate gamble, and it failed, Mohammed realized, momentarily forgetting about the dozens of bullets and the stake in his body. *Now I must make them pay, no matter how much it hurts.*

This is war!

Owain fairly threw open the lid to his luxurious coffin on New Year's Eve. Sometimes he just lay there for hours, even after he'd awoken, lacking the energy and the will to rise and face another night. But not this night. The first notes of the siren's song had coaxed him from his slumber.

How is it, he wondered, *that even in my resting place I can hear her? How does she do it? I must find out.*

Even Owain's remarkable hearing did not explain the fact. Chances that he would discover the answer tonight, however, were slim. Owain's objective investigation of the siren had long since given over to total immersion in her song. Certainly he still possessed intellectual curiosity about what was happening, as when he had first stumbled across the rites over a month ago, but once the music took hold, the visceral emotions it stirred were undeniable. Emotions that Owain had not felt the twinge of in tens of years were making themselves known, and suddenly Atlanta, and unlife in general, was not such a dreadful place.

No time for a shave. He would just have to live with stubble tonight. Owain grabbed a shirt and vest and slacks from his closet.

He was amazed by the energy he felt. He had not exercised such vigor since…he couldn't remember when. A vampire's habits formed over tens and hundreds of years. Left sock, left shoe. Right sock, right shoe. Even minor changes in routine did not normally occur overnight, but Owain had felt so very different the past weeks. Last night, he had thought he'd felt a twinge of actual hunger. That hadn't happened in…again, he couldn't remember how long. Of course he had always fed regularly, because he knew he needed to, and that was the type of thing that a ghoul like Randal tended to keep track of like an overprotective mother. But

Owain had not been driven by a powerful appetite for blood in years. The sensation last night had caught him so off guard that he had even gone hunting, prowling the shadows outside a debutante ball until a luscious high-society snack had wandered his way.

Owain quickly made his way downstairs. "Randal!" he called the ghoul. "Have Ms. Jackson bring the car!"

"Good evening, sir." Randal was always prepared when Owain came down—well-groomed, every red hair in place, white shirt starched and ironed, black tie and vest immaculate. "News from the State Supreme Court today, sir. They have refused to hear the zoning appeal by the Citizens Empowerment Union." Randal paused, his expression growing concerned. "Did you forget to shave, sir?"

"No. I did not forget."

"But, sir…"

"Randal, do not dote on me this evening. Or ever. Do you understand?"

Randal paused again. He knew to steer clear of Owain in his black moods, but this was different. "Yes, sir."

"Have you called Ms. Jackson?"

"Pardon me, sir?" Randal was still a sentence behind.

"Have you called Ms. Jackson as I asked you to?"

"Not yet, sir."

"And why, exactly, not?"

"Yes, sir. Right away, sir." Randal turned without comment and left the room.

Definitely time for a change, Owain decided. *High time.*

There were a slew of details that needed taking care of. Lorenzo Giovanni had requested information on several Atlanta Kindred, and Owain supposed that he should thank Benjamin for seeing to it that Justice Chamberlain and then the State Supreme Court had made such wise decisions. A dose of sweet wine to ease the burn of Benjamin's wormwood was not uncalled for. But there would be time for all of that later. Legal affairs had a way of dragging out until Owain was glad he had the lifespan of a vampire to see them through. And Giovanni had not sounded as if he were in too much of a rush.

Again, Owain caught a hint of the siren's song. He was looking forward to glimpses of familiar lands. *Adref.* His thoughts turned homeward. But unlike those mortals, and perhaps Albert and Roger, Owain told himself, he was not compelled to attend the rites at the church. He could ignore the song if he chose to do so. He simply did not chose to do so.

Owain needed a peaceful, relaxing evening, he reminded himself. The past several days, his rest had been dogged by visions. Always the mist and the menacing tree taking shape from the staff, and all the rest.

What better way to relax than to satisfy his intellectual curiosity?

"Sir." Randal came back into the study carrying a small piece of paper. "This message just arrived from Prince Benison. He is requesting your presence at an emergency council meeting of the primogen tonight."

Owain's first reaction was that he didn't remember having given Randal leave to open official correspondences. Then the content of the message registered. "Tonight." Owain grimaced. The prince had been increasingly distraught for weeks now, and even though the epistle was worded as a *request,* it was in effect a summons.

The lilting notes of the siren's song were growing stronger, like the first light droplets of a spring shower belying the magnitude of the approaching stormclouds.

Damnation! He couldn't even claim he hadn't received the message, for Benison's ghoul passenger pigeons were as dependable as the sunrise. Although the letter had been left with Randal and not directly with Owain.

There had to be some way. Owain thought. This conflict between duty and desire had constantly plagued him as a mortal, and through the early years after his Embrace. Shortly thereafter, however, he had decided that his duty was to fulfill his own desires. From that point on, he had mostly done what he wanted, though in recent history, there were very few instances that he had actually *wanted* anything. That was the difference this New Year's Eve.

Technically, Owain was not primogen. Eleanor represented the Ventrue, and she would be happy not to see Owain. It still amazed him that such a model of propriety should be indulging herself with Benjamin. How did the younger Ventrue excite her, by reading case studies from his law books?

That decided it. Owing Benjamin a favor, Owain would put Eleanor in a better frame of mind by not attending the meeting. Maybe she would be inspired to what Owain had always thought she really needed, Kindred or not—a good oldfashioned orgiastic screw.

"Shouldn't you shave before attending the council, sir?" Randal asked.

Owain handed the paper back to his ghoul. "I won't be going."

Randal couldn't believe what he was hearing. "But, sir, the prince…"

That was almost enough for Owain. "Would you like to approve my itinerary for the night, Randal? Should I submit a weekly schedule for your edification?"

Randal knew when he had pressed too far. "No,

sir," he said, the picture of deference.

"I thought not." Owain took his gilded dagger and placed it in his belt sheath. The stiletto was already in place. "Don't wait up, Randal." The Rolls was idling out front, and a moment later Owain and Ms. Jackson were speeding away toward Oakland Cemetery.

TWELVE

Benison stalked around the parlor. *Where on God's green earth is Evans?* The primogen were all present and waiting in the conference room for the prince. Owain wasn't even an actual member of the primogen. He held no voting privileges, but the prince had wanted him here as Benison instructed his followers how he was about to save his city from the curse which had almost destroyed it.

A disturbing thought crossed Benison's mind. Owain might have fallen victim to the curse. What other reason could there be for his absence? At any rate, Benison's patience was at an end. He would find out about Owain later.

As the prince made his way to the conference room, he could not help hearing the noise of the workmen repairing the wall in the living room. The lamp, pictures, and oriental rug had been replaced, the couch reupholstered. Another hour or two and every trace that Roger had ever existed would be removed. Benison grimaced at the thought of his only childe. The entire episode had been one long mistake. If Benison Embraced again, he would crush the childe in his own hands at the first sign of trouble rather than allowing the vexation to drag on for years.

Spare the rod, spoil the childe, he thought. It was another case of his leniency contradicting Divine will. It would not happen again.

The primogen awaited, seated around the large mahogany table within the conference room. Benison joined them. Bedelia, resting comfortably in her ornate wheelchair, represented Clan Malkavian, since Benison was prince. His faithful wife Eleanor wielded the Ventrue vote. Thelonious, with whom Benison had engaged in so many spirited debates, represented the Brujah; Marlene and Hannah the Toreador and Tremere respectively. Even Aurelius, the slimy, warted Nosferatu, had crawled from under his rock in response to the prince's summons. There was no Gangrel primogen in Atlanta, not that there weren't several clan members among the anarchs.

The casual conversation that had been limping along ceased as Benison entered the room. Deliberately, he walked around the table to his seat at the head, but did not sit. He leaned forward on his fists, looking up through his bushy auburn eyebrows at those assembled.

Speaking calmly and quietly, he began without preamble. All present were well aware of the crisis. "We, the Kindred of Atlanta, have always endeavored to remain faithful to our Creator above. It was through the legacy of one of the earliest sins, the first murder, that we are what we are. Our duty, therefore, is to seek redemption, to bring ourselves again in line with the wishes of our heavenly Father."

Benison paused, surveying the faces around the table. He knew there were those among the primogen who did not share his view of the Cainite's role and duties within the grand scheme of the universe, but he was determined that, even if they did not accept his rationale, they would endorse his measures. "Being more than mortal, yet less than divine, ever fallible, we have strayed from the path of redemption. Our Lord is displeased, and the Kindred of Atlanta suffer."

Eleanor and Marlene watched him closely. Thelonious stared at his own clasped hands, Hannah at the table, neither betraying any reaction to what was being said. This bothered the prince. Bedelia snored softly, while Aurelius' expression was unreadable through those bulbous rheumy eyes. The primogen of Atlanta were a guarded, stoic lot. Benison was hesitant to predict their responses.

"This curse laid upon us," he continued, "is a telling reflection of our transgressions. Because the young of our city flaunt our Father's wishes so willfully, because they take such pleasure in doing that which they are told not to, they suffer the greatest torment.

"I offer them no pity."

There was stirring and shifting of weight among the primogen. Thelonious, studied but Brujah through and through, held definite sympathies toward the younger Kindred. It was possible he might have guessed where Benison's thoughts were progressing. Marlene, too, through the "centers of recreation" she controlled—strip joints and sex clubs—dealt extensively with the more restless Cainites. She stood to lose a great deal from a disgruntled clientele.

They must see the greater danger! Benison thought.

"The younger Kindred revel in bending to the point of breaking the Masquerade, that which keeps us all safe in this world of mortals. They ignore hunting boundaries and sow their chaos throughout the city without a thought for any other but themselves." Recounting the indignities he suffered infuriated the prince. He grew more animated as his agitation mounted. His voice grew thunderous. "They abuse the latitude which, graciously, I grant them!"

Benison slammed his fist onto the table. "No more!"

Marlene jumped in her seat. Bedelia blinked awake and smacked her lips noisily.

"The Traditions that they ridicule," the prince continued, his pique still rising, "are the cement of Kindred civilization, that which sets us above foul beasts, they are the bulwark of the order mandated by our Creator at the beginning of time. And whereas I have tried to allow leeway so that each may follow his or her own conscience, I will no longer stand aside and watch the home which we have built, the society of which we are each irrevocably a part, torn apart for the selfish enjoyment of a few!" He pounded the table again, punctuating his point.

Benison took a moment to calm himself. No one yet dared to interrupt him by offering comment. Again he spoke in a low voice. "From this point forward, the Traditions shall be enforced. To the letter of the law. The so-called anarchs may live in my city, but anarchy shall not reign. They will obey the Traditions and the pronouncements of this council. Otherwise, they will face exile…or final death."

Thelonious could remain silent no longer. Benison was almost surprised that the Brujah had held his tongue to this point. "But our city flourishes because of our freedom, Prince Benison. The Kindred will not submit to a police state. You will have a second Anarch Revolt, and they will have many sympathizers."

Benison glared at Thelonious. *Get behind me, Satan*, the prince wanted to shout, but he restrained the impulse. Thelonious argued from conviction, not from maliciousness. But, still, Benison wished for a world without the misplaced loyalties of the Brujah clan.

"Our city flourishes because of freedom?" the prince asked mockingly. "Is a Kindred who feeds and feeds but cannot satisfy his hunger, no matter how much blood he consumes, flourishing? Is a Kindred who follows the path of his blood back through the lives of his ancestors until insanity takes hold of his mind and body flourishing? Is a Kindred attacked by his own hunger-crazed childe flourishing?"

Thelonious looked away. All knew of Roger's demise, and none wished to press Benison on that point. His fits of rage were as legendary as they were deadly.

"I...think...not!" The prince's fist against the table underlined each word. "The Traditions and the Laws shall be obeyed!" His eyes, dancing emerald fire, challenged any to deny him. Silence hung over the table, Thelonious again staring at his hands.

"That is my first decree of three," Benison went on, "and the very fact that I must *argue* that the Traditions should be upheld," he shot a fierce glance at Thelonious, "shows just how dark the nights have become." Normally, the prince welcomed, even encouraged, spirited debate among the primogen. Many were the dawns that he and Eleanor or Thelonious had paused in their contention over politics or finance or civil rights only because of the emergence of the sun. Tonight, however, his messianic fervor was stoked to a fever pitch, and there were only the righteous and the corrupt. The prince did not consider this gathering a deliberative forum, but rather an opportunity for the leaders of his community to sanction the course he had chosen.

"My second decree," Benison enumerated, "is this: that the Clanless among us, the Caitiff, shall choose their own clan to become a part of, or I will assign them to a clan, expecting them to fulfill all duties and responsibilities accorded a member." There was shock around the table now. Not even Eleanor had seen this coming.

But there was more. "If a Kindred should reject his or her incorporation into a clan, then he or she shall be banished from this city, and if he or she should defy exile, the punishment shall be final death."

There were several gasps. "But Prince Benison," said Eleanor, always careful to address her husband formally in public, "the anarchs will certainly never submit to such a law."

"I do not seek their consent," he shot back, obviously irritated to be questioned from that quarter. "They reject our instruments of governance, therefore I do not seek their advice on the laws we must live by."

"But this will mean war," Thelonious insisted. "They will rebel before submitting to this."

"Then they will die!" Benison snapped.

Thelonious refused to back down. "Do you want the Justicars to intervene? Because that is what will result of such arbitrary pronouncements. Do you want them here to govern because you cannot?"

Benison's face was reddening. Thelonious was pushing him very close to a violent rage, as all were aware. Both Marlene and Aurelius edged their chairs back from the table. Thelonius, sensing the precipice he approached, fell silent.

Benison's fingers were digging into the mahogany. A furious trembling took hold of him momentarily, but he struggled to maintain control. "These pronouncements are anything but arbitrary, Thelonious." The prince forced himself to smile as he said the name of the Brujah, but the result was more of a snarl. "For weeks, I have watched my city falling apart. I have watched as crazed Kindred ripped their brothers apart. I have watched as dementia led them to suicide. I have watched as the Masquerade verged on dissolution. Only because I have influence among the police, and because you, Thelonious, control the newspapers and other media, only for those reasons is our Kindred society not completely destroyed."

There were none who could deny the catastrophes which had befallen the city, none who had not witnessed the deterioration, the rot.

"I have watched," said Benison, "and as I have wrung my hands, I have studied. For there is not the first action among Kindred and kine that is not foretold. Though we act according to the free will our Creator endowed upon us, our every action, and every disaster that will befall us, is known.

"'This is the Endtime,'" he quoted. "This is the Falling of the Blood. This is the Winnowing.'"

Silence again held sway at the table. All had heard the prince, at his formerly weekly prayer meetings, recite or read from the fragments of the *Book of Nod* that he had acquired. Only, before, he had always shared the Law, the Traditions, the foundations of Camarilla society, never the darker prophecies which spelled out the doom of the Kindred.

"The Time of Fallen Blood is at hand," Benison

said. "There are the youngest of Kindred whose blood is too weak to create progeny." He continued:

"'And in the last days the Master will once again take up his Tools. The Firmament will tremble and the Earth itself will be split assunder. The secret places of the Earth will be cast up into the air and the creatures of darkness will shriek in the light of day. For it is written that Abel was a keeper of sheep but Caine a tiller of the ground.

"'The First-Born comes in fury. He harrows his children from their graves. His wrath is a hammer, an unhewn cudgel wet with the blood of the Kinslaying. He drives the lightning before him.'"

Benison paused. The words he spoke carried the weight of ages, and none who heard them considered them lightly, not even Brujah. "We have not only offended our God," said Benison gravely, "we have angered the Dark Father."

"'His voice is a dark wind scouring the plain. At his word, the sky opens, raining blood upon the furrows he has prepared. His children raise expectant faces to the Heavens, but they are choked and drowned in the torrent of spilling life. Such is the price of their hungers.'"

None of the primogen met the prince's gaze. Hearing the words, the declarations attributed to the scribe of the ancient First City, it was not so far-fetched that God or Caine had seen fit to shower wrathful destruction upon the Kindred.

"We have forgotten the ageless edicts, the ordained forms that define our existence," Benison insisted. "And the very blood that should give us life…" He raised his hand to his teeth and tore a gash in his palm, and as he clenched his fist, the blood ran down his arm and dripped onto the table. "…it is our curse."

The prince could see that there were still those who would oppose him, those who would lack his vision and courage. Thelonious, momentarily cowed but unpersuaded, glared at the table in front of his seat. Aurelius would never look beyond perceived slights of the past, regardless of the needs of the city. Marlene was frightened by such apocalyptic notions, while Hannah's loyalties lay primarily with her masters within the Tremere.

How, Benison wondered, *can they be so blind? They must see the truth!* He looked from face to face around the table. It was all so clear to him. "We are hastening the Endtime! We are calling destruction down upon our own heads! These decisions are far from arbitrary," he again assured the primogen. "If anything, they are preordained. I do not believe it is yet too late to return to the path of righteousness. We will lead the way for all Kindred. This city will be a beacon on the hill, leading them through the Dark Times."

There was silence.

"The Clanless must be brought to heel; they must integrate themselves into a clan, or face the consequences. We must restore the rightful order, or face the Endtime. *'Then shall Caine unyoke his red-eyed ox, whose name is called Gehenna, for none may abide its countenance.'"*

Eleanor watched her husband closely, moved by the intensity of his conviction. Marlene removed her hands from the table, trying to hide her trembling from the others.

Finally it was Thelonious who spoke in a quietly defiant tone:

"As primogen, we must vote on these matters."

Benison fumed. Full of pride and righteous indignation, he scowled at the Brujah. "We will vote on the decrees *in toto*. That is my right."

Benison looked around the table. He had deluded himself, he realized, into hoping for the unamimous backing of the primogen. In reality, he was not even assured the four votes required for victory.

But there was still his third decree.

"A holy place of worship has been defiled." Benison continued, gazing slowly around the table at each of the primogen, searching for any flash of recognition. He saw none. Even foul, flat-nosed Aurelius looked perplexed. "This, of course, happened without my knowledge but has recently come to my attention. Not far to the east of here, an unknown vampire of rare bloodline secretly took haven in an abandoned church. There, on consecrated ground, she not only fed without permission upon mortals of this city, but also performed heinous demonic rituals! She may even have created progeny without my consent or the consent of any elder." Still the prince watched their faces. "I will ask this once of you as primogen. Only once." He waited a moment to let them absorb the implication of that statement, then asked, "Did any in this room know of this violation of Tradition, of Law, of holy will?"

Not often was a prince able to put the entire primogen of his city to such scrutiny. Times were desperate, however, and none of the elders balked at the implicit accusation. To object to the prince's audacity might be interpreted as guilt, and in his current state of mind, Benison was not likely to forgive or to forget any admission, real or imagined.

The silence hung heavy over the table.

"Very well," said Benison finally. "I will tell you what I will tell all of the Kindred of Atlanta tomorrow night. Having been given one opportunity of confession, there will be no mercy." Benison stared hard around the table. "I will take care of this Daughter of Cacophony. After tonight, her siren's song will not curse this city, or any other."

Roger had not given the prince so much information. Benison wasn't even sure from the final rantings if his departed childe had even realized that his pale vocalist was a vampire. But Roger had let Benison know what was going on, and the prince had other sources of information.

No mere eccentricity, Benison's seemingly one-sided conversations were a powerful tool in his ruling the city. There were countless spirits roaming the streets and halls of Benison's city. The restless dead of slavery, of the War Between the States, of the civil rights crusade all haunted Atlanta. From his sire Bedelia, Benison had learned the art—or perhaps curse—of seeing and conversing with those spirits.

After Roger had passed beyond, Benison had spoken with one member of the Anacreon, the spirit counterpart to the Kindred primogen. It was at the request of the Anacreon that Benison had set Oakland Cemetery off limits to all Kindred. The spirit had made inquiries among her kind and reported back to Benison. Between the facts provided by Roger and the spirits, Benison had figured out the rest. And armed with that knowledge, he was determined to rectify the situation.

"Song? What's wrong with a song?" All eyes turned toward Aunt Bedelia, who had suddenly become unusually animated, her eyes bright and curious. "I like a good song now and then. Quite a dancer I am," she said, tapping her feet on the footrest of her wheelchair.

Benison was taken aback by her outburst.

Bedelia's word was law to him, and even her off-hand questioning of his decree eroded the prince's certainty. Maybe he had overreacted. Perhaps the Daughter of Cacophony's song was not a curse upon the city. Benison felt his knees buckling. Only his sire could have shaken him so.

"Perhaps, then, we should go ahead and vote," suggested Thelonious, emboldened by the prince's distress, "while we're all...attentive." He glanced over at Bedelia, who had a wide grin on her face.

Benison licked his dry lips. "Very well." He looked nervously around the table. "We will vote on the decrees. Three as one."

Thelonious stood. "I vote against the decrees," he announced defiantly, but then nodded deferentially to Benison. "Though I admire Prince Benison's motives, I feel these measures will only worsen the situation, aggravating an already tenuous situation with the anarchs. As for the intruding vampire, I believe she can be dealt with in accordance with existing law regarding violation of the Traditions." Thelonious sat.

"I, too, vote against," muttered Aurelius in a low gravelly voice that reminded Benison of a growl in the back of a wild dog's throat. Unlike Thelonious, the Nosferatu offered no explanation for his decision.

Eleanor stood. "I support the decrees," she said with enough hesitation to betray less than utter confidence. For an instant, she looked as if she were about to qualify her statement, but she said nothing else and retook her seat.

"I vote for the decrees," said Marlene, still clenching her hands together and smiling half-heartedly at the prince.

Hannah stared at the table, not meeting anyone's gaze, not yet saying anything.

Benison looked toward Aunt Bedelia. She was still very interested in the proceedings around her. "Mother?" the prince prompted her expectantly.

She smiled broadly at her childe. "What are we voting on?"

Benison sighed in exasperation. Others restrained irritated mutterings. The prince rubbed his face then vigorously scratched his bearded chin. "We're voting on the decrees," he patiently explained. "The decrees to hold Kindred accountable for violations of the Traditions; to compel marauding, looting Caitiff to adopt the customs of respectable clans; and to destroy a villainous wretch who has trespassed and brought the wrath of God down on our city."

Bedelia nodded enthusiastically. "Yes, that's right. About the song. I like singing. I vote against the decrees." She positively beamed at Benison, she was so proud of herself.

The prince braced himself against the table and swallowed hard. "But, mother, do you understand…"

"That's how I vote," she snapped, her good humor suddenly at an end. "Is it morning?" She looked around the room searching for a nonexistent window. "I'm tired. Could you brush my hair for me, J. Benison?"

The prince did not hear his sire. He had sunk down into his chair. How, he wondered, could this be happening? His heartfelt convictions and decisive course of action all going terribly awry. Hopelessness took hold of him, squeezing his heart to the point of physical pain.

"I vote for the decrees."

Benison's head snapped up. "Pardon?"

Hannah still looked only at the table, uncomfortable that so many eyes were focused on her. "I vote for the decrees," she repeated quietly and said no more.

Thelonious, shocked, turned to Hannah, but no words escaped his open mouth.

Benison felt the power of conviction flooding back into his body. He practically bounded out of his chair. "Of course you do. As do I. The New Year's Writ of Three is approved by the primogen of Atlanta, to be carried out by myself, J. Benison Hodge, prince of Atlanta, on this…" he pulled out his gold pocket watch which showed twelve minutes past midnight, "first day of January, the year of our Lord nineteen hundred and ninety-nine."

Benison triumphantly snapped his watch shut

and began around the table toward the door, his brief crisis of confidence utterly annihilated. "There's little time to spare. You each have a task: to inform every member of your clan, and every anarch, every Kindred in the city—tomorrow night at midnight, we gather at the abandoned warehouse across from the Oakland Cemetery. No exceptions. *Every* Kindred is to be present." Benison stopped for a brief moment at the door. "Eleanor, dearest, could you see the guests out. I have business to take care of."

And with that, the prince was gone.

The quaint little village, the inhabitants doubtlessly sleeping under their roofs of heavy thatch, had no warning of Ragnar Nordstrom's approaching Viking longboat. The Norsemen were silent as the grave as their craft slowly ground to a halt near shore, sending rings of concentric ripples to distort the reflection of the full moon upon the water.

The raiders had their orders. There was room on the boat for twelve slaves. They could take places at the oars, spelling the crew, until Ragnar grew hungry and summoned the captives, first one, then another, and another. The crucial calculation was not draining them so frequently as to run out of slaves before finding another suitable village.

This place, Ice Land, strangely named with its

hot springs and greenery, was farther than most of Ragnar's men had travelled before. The last few nights had been a close thing, with no land sighted in many days, and the last of the Irish slaves used up. The crew, fearing for their own lives, from starvation and from Ragnar, could have mutinied during the day when he would have been helpless to stop them. They could have overpowered the three mates Ragnar had ghouled for just such daylight protection, and cast their vampire master into the sea.

Possibly he could have dived deep into the murky depths away from the sunlight. Possibly he could even have caught up with the longboat that night and exacted his revenge. But most likely he would have languished in the cruel sea like the day's catch in the stewpot.

Even had the crew succeeded in destroying Ragnar, they would have had no chance of turning back. They had come too far from familiar land. They still would have faced the same expanse of sea with diminishing supplies and no exquisite killer to aid them in battle should they find civilization.

Ragnar would continue to the west. There were reports of a Green Land, and of a vast land of rivers and trees beyond that. The vampiric blood that flowed through Ragnar's veins drove him ever onward. Even the shores of Ireland and the rugged mountains of Wales were too crowded for him. *The blood will change you*, the beast that had taken him had growled. And so it had. The sea was all Ragnar had known, but already the confines of a ship were preying on his nerves. Maybe he would slip away from his crew at Green Land if it was half as lush as this Ice Land. If not, he would continue westward until he found a land large and wide enough for him, and then he would run and hunt beneath the moon and revel in the freedom of open spaces.

For now, however, there was the village.

A portion of Ragnar's men moved stealthily to the far side of the village to cut off the most likely route of escape. The raiders had their orders. Twelve slaves. Everything else was ripe for plunder.

Ragnar had an epiphanous thought and turned to Sven, the closest ghoul. "Two extra slaves, Sven," Ragnar whispered. He would sate himself before they set out to sea again, to make the twelve slaves last as long as possible. Sven nodded acknowledgement and passed word to those nearby.

All was in place. The village slept peacefully.

Ragnar lit and raised a torch—the signal. With a thunderous roar, the attack began.

The inhabitants of the huts closest to the sea were caught unaware, sleeping. In just a few minutes the requisite fourteen captives were bound and a hut set aflame—the signal that all booty was now fair game. A lusty cheer arose from the Norsemen.

Smoke and cinders filled the air as the thatch roofs of one hut after another were put to the torch. The fleeing villagers offered only token resistance. The Vikings were too well armed, and with the advantage of complete surprise were terrorizing and slaughtering the villagers before any real defense could be mounted. The men the Norsemen killed. The women and boys they sometimes stopped to rape, but otherwise dispatched just as brutally. There was little hard wealth to be had in this sleepy hamlet, so more often than not the wives and sisters of the village received the attentions of at least one of the raiders before a merciful death.

The screams of his men's victims rang in Ragnar's ears, and he smiled. Only the strong and ruthless survived in this life, and only a chosen few, he had discovered, lived beyond the mortal veil, kings among men. Each scream, each vial of life's blood spilled onto the rocky soil, was a tribute to Ragnar's mastery over life…and over death.

To his surprise, three villagers with swords had somehow managed to find one another and, facing outward, were protecting one another's backs. Several Norsemen circled, feinting or lunging with their weapons, but none had broken through.

Ragnar frowned. *What do they hope to accomplish? They cannot save their women, or their homes, or even their lives, but still they fight rather than flee. Futile.*

But he knew it was exactly what he or any of his men would do in the same situation.

Not particularly wanting to lose any of his men before the journey ahead, Ragnar strode over to the contested melee. He motioned for the Norsemen to back away, which they did.

Two of the villagers shifted to face him. The third, facing the other way, guarded their backs.

"Tell your friend to join us," said Ragnar. "The others will not attack."

One of the duo facing Ragnar spat in his direction and spoke in a strange, thick accent that Ragnar only understood as being defiant. They held their ground, swords poised, ready for attacks from any direction.

All around, the last of the villagers who had been kept from fleeing were dying.

Ragnar set his shield on the ground and stepped forward. He would face them with sword only. It was more than he expected he would need, but why take chances?

Ragnar feinted with his sword, and as his two opponents reacted, with blinding speed he reached between their shoulders, digging with clawed fingers into the back of the head of the man guarding their backs. Ragnar jerked the man through, out of the reach of his friends, and crushed his skull as all looked on.

The two remaining villagers stared at Ragnar and

their friend's slumped body in disbelief. A disarming flick of Ragnar's sword and a claw through the hamstring, and the second man was down.

The third lowered his sword, certain that he could not prevail. Ragnar tore out his throat, granting a quick death.

"Not bad," came a voice from behind him. "But can you take an evergreen?"

Slowly, Ragnar turned.

The world shifted suddenly, spinning uncontrollably. Ragnar struggled to keep his feet. He was surrounded not by his Norsemen and the gratifying smell of burning thatch on the sea air, but by the blurry forms of trees and the babble of runnng water.

"What is your name, oh ravager of trees?" asked the figure before him.

Still the world rocked beneath his feet. Gradually his vision cleared. "My name…my name is Nicholas."

The newcomer was Kindred, Gangrel as well, Nicholas could tell at first glance by his wolf-like features. That, and he did not smell enough to be lupine.

"My name is Edward Blackfeather," said the other Gangrel. "Will you try your hand against one less rooted to a single spot?"

Nicholas glanced behind him. Huge gouges were ripped out of two trees, and another, a thin sapling, was completely uprooted and lying at his feet.

"Or do you only sully your claws with sap?" asked Blackfeather, squatting atop a boulder.

Nicholas smiled, and launched himself at his new acquaintance.

Blackfeather leapt into the tree branches above him as Nicholas sailed past. Nicholas landed and turned, ready for an attack from behind, but there was no sign of Blackfeather...until he tackled Nicholas from the other side.

Nicholas tried to roll and scramble away, but Blackfeather's incredibly strong grip was unbreakable, and he quickly had Nicholas pinned beneath him. This close, Nicholas realized that much of Blackfeather's body was covered with dark fur. His ears, partially hidden by his long black hair, were wolfen, and his fangs shone in the moonlight. Aside from barely managing to scratch his assailant's wrists, Nicholas could accomplish nothing from his position.

"I give up," said Nicholas.

"Probably not a bad call." Blackfeather winked, then got off and allowed Nicholas up.

Their mettle tested against one another and relative prestige determined, this meeting between Gangrel proceeded on friendly terms. "I am of the Cherokee nation," said Blackfeather. "The Blue Ridge Mountains are my province, from Georgia to Virginia. I am Garou-friend," he proclaimed proudly, then shrugged his shoulders, "except when I am Garou-enemy. They are an unpredictable lot."

"I am Gangrel of the wide open spaces," Nicholas responded. "From Russia as a mortal I fled after the Revolution, a Menshevik without a home. These nights, both the forests of Europe and the American plains call loudly to me."

Normally among the Gangrel, introductions would evolve into story after story, each spinner of tales attempting to outdo his companion until the tales reached epic and mythological proportions, and Nicholas in particular could have wound many a yarn of his ancestors feats—all too familiar to him—but this night other matters loomed.

"Have you heard," Blackfeather asked, "of the blood curse that strikes down the Kindred?"

Nicholas stiffened. "I have heard." He wanted to say, *I have felt it! I hunger always! I spend as many nights not knowing who I am as knowing—if I am myself, or my sire, or his sire, or his sire before him!* But he feared he would drive away the only real companionship he had found in months. "It is that curse in the city I am fleeing," Nicholas explained.

"Then you have seen the carnage?" Blackfeather was intrigued to have a first-hand account. He had heard stories from various quarters but avoided the cities himself, where the concentrations of Kindred were found, and where the curse had wrought the greatest destruction.

Nicholas told him what he could remember from the stupor-filled weeks he had spent in Atlanta—anarchs and others going mad with hunger, Cainites refusing out of fear to leave their havens except when they were forced to hunt. He did not mention the delusions, the ancestral regression which was becoming widespread. He did not want to remind Blackfeather of the earlier battle with the trees he had witnessed.

For his part, Blackfeather related stories that he had heard of Cainite wars breaking out in city after city as existing power structures were ripped asunder, and those ambitious or insane enough rushed in to fill the void.

"Another reason to stay out of the cities, I say," Blackfeather suggested.

Nicholas nodded agreement. He was headed for the wide open spaces. He'd only been in the city for an errand, and now that, thankfully, was completed.

The two Gangrel talked until near sun-up, then sank into the ground to rest through the day and go their separate ways the next night.

THIRTEEN

It was a clear crisp night, and Owain could see stars through the holes above him in the belfry. He was growing impatient. The prelude was continuing much longer tonight than it normally did. What was the siren waiting for? There were a handful of mortals kneeling in the sanctuary already. How many did she and her brood need?

Owain peered down through the hole. Even after using his vampiric gifts to shield his presence, he remained leery of being too obvious. He was not worried about the mortals. He had years and years of experience walking before their eyes without beeing seen, but with other Cainites, one never knew the extent of their power. There were supposedly ancient vampires in the world whose powers would dwarf Owain's, and there would be no way to know he was confronting one until it was too late.

The siren below, the beautiful creature who had brought emotion back into Owain's unlife, appeared to be a mere teenager, but Owain himself looked barely more than twenty years of age. He had felt at times that perhaps she did know he was lurking in the shadows, voyeuristically taking part in the ritual frenzies below. And it was possible that she did know. But why would she continue as if she didn't? Maybe she didn't care, as long as she and her brood were sufficiently nourished at the conclusion of the rites.

There was no way for Owain to know, short of confronting her.

Uncertainties abounded. There had been the one night that Albert had looked right at Owain. Had Albert seen Owain despite the Ventrue's precautions? Could Owain guess with any hope of accuracy what went on in the Malkavian's mind? Probably there was little for Albert to gain, if he even knew, in revealing Owain's presence.

There would be much greater risk for Owain in pursuing any of these questions, which would mean confronting those involved, than in hoping the questions would never attain relevance. As long as the siren continued to sing, Owain didn't care if she did know, somehow, that he was there. As long as the rites were not common knowledge, it did not matter if Albert thought he might have seen Owain in the church once.

The uncertainty, Owain realized, exhilarated him. The danger made the nights intriguing. What had been the thrill of being shut away on his estate? Manipulating a stock deal for a few more dollars? Secretly buying another company?

As long as he didn't act *too* rashly, he cautioned himself. No sense throwing away nearly a thousand years of survival for a fleeting joy ride. Still, he appreciated his reacquaintance with the thrill of life.

Below, the front door of the church opened, and Albert sauntered in. This was the only place that Owain had ever seen the Malkavian behave even semirespectfully. It was quite unusual to see Albert regard the reverence of any place or person, but the siren's song apparently gave him pause as nothing else Owain had observed. He noticed, too, that Roger was not with Albert.

Owain sat back in his hiding place. If the siren wished to draw out her invitation, there was nothing he could do about it, and he didn't wish to parade himself before Albert. Instead, Owain let the siren's music wash over him without resistance.

She sang so easily, as if there were no other desire in her heart. With his eyes closed, Owain could picture her delicate face upturned, mouth open, jaw and throat relaxed. Her nostrils flared just slightly as she drew in breath needed only for her song. Mirroring her soul, every breath she took existed wholly for her music.

The lofty notes took hold of Owain, feeding in him the need for warmth, and acceptance, and comfort. With ease, Owain found the strain of the song that was hers, and that which was his, and he willingly followed where they took him.

☥

Antwuan hurried down the street. He had been at a movie with Little Johnnie when he heard the angel's song. At least he hadn't had to run out on a date. Didn't really need a date when he was going to come back here to Shaquanna at the church. Away from there, he and Shaquanna exchanged glances and smiles, neither mentioning those incredible nights. But once the magical music began, Shaquanna was insatiable, wanting Antwuan again and again, until finally he stumbled home barely able to stand. Already he could feel her warm body against him, could smell her scent, could taste her neck, her shoulder, her breast. The angel had answered Antwuan's prayers.

At the church, Antwuan came up short, surprised by the large white man standing on the walk in front of the old building. The guy's hair was spiked and dyed nearly fluorescent blond. It practically glowed in the dark. The man dwarfed Antwuan, and Antwuan wasn't that scrawny. This wasn't someone Antwuan had seen before, but no one had ever noticed the church who wasn't there following the song. So it took all types.

Antwuan walked up to the man ready to nod and keep going on in, but the huge stranger held out a hand for Antwuan to stop.

"Are you going in here, friend?" the man asked in a deep throaty voice.

"Yeah." Antwuan was anxious to get inside.

The man smiled as Antwuan stepped past, then grabbed him from behind and snapped his neck as casually as if he were swatting a fly.

Xavier Kline stood before the abandoned church, a long axe strapped to his hulking back, a body at his feet.

So this is it, he thought. *This is what the prince is so upset about. Wants me to take care of some choir girls.* He laughed aloud. *What the prince wants, the prince gets.*

Kline waved for his friends. Jacko and Damion joined him out front. It was common knowledge that Prince Benison didn't care for Brujah, but when he wanted dirty work done, he didn't hesitate to come calling.

"The others spread around, in case we need them?" He snorted at the thought that he would need help at all. Jacko and Damion nodded. Kline had brought four other Brujah with him as well, two of whom were actually his childer, but the prince didn't need to know about that. Kline had had another childe before the curse had struck, but only the strong survive.

"All right. Let's go."

Jacko and Damion flanked him up the walk toward the church.

The song had taken a strange turn tonight. Or maybe it was Owain and not the song at all that had taken the turn.

Owain had allowed himself to drift along with the siren's strand of music, the main theme that wove in and out of all the other notes, binding them together, bringing the tunes into one heavenly melody. Through the sounds, he could feel the depth of her loss, the poignancy with which that she had lost still moved her. She lamented that which had once made her whole, that which had fulfilled her and flooded her life with meaning, that which had been taken from her.

Owain wanted to discover what it was of which she had been so cruelly robbed. What could engender such a touching melancholy to endure over so many years? For Owain could feel the age of the song. He could glimpse the years through which the loss had persisted and become richer and more textured in its grief, yet still not lost a scintilla of the vitality from the first night it was voiced.

He had spent centuries lamenting his own past, at least until his ability to lament had withered away, all the while hearing the sobs of others who couldn't know what true suffering was. Now he was touched by this song, by the depth of loss it conveyed, and he wished to know this suffering that rivalled his own. He wanted to learn the siren's story, because he could feel a oneness in their loss, a bond that, once completely revealed, would never be severed.

As the notes of the song pried open his dark soul, Owain saw in the distance of his mind a small village tucked among the green Irish hills. The sun shone brilliantly on the sparkling countryside, the afternoon rains having recently passed. Not far from the village, stood the remains of an old stone church, long since abandoned, much of its roof collapsed. Within the partial shelter of the church was the siren, slight and pale even then, but full of life and love. She was not alone. She and the young man she fancied, their afternoon courting interrupted by the storm, had taken refuge from the rain. It was the sudden inconvenience for which every young lover hopes. They lay entwined upon the grass that over the years had tenaciously battled its way through the cracked stone floor. He kneaded her youthful, bared breasts, as she fondled him, engendering again his desire for her. Their world was that moment, spiritual fulfillment consummated with a completeness only hinted at by their sexual appetites.

So entranced by each other were they that neither noticed the man who stood over them. Not until he physically ripped away her lover did she see her father and the rage burning within him. As she covered her nakedness, her father struck the boy. Her lover stumbled and fell, his head striking the stone floor. He lay still. And as she wailed and sobbed over his body, her father dragged her away, and sent her away, never to set eyes upon her again.

While she knew only shame, Owain felt anger for her. Hatred grew within him, and he wished he could lay hands upon the dirty farmer, throttle him and watch his eyes bulge out, for what he had done. Owain felt anger, and for the first time in centuries, he felt pity. Ill-fated love creating a life of exile and regret.

How different was Owain? Not very. His brother Rhys had sensed Owain's love for Angharad—had sensed that love and sent Owain to die and later Angharad to waste away and grow old, as Owain's hollow youth lived on and on. His exile had been as real as the siren's. He'd struggled on for two hundred years, but the Norman Ventrue overrunning Britain had chased him out in the end. And though he had suffered for centuries, only now through the siren did he feel the full tragedy of his loss, beyond the anger, beyond the thirst for vengeance.

The healing catharsis was not to be prolonged, however. Though Owain clung to this bond of pain through the song, he was carried somewhere very different. He struggled to remain with the siren, but was helpless against the different images that assaulted him.

As the music rose in intensity and the maenads began their dance, visions he had seen before, but that had nothing to do with the siren, formed in Owain's mind.

The mist. It chilled his body. Nothingness. Negation. Only cold. The warmth of life nowhere to be found.

The mists began to swirl, as he knew they would. First motion. That which must have come before all else.

And as the hillside rose from the swirling mists, Owain stood upon it. He gazed upon the wooden staff which shone with the brilliance of life. Its warmth radiated over the hillside and kept the mists at bay. And as Owain stood by the staff, a voice spoke to him, a voice all around him but nowhere, a voice neither near nor far, a voice familiar yet distant and strange, and it said:

Hoard the nights that have fallen unto you.

Owain faced the staff as if it had spoken, and as the staff's warmth reached out for Owain, he backed away, afraid to be burned by the touch of the living wood.

And it was living. For as Owain backed away, the staff twisted, grains separating and forming branches that reached in every direction—to the east, to the west, to the north, to the south, to the sky, to the earth. They reached for Owain.

The branches came for him, and Owain ran.

He fled down the hillside, into the mists, away from the staff, away from the living tree. Again the voice spoke, from everywhere and from nowhere:

Hoard the nights that have fallen unto you.

I tell you, it avails you nothing.

Owain fled blindly through the mists. From behind the branches grasped for him, snagged his cloak and his hair, caught his feet and knocked him to the ground. But time and again he climbed back to his feet and ran onward.

The voice whispered in his ear:

This is the Endtime.

On and on through the mists he ran, the branches of the staff turned living tree ever-present, ever-reaching, ever-desirous.

Soon a shadow fell over Owain, but still he ran.

He ran onward, and then upward, the ground rising to meet his feet like a lover whose sweet has long been absent.

Steeper the ground became, terrace walls dividing the hillside. But still upward he clambered, the living tree behind him, following, hungering.

He ran and climbed until he was atop the high mound that had cast its shadow over him.

This is the Endtime, spoke the voice.

Atop the mound stood a stone tower, a shrine circled by ravens. The clouds lay heavy and thick around the tower. Lightning slashed through the churning vapor. Thunder shook the ground.

Owain ran into the tower, but no doors stood to shield him. There was only altar and cross; and call on the grace of God he was loath to do.

The branches of the tree snaked their way up the mound. They stretched to the tower threshhold, but did not enter. Slowly, they turned, gripping the side of the tower, wrapping ever 'round, upwards to the stormy sky. The branches held tight to the stone and grew thick. Soon there were doors enclosing Owain, doors of living wood, leaves and blossoms bursting forth, filling his tomb with a sweet fragrance.

This is the Endtime.

This is the fading of the Blood.

This is the Winnowing.

The shadow of Time is not so long that you might shelter beneath it.

Again thunder shook the earth, and then the earth was moving of its own accord, rumbling and quaking. The cross crashed from the altar, smashing...

The church doors crashed open, one tearing from its hinges and smashing to the floor.

Xavier Kline marched in, flanked by Jacko and Damion.

The maenads, three as one, turned and hissed like trapped animals at the intruders. The mortals, as well as Albert, looked around, dazed, unsure why the music had so suddenly stopped. Owain shook his head. Disoriented, dizzy, he tried to gain his bearings.

Her face twisted in anger, the siren jerked open her mouth, emitting a single note of rage.

Owain was knocked backward against the wall. The mortals were all thrown to the ground. But none of them were the target of the eruption. Kline and his henchmen were blasted backward out of the building, Jacko going through the wall by the door.

Every pane of glass shattered with such force that most of the boards were ripped from the windows and clattered to the ground outside.

Owain could see that many of the mortals were bleeding from their ears, and touching his own face he realized he was as well. Sharp, painful tinnitus wracked his skull.

A moment later, two more Kindred came bursting through the empty windows on one side of the sanctuary, Uzis blazing. Another two leapt to perches in opposite window sills. They, too, opened fire on those below.

The mortals and maenads were caught in a withering crossfire. The force of the bullets striking their bodies from different directions whipped them around like ragdolls in a tempest. The siren was struck by dozens of bullets and stumbled backward.

All this, Owain watched from above as he slowly regained his senses after both the visions and the concussive force of the siren's scream. His gilded dagger was in hand, but he stopped himself from leaping into the fray. What could he do but join those dying? One dagger would not make the difference against so many guns.

But as he saw his lovely siren riddled with bullets, her body torn and bloodied, such logic meant very little. He wanted more than anything to save her, to tear apart those who threatened her and then whisk her away to safety. He wanted to…but he did not.

Fallen to one knee, blood pouring from wounds all over her body, including one where a bullet had passed through her cheeks, the siren turned to the two Kindred closest to her and again released a piercing wail.

They were not far away, and when the sound hit them, heads snapped back, limbs separated from bodies, bullets exploded in chambers setting off more explosions. As the wall behind gave way in a maelstrom of sound and fire, the two Kindred ceased to be.

The entire building quaked from the blast, and one of the remaining two Kindred lost his footing and fell from his window perch. The siren turned toward the intact side of the church and her two attackers there.

As she opened her mouth, a fire axe launched through the air from the front door thudded into her face and neck. The axe knocked her backward to the floor.

Seeing the axe strike true, Owain slammed his dagger into the floor. He bit down into his lip to suppress a cry of horror. It couldn't end like this for the siren, she who had brought feeling back into Owain's existence. And how had he repaid her? By watching her slaughtered like a lamb and not lifting a finger to help.

Below, Xavier Kline, weaving and struggling to remain upright, staggered through the sanctuary, which was now silent except for the moaning of one mortal. He made his way toward the siren. The axe protruding into the air from her head and neck, she feebly grabbed at the handle but lacked the strength to pull it free.

There's still time! Owain tried to convince himself. *Save her!* But he couldn't even hold himself upright. He was too dizzy from the blasts of sound. How Kline was even managing to stand, Owain could not imagine.

Owain could not bring himself to the siren's aid,

but neither could he look away as Kline stood above her, reeling, but with the upper hand. With a violent jerk of his arm, the Brujah ripped the axe from her body. Owain thought he heard his siren gasp in pain, but she was no longer capable of song.

Take him! a voice within Owain screamed. *There's still time!*

Kline's two accomplices were sifting through the mortals' remains, finishing off the member of the congregation who had miraculously survived the deadly gunfire and the siren's attack. They were distracted.

But Owain was frozen. Fist quivering, he watched as Kline raised the axe high above him, where it seemed to pause for a horrific eternity, and then brought it crashing down onto the siren's neck. Owain didn't see the second blow which actually severed the head from the body, cutting through the last ragged adjoining tissue and digging deep into the floor.

He was crawling away like a beaten whelp, sick with himself, his head full of pain and ringing, wishing for nothing more than that the sun would rise that instant and take them all, burning, to hell.

Joining the pain, a voice echoed in his mind:

This is the Endtime.

FOURTEEN

The siren came to Owain. He heard her delicate footsteps as she slipped through the door to his room. She padded across the floor and gently lifted the lid to his resting place.

Owain looked up as she leaned seductively over him in the dim light—skyblue eyes and alabaster skin, dark black hair, gown hanging loosely exposing the slight swell of breast and palest hint of areola. She opened her mouth to weave him a lovesong, a melodious catharsis through which they could both at last overcome the sadness and loss that had clung to them over sea and mountain and everpassing years.

But no sound flowed from her mouth. No song

of beauty, no enchanting lullaby. Her tongue caressed the notes, yet sound eluded her.

Then she turned her head, and Owain saw the wound, the gaping chasm in face and neck. Shattered bone and jagged sinew lay exposed. She tried to cover the opening with a narrow hand so the air might flow properly and again she might sing, but the space dwarfed her thin fingers.

Owain raised his hand to help her. He craved the tender mercies of her song. But as he touched her flesh, blood began to seep from the wound and then to pour. Their hands together could not staunch the flow. It streamed into his coffin.

He tried to call for help but evoked no sound. A mere touch revealed a wound marring his face and neck. His blood poured forth, joining the pool collected in his coffin. Still the blood of the siren flowed freely, and as Owain struggled to escape, only to slip and lose his grip, the vitæ rose around him.

From the bottom of a deep well, Owain looked up at the siren, his entreaties as soundless as her song. And as the blood rose up and over him, she closed the lid and there was darkness.

"The usurper wants to meet with me! Ha!" Gustav's laugh was full of derision, not humor. His gray eyes betrayed no amusement. "Can you believe it, Edward?"

Edward Hyde adjusted his top hat, using the large silver head of his antique cane. "Meeting sounds good," he said, as he adjusted his position in the exquisite leather chair in Gustav's haven at the Berlin Palace. "If you don't meet with him, you can't kick in his teeth. He's always so damned proper and friendly. 'So good to see you. I do hope everything is well with you. I agree with everything you say. Goodness, look at the time. I must run.'" Hyde polished his cane on his flowing black opera cloak. "I hope I'm there when you kill him, Gustav."

Gustav rose from behind his desk and began stalking around the room, past the portrait of Frederick the Great, past the photograph of German troops marching through Paris. "Do not worry. All of Berlin…no, all of the world, will know when I destroy him," Gustav promised. "And Berlin will be mine, solely mine, again." He continued pacing back and forth behind his desk. "This is the height of arrogance, to ask for a meeting with me."

"You know what it means?" Hyde asked gruffly without looking up from his polishing.

Gustav halted his pacing. "Of course I know what it means. It means he is desperate."

"Or," Hyde pointed out, "it could be a trap for you."

"Ha!" Gustav resumed pacing, a sneer almost permanently creased on his jowly face. "Wilhelm?

Set a trap for me? Ha! He runs from me! His night is happy when he avoids me. He has more 'important' friends right now than do I. Otherwise, I crush him. But that will all change, and when the city is mine, those 'important' friends will beg for mercy, and I will crush *them*!" Gustav shook his fist, as if he held Wilhelm's friends in his hand already. "He does not try to trap me. He is not so devious. He is *sneaky*. How else could he have taken my city from me? But he is not devious."

As he again sat behind his desk, he ran his fingers through his steely gray hair, nearly an identical shade to his eyes. "He is desperate because his friends who keep him in power shrivel away and die. He is nothing without them. Nothing! He will be as a naked child soon."

"But your friends die too," said Hyde.

"But I," Gustav raised his finger triumphantly, "I rule by *my* power, not the power of my friends. Quite a different thing." He waggled his finger at Hyde.

"Hmph." Hyde, a rough, burly man, was somewhat obsessed with the intricate engravings on the head of his cane. The silver shone as brightly as the night he had taken the walking stick from the body outside the opera house, but still he polished. "He wants to meet. So you meet him and kill him."

Gustav dismissed the simplistic idea with a scornful glance. "He will not meet me where I can crush him," the erstwhile prince explained. "It will all be very formal and very proper. He will be friendly, and there will be many other Kindred around."

"So kill them all," Hyde grunted.

"Kill them all! Ha!" This time Gustav *was* amused. He could barely speak for his hearty laughter. "Edward...you say...kill them all...you say the most absurd..." But slowly Gustav's laughter died away. The absurd, as he called it, seemed incredibly attractive. "Kill them all," he said quietly.

The feud between Gustav and Wilhelm had been raging for over eighty years. Recently, at least, they had both eschewed open violence for fear of dragging the Camarilla Inner Council into Berlin politics. The Council or its Justicars might support one prince claimant over the offender if too much violence and chaos occurred, or the Camarilla officials might administer the city themselves or bring in a new prince, disenfranchising both Gustav and Wilhelm.

But with chaos breaking out everywhere as established balances of power listed like small boats in a raging storm, Gustav realized, thanks to Hyde's prompting, the Inner Council would have little time to spare for one city's political contentions. By the time an inquiry might be mounted, Gustav would have cemented his hold on power, and the Council was unlikely to risk more instability by removing a de facto prince.

Gustav stood abruptly and slapped his palm against the desk. "Wilhelm is right. We should meet and speak like civilized Kindred. This curse of boiling blood endangers all our city."

Now Hyde, his head cocked quizzically, looked up from his cane. "What did you say?"

Gustav, rubbing his chin, ignored the Malkavian primogen of East Berlin. "Then I should change my thinking about the messenger," he said aloud to himself, then turned to Hyde. "Did you know, Edward, that he sent his own childe, Henriette, a slim delicate flower, as messenger? This as a sign of good will."

"You sent her back?" Hyde asked.

"Oh, no," said Gustav. "She is downstairs with a stake through her heart." Hyde nodded. "I had planned to send her head back to her sire, perhaps with some western Kindred's genitalia clenched between her teeth. But I suppose that would complicate this whole meeting business."

Again, Hyde nodded sympathetically. "Why not," he asked, "keep her three nights, blood-bond her, and send her back with the message and have *her* kill Wilhelm?"

Gustav opened his mouth to deride his visitor, but then closed his mouth without speaking. Wilhelm did not regularly bond his supporters or childer, so there would be no conditioning to overcome, and Gustav could always deny that he'd had any hand in the matter at all if the girl failed. With a little Tremere magic to remove all traces of his handiwork, he could have the best of both worlds—an assassination attempt and a diplomatic meeting.

"You are a true genius, Edward Hyde."

"I keep telling you this, Gustav."

"Come," said the self-proclaimed once and future prince. "Let us attend to our messenger."

Owain ignored the knocking at his door. Darkness had fallen hours before, he knew, but he could not bring himself to face the night. Last night he had wanted nothing more than to greet the sun, to let it cook his flesh, to sear the cowardice from him until the relief of final death took his soul from the torment that was unlife.

So complete was that cowardice, however, that he had sought the shelter of his haven even before the first rays of cleansing light had crested the horizon and ravaged his cold flesh.

Survival is not cowardice, he kept telling himself, but never quite believing.

At least the insistent knocking distracted him from his dreams. All day he had been plagued by dreams—not visions of home or even of a vengeful living tree that stretched after him for miles until finally it trapped him in a collapsing tower.

Nightmares. Shades from boyhood.

He wanted none of the dreams. He wanted nothing to do with the visions. He wanted to lie in darkness, to not think, to not be. And before long, the knocking, which did not cease or even pause for any length of time, began to grate at his already ragged nerves.

It was Randal at the door of Owain's room. Owain knew the tenor of those particular knuckles against wood. Then the ghoul was calling through the door, knowing his domitor could hear him, but Owain refused to listen. He heard the sounds, but he refused to allow them to form words in his mind. Randal's voice was no more than the noise of his knocking. Sound without form.

Like the song without sound of the siren as she had stared at Owain through mangled flesh. He might as well have hacked apart her face himself. He had sat and watched it all, not lifted a finger to save her. Her song had brought him in touch with humanity long vanquished, and he had sacrificed her for nothing more than that he might continue his hollow, meaningless existence.

But what is there without existence? he wondered. "By God! What is there *with* it?"

The sound of Owain's voice lent renewed vigor to Randal's knocking. "Sir? Sir? It's quite important, sir."

No, Owain determined, *I will not acknowledge the*

world. *I will not let myself be dragged into caring.* At least the past few centuries of boredom had lacked that torment. It had been so long since Owain had truly cared about anything.

Perhaps, he pondered, torpor was calling for him again. It had, after all, been almost three hundred years since his last extended rest. Randal could take care of the household details. Except there was no blood supply for him or for the other ghouls. Without the periodic nourishment of Owain's vitæ, they would age hours in but minutes and wither away to little more than dried husks, much as many of the Kindred of Atlanta had recently. Señor and Señora Rodriguez's two hundred years would catch up with them quite rapidly. Randal would last little longer. Ms. Jackson would probably survive, as might the security team Arden and his nephew Mike, but the withdrawal effects of being cut off from vampiric blood would not be pretty.

From the hallway beyond, a new sound caught Owain's ear—the jingle of metal against metal, keys clinking against one another. In the back of his mind, Owain had known that it would come to this.

The key turned in the antique brass lock and the mechanism clicked over. The door swung inward. For a moment there was silence, then Owain heard Randal take a deep breath and cross the room to the coffin. Owain could have locked himself in from the inside if he had wished to press the issue, but probably the ghoul still would have refused to let his master rest.

Fingers made contact with the lid, and then it was opening.

Owain's hand shot up. His fingers latched onto Randal's throat, nails digging into flesh. The lid, before Owain flung it completely open, crashed down on the ghoul's head. Randal tried to call out, for whatever good it might have done him, but the crushing pressure on his larynx cut his air.

Owain pulled his servant backward halfway into the coffin. "Did you ever have one of those days, Randal, when you just didn't want to see anyone?" The vampire loosened his grip just enough that Randal could struggle to speak.

He choked out a desperate whisper: *"Forgive me, sir."*

Owain loosened his grip a bit more. "There is no forgiveness, Randall. Not in this world nor the next." Owain tore into his retainer's throat, gnawing through flesh until he hit upon the carotid artery.

The fear and pain in Randal's eyes were soon outweighed by the ecstacy of the kiss. He fell limp, and though he whimpered with sorrow as his life's blood drained out of his body, he could force not a single muscle to resist.

The blood was a richer vintage than that of a

mere mortal, as it had been mixed with Owain's own blood for many years now, but it lacked the potency of the fragrant vitæ Owain had drunk from full vampires back in his days of naked ambition among the mortal world.

Randal's whimpers died away. Owain, feeding from anger rather than hunger, released the body, which slid down the side of the coffin to the floor. How, Owain wondered, had he abided such impudence for so long? Had his senses as well as his emotions been so dulled?

Ms. Jackson's duties would have to be expanded, at least until Owain could find a replacement to conduct his household affairs. It was not as simple a task, replacing one's personal servant, as it sounded. There was no service to contact for ghouls in waiting. Luckily, Owain imagined Ms. Jackson would have little trouble filling Randal's shoes. Perhaps an increase in staff would not even be necessary.

Again contemplating the attractiveness of torpor, Owain decided that, if he went that route, he would provide blood enough to maintain Ms. Jackson, and let the others go. Of course, there would be many other details needing his attention. Since there was no way to gauge exactly how long torpor might last, he would need a more secure and less ostentatious resting place than this estate, and there were so many business interests to be safeguarded or placed in escrow.

Then there was always the chance that he would lapse into years of inactivity without actually meaning to do so. That would be the simplest way, drifting away from the conundrums of nightly unlife, and preparations be damned; but also the risks of eventual discovery and harm, if not final death, would be considerable.

How much did Owain care? How strongly did the urge for release outweigh the survival instinct?

It was that precarious balance he was contemplating when he saw the small slip of paper on the floor not far from Randal's body. The paper was a distinctive personalized stationary that Owain was sure had been delivered within the past few hours by a ghouled passenger pigeon that any mortal ornithologist would be shocked to see. A voice of receding influence within Owain's mind wanted him to leave the message be, to lie back in his coffin and pull the lid shut, closing out the world beyond. He could make excuses later if need be. Correspondences intercepted, a treacherous servant now chastened—that would most likely be his best excuse for failing to respond to last night's summons.

Owain considered that course, but acted otherwise. His risen ire and the recent feeding had snapped him out of his nihilistic doldrums, for the time being at least. He leaned over the edge of the coffin and snatched up the paper. As he knew it would be, the message was rendered in the prince's practiced script:

1 January

Mr. Owain Evans:

Your presence is required tonight at midnight at the abandoned factory opposite Oakland Cemetery.

This gathering is of utmost importance in ensuring the continued prosperity of all the Kindred of our fair city. I shall brook no failure to attend.

Your obt. svt.

J. Benison Hodge

Prince of Atlanta

Owain crumpled the paper and dropped it to the floor. *Not much room for misinterpretation there*, he noted.

He could still ignore the summons and make excuses later, but it sounded as if Benison might not be interested in hearing excuses, valid or otherwise. Besides, Owain decided, the prince had always treated him respectfully, and there was little sense in offending the ruler of the city without reason. There might also be a way to find out what had led Xavier Kline and his henchmen to the church. Certainly Thelonious, the Brujah primogen, had not ordered the attack. Had Kline acted of his own accord?

The very thought of Kline and what the mindless brute had done to the siren nearly drove Owain to violence. Could he face the Brujah if he were at the gathering? Could Owain trust himself not to fly into a rage and attack the destroyer of the peace and meaning that Owain had finally discovered? But what was the last official Kindred function Kline had attended? Owain could not think of one. *Probably another meeting of the primogen and the prince wants a bit of extra advice. Strange, though to call them two nights running.*

Owain glanced at the grandfather clock in the corner. *Eleven thirty-five!* Less than half an hour to be there. *Wouldn't do to miss one meeting and be late for the next.* Quickly, he stepped over Randal's body and prepared to go, again not shaving—the stubble would never grow any longer than it already was. Within two minutes, he was hurrying down the steps and yelling for Ms. Jackson.

Benison sat toward the back of the cavernous building. The Fulton Bag Factory, abandoned for years but now scheduled for renovation into loft apartments. The prince knew the Anacreons would never stand for that, not so close to the cemetery that they had demanded remain off-limits to Kin-

Gherbod Fleming

dred. The wraith leaders had already told him as much, but as of yet he had taken no action on these latest requests. It wouldn't do for the prince of Atlanta to appear to be taking orders from the spirit world denizens. They needed to know that he was in command.

Unless the haunting began again.

Before agreeing to the Oakland Cemetery designation, Benison had alternately fought the mindless shades with his sword throughout Rhodes Hall, and cowered from them, locked tightly in his coffin when the sensation of spirits pressing around him from every direction had become too much to bear. Once he had agreed to the Anacreons' request, the hauntings had ceased.

So Benison would hold out long enough to assert his control, but not so long that the shadows might return to his home before derailing the construction plans as surely as Nathan Bedfor Forrest had disrupted Federal rail support.

That business had been planned out for quite some time now, though. What bothered Benison tonight was the tardy arrival of numerous Kindred. He had planned to begin promptly at midnight, capturing the symbolic beginning of a new day just as his proclamations would deliver the city from its present panic and usher in a new era of abundance.

Already, however, it was nearly half past, and his subjects were still straggling in, mostly the ancillae.

The primogen were all present. They knew the importance of the decrees to be handed down. Hannah was present with her two chantry neonates. Noticably absent were the two she had "disciplined." Of course Eleanor was present, and Benjamin, and Owain had arrived a few minutes late. That accounted for the Ventrue—although Benison would have to remember to find out why Owain had missed the meeting last night. Foul Aurelius was lurking in the damp shadows, as was his younger Nosferatu whose name always escaped the prince's mind. Bedelia, Thelonious, Marlene and her hangers-on were all at hand. Nearly a score of recognized Kindred all told.

Even Xavier Kline, who occupied that gray area between fully recognized Kindred and anarch, was present, though he appeared a bit worse for wear from his encounter the night before. Wads of cotton were stuffed in his ears, and the once or twice he grew frustrated with them and removed them, he winced in pain at each sound above a whisper and was forced to put them back. It was a rare injury that didn't heal quickly for a Kindred. *Kline must have taken quite a beating*, Benison noted. *I must reward him for his faithful service.*

Maybe a half-dozen of the anarchs were present, some still wandering in. There must be more, Benison knew, but how many had perished from the curse? He shouldn't be surprised they were late.

Why should they show any more respect to the prince than they did the Traditions?

Lorenzo Giovanni, the ghoul, with his bodyguard had arrived punctually at five 'til midnight. Even the temporary guest in the city keeping account of his family-clan's holdings paid Benison more respect than the anarchs who resided here.

No longer, Benison promised himself, *will I tolerate such impertinence. No longer.*

The prince was almost ready to begin, and those not present be damned. But he and they were *already* damned, Benison mused. Worse yet, though, they would feel his wrath.

Eleanor was amazed at how many were present. There were very few Kindred she didn't know well by sight in the city, but as far as she knew, never before had so many been gathered in one place. A quick count of heads totalled over thirty, and that after reportedly at least that number had succumbed to the curse! How had they allowed the city to grow so overpopulated? Perhaps the plague had done them a favor. After all, to a remarkable degree the younger Kindred, recognized and anarch, were those stricken. Perhaps that, along with Benison's upcoming fire and brimstone sermon, would restore a greater degree of order to the city.

She glanced over toward Benjamin. She would have to ask him about that concept of the curse as a necessary means of population control. Had it indeed been visited upon their city by God, as Benison contended? But it had affected more than just this city. Benison had been too concerned about appearing weak to communicate with other princes, but Eleanor had received reports from her sire Baylor of the widespread carnage. Was the overpopulation problem so widespread?

Again she glanced at Benjamin. His mind was so refined, so perfect. He would undoubtedly provide valuable insights on the subject. They had to take pains to show not even a passing interest in one another in public. She had not betrayed her husband in a sexual sense, not entirely, but still if he were to discover the emotional and intellectual bond between her and her secret childe...That damnable Owain Evans had somehow. Where was the scoundrel? Lying low, spying on all those around him, no doubt. *The man is more Nosferatu than Ventrue*, Eleanor was convinced. Before long, she needed to discover just how much he did know. If he had merely seen Benjamin and her together and connected the pieces, then he wouldn't know that she was Benjamin's sire as well as lover. Either way, he needed to be dealt with. She couldn't allow him to manipulate Benjamin that way. She couldn't take the chance that Benjamin would grow to resent their relationship as a cause of danger more than he resented Evans.

And heaven forbid that Marlene, the tabloid incarnate of Kindred society, should find out. It still stung Eleanor that Benison allowed the semi-reformed harlot to remain in the city. Some pressure might just be required on that front as well.

The factory was full of a quiet murmuring as Kindred milled about and speculated about what was to come. The sound was quiet to the enhanced senses of a Cainite, but would be virtually silent, Eleanor knew, to a passing mortal. Only the ancillae burst out in occasional laughter, calculatedly brash to hide their unease. Each time the young upstarts forgot their place, the elders stared them down.

Even the low murmurings died away, however, as the prince rose from his seat and approached the gathering. He paused for a moment, gazing over his assembled subjects. "Kindred of Atlanta," he began, "seldom have so many of us gathered together, and it saddens me that a great tragedy is the cause. But like the people of Israel who grew strong in their exile, from disaster is greatness often born."

Eleanor took pride in the majestic aura of her husband. His black suit was the height of 1890s fashion, as was her dark red gown. He stood tall and straight, a monolithic symbol of strength in the troubling times. There were those who disagreed with him, some on principled grounds, such as Thelonious. Others schemed amongst the shadows. But none could stand against him once his mind was set, and tonight he was as determined in his course as ever she had seen him.

His words inspired her. "We have all felt the hand of the curse in one way or another. We may try to hide the ways, for fear that others will ascribe to us weakness in our loss, but we all have been touched. For me, I have lost my only childe. He found his final death before my eyes."

There was a great silence among the Kindred. It was unheard of for the prince to discuss so personal a tragedy in such a public forum. Even in the Bible classes he led, his sermonettes and diatribes were of a rather philosophical bent: detached, not personal.

"Just as painful for me has been to watch the community which I am entrusted to protect torn apart from within, none sure of what is happening, all afraid to associate with another who might be cursed or demented with hunger.

"Tonight I will reveal to you how it is that we have come to be cursed." Whispers of surprise and disbelief broke through the Kindred at this news. "And I will tell you how we will set ourselves on the road to salvation. With the help of all gathered here, we will remove this curse."

The noise quickly died down as all listened carefully, some full of incredulous awe, others skeptical, still others sure that this was the Malkavian in the prince coming out, the mad priest-king.

As for Benison, he had a narrow line to walk. He spoke with the conviction of his beliefs, but there were many he would need to convince that he spoke authoritatively, not in the sense of power but of knowledge. In that same vein, he could not reveal the source of much of his information.

Many of the details he recited of how the curse had struck were too painfully common knowledge—the hunger that ate at the Cainites, turning their nightly requirements into obsessive and uncontrollable urges; the madness that took them, creating sometimes raving lunatics, sometimes slavering killers.

But the prince had discovered more. In his discussion last night with his Anacreon allies, he had learned that the madness visited upon the accursed Kindred was no random insanity. The wraiths could feel the lure of the madness in the Shadowlands of the restless dead. There was a force of entropy at work, a regressive energy, they explained, and to their spirit eyes the source of the curse was evident—blood.

The Cainites' blood was not weakened. It had lost none of its potency. Quite the contrary. It had *increased* in potency, so much so that the curse literally transformed the blood to that of an earlier generation, and earlier, and earlier. For some, the regression involved becoming the vampire of earlier generation through whom the blood had flowed, reliving certain events, fighting certain dangers. Whether the accursed experienced ancestral memories or not, the physical eventualities were the same. The body and mind of the Cainite could not adjust to the rapidly increasing potency of the blood. The mind broke down. The flesh broke down. And always there was the hunger. No amount of feeding could satisfy the shifting needs of the body.

Madness. Starvation. Death.

All this Benison had constructed through his conversation with the Anacreons. But he could not inform the Kindred of Atlanta of those discussions. Not only would the Anacreons themselves not want it so, the prince's ability to learn that which no Cainite or mortal had seen was an important handhold for his grip on power.

"The curse," he explained to his subjects, "is the call back to our beginnings—to our sires, and our sires' sires, and their sires before them. Back to the very beginning. Unless we can lift the curse, it is our call back to the most ancient of ancients. To the antediluvians. *To Gehenna.*"

Eleanor winced at the word, and startled comments rang out all over. Officially, the Camarilla disavowed any belief that the antediluvians, grandchilder of Caine, even existed, much less would return at the Endtime, Gehenna, to consume all those Cainites of more recent generations. There were cults and mystics and doom-mongers, even within the Camarilla, who said otherwise. But a prince making such a public pronouncement, Eleanor knew only too well, as a former archon, would normally bring the full fury of the Camarilla down on his city.

But times were far from normal.

The prince might have some room to maneuver, if situations elsewhere continued as chaotically as they seemed. Benison had not spoken lightly. He had determined a course of action, and he might just have time to implement it.

"*This is the Endtime,*" the prince again recited. "*This is the Falling of the Blood. This is the Winnowing.*"

Again, as with the primogen the night before, the reaction of the assembled Kindred to the prophetic passages from the *Book of Nod* was utter solemnity. The sacrosanct words carried a nearly tangible force; they lent credence and power to the unwavering convictions of the prince.

"*The First-Born comes in fury. He harrows his children from their graves. His wrath is a hammer, an unhewn cudgel wet with the blood of the Kinslaying. He drives the lightning before him.*"

Despite the compelling nature of the prince's oratory, several anarchs quickly grew restless. Aside from the initial shock value, they afforded little significance to the portentous words of the ancients. The younger Kindred fidgeted like so many children in church but, surrounded by their elders, did not interrupt. Thelonious observed and took note of the anarchs' growing unease.

"Even for the Cainite," Benison continued, "there is a place and an order. Just as the kine are placed in dominion over the beasts, the Kindred are placed in dominion over the kine, and with dominion comes responsibility for the well-being of the lesser being. Among us, our Traditions ensure that we are able to live with one another, so that our society may function harmoniously, and we may more efficiently shepherd our mortal charges."

As Benison enumerated the importance of the six Traditions and the ways that many Kindred had strayed from the natural order commissioned by God and consecrated by the Dark Father Caine on behalf of all those who bore his stain, a distinct division developed among the Cainites. Many of the older vampires, those more indoctrinated in the ways of the Camarilla, grew openly supportive of what the prince said. They could agree that they might have errored, and that, with only minor adjustments, they could comply more fully with the authoritative prescriptions of which Benison spoke.

On the other hand, some of the younger Kindred and many of the anarchs grew increasingly edgy.

"I have decreed," Benison announced, "and the primogen have approved the New Year's Writ of Three. Measures by which we may remove from our city the curse which our divine Creator has justly visited upon us in retribution for our recalcitrance in observing the ordained ways. First, the Kindred of Atlanta will cease, from this point onward, their laxity in observing the Six Traditions and the proclamations of prince and primogen. Violations of the spirit, as well as the letter, of the Law will be dealt with in a vigorous and just manner."

None spoke out against the prince. Many weighed the implications of the his decree. The situation in the city had grown so desperate and the need for *some* drastic course of action was so apparent, that many skeptics were cowed into submission. There were grumblers among the anarchs, but they assumed that once away from this gathering they could again pay lip service to the Traditions and do as they pleased. For the time being, standing close to the elders of the city and listening to the prince, the ancillae opted for subversion over confrontation. Not even Thelonious spoke out. Having said his piece among the primogen, he knew when he was beaten and planned for the future.

"Second," said the prince, "those of you without

clan will choose one to seek adoption into. And those of you who are of a clan but leave unfulfilled your duty as a clan member, you will take up your responsibilities. There will be order in this city again! The ordained association between ancilla and elder will not be blurred!"

This decree shocked the assemblage to silence. Whether resigned or irritated, they had all seen the first coming, but this second decree...this verged on heresy against the accepted tenets of the Camarilla.

Eleanor watched closely the assembled Kindred. It would be her responsibility to aide her husband in maintaining order, and while he was quite able to command through sheer force of will and intimidation, her eye was the more trained for less overt signs of trouble. Why crush a revolt if the leaders could be coopted before it even began?

To some extent, Benison practiced intrigue instinctively. For a time now, he had been enlisting the help of Xavier Kline, the most potentially hostile of the anarchs and perhaps the most dangerous, in situations that allowed the neolithic churl to act upon his aggressive tendencies in a manner beneficial to the prince. Among the others, Eleanor could pinpoint no glaring dangers. The primogen would fall in line, and the other recognized Kindred would follow that lead. Hannah had voted for the decrees, so the Tremere should be nominal allies—all the better to keep an eye on them. The anarchs would cause minor trouble. Surely Benison would be forced to have Kline put one or two of them down, but that would serve as a signal to the rest, and they would comply or move on to other cities. *Bringing the anarchs to heel and controlling the population of his city.* Perhaps her husband's strategy was more insightful than she had originally given him credit for.

It all hinged, however, on one condition: *the blood curse.* What would happen if the curse suddenly abated somehow? The Camarilla would redirect its time and resources to respond to this radical decree. *Benison must have thought of that and bulled ahead regardless*, Eleanor suspected. *That would be like him.*

The shocked silence shortly gave way to muttering and debate. Some elders had no desire to associate with anarchs. Others, sensing that their clans might be invigorated by increased numbers, wished to make subtle connections with the Clanless most likely ripe for recruitment.

Eleanor was impressed by the audacity of her husband's actions, if not completely convinced of their inherent wisdom. The first decree, reasserting the relevance of the Traditions, was merely an ultraconservative interpretation of existing law. The second decree, however, basically disenfranchised the Clanless, the most rapidly growing portion of Kindred society. If that practice were successful and spread to other cities, it could inflame young Cainites to the point of a second Anarch Revolt. Thelonious had been correct on that count. And where would the anarchs turn? Either, ironically enough, to the Camarilla itself for protection, or into the waiting arms of the Sabbat.

Cloaked in bold action, it was a fragile hand the prince played.

The problem with attending a large gathering of Kindred, Owain decided, was that at least half of those present wanted to hide in the shadows and skulk about. He certainly did, and he kept bumping into the two Nosferatu, Aurelius and that other one whose name escaped Owain's memory. They were all so busy obfuscating within an inch of their unlives that they didn't see one another. So far Owain had been stepped on and elbowed, and he had accidentally stuck his finger in someone's eye. At least he hoped it was an eye and not one of Aurelius' draining boils.

In this place so close to the site of his lovely siren's murder, Owain looked on as the prince delivered his decrees with equal parts conviction, apocalyptic fervor, and drama. *That must be what I missed last night*, Owain realized, *the primogen approving Benison's plans*.

The first of the decrees had been fairly unremarkable. The second was somewhat of a surprise. Owain had watched with interest the varying reactions around the room. He was surprised that Thelonious, among others, had not offered at least a token protest, but perhaps that had all played out the night before.

Most interesting, though, was Benison's explanation of the curse. Aside from wondering how the prince had come to acquire such knowledge, Owain was intrigued by the idea of ancestral memories. Until now, as the city had plunged into chaos around him, Owain had been somewhat insulated from the crisis. He dealt directly with very few Kindred, which was how he liked to maintain his affairs, and none of his ghouls had suffered from the curse. In fact, he had spent more time enamored by the siren, and now the tragedy of her death, and had spared little thought for the malady that had claimed nearly half the Kindred of Atlanta.

Hearing Benison, however, Owain wondered if there might not be some connection. The vision. The tree, the tower—could this be akin to the dementia brought on by the curse? He had found himself wandering among vague memories of the Middle Ages. He had fed more often than was the norm for him. Were these the beginnings of the curse? Would his blood visit upon him the final release he lacked the courage to inflict upon himself?

The noise around Owain lessened as the prince moved on to his third decree.

"...and I can only take responsibility for the sacrilege which has transpired," said Benison. "Less than two miles from here stands a church, long since deserted by its mortal parishioners."

Owain felt a knot in the pit of his stomach.

"Unbeknownst to myself, a Cainite of foul design occupied that place of worship."

Owain stared straight ahead, knowing what was coming, not wanting to hear it, not wanting to believe it.

"She performed rituals, invoking demons and paying homage to pagan gods, and in doing so intensified the divine wrath called down upon us, perhaps even was first in drawing the anger of our divine Creator!"

Still reeling from the previous decree, the Kindred of Atlanta accepted this one without comment. With a supreme effort of will, Owain held himself steady, though he wanted to scream and rage, to throw himself at the prince.

"The problem," said Benison, "has been rectified."

Rectified.

The word rang in Owain's ears. The first beauty that had wound its way into his life in hundreds of years, like a ray of light through a maelstrom of stormclouds.

Rectified.

She was butchered! he wanted to yell. *Hacked apart with an axe by a conscienceless killer.*

Conscienceless killer. Owain had been called that before. He had *been* that. Had he not done worse in his day? The prince was still speaking. Owain forced himself to listen, to focus.

"I ask of each of you a question. I will ask it only once, and within the quarter hour I must have your answers." The prince turned to the side. "Kline, bring him."

Someone had to relay the message, as Kline had not heard, but slowly the crowd parted, making way for the Brujah behemoth. He led a figure covered by a black hood, hands tied. But despite the hood, Owain recognized him.

When Kline reached the center, before Benison, the Brujah withdrew and the prince approached the prisoner.

"This Cainite," said Benison, "has consorted with infernalists. He has broken Kindred law and holy law. In part the curse that ravages our city is on his head." The prince slowly surveyed the assembled Kindred, his green eyes imparting severe meaning. "My question to you all is this: Have any others taken part in these demonic rites? Do any others bear the stain?"

Silence. The silence of the grave.

"Think well," said the prince, "for after tonight, there will be no mercy."

Kindred shuffled their feet, looked at the floor, did anything they could to avoid making eye contact with anyone else. Owain stared at the hooded figure.

"Speak now," the prince urged, "and you will be treated leniently."

Leniently? Owain wondered. *A quick death?* But no, that was not like the prince. He was not an intentionally cruel man. He would hand down a just sentence. *Like the just sentence he handed down to the siren?* Owain gnashed his teeth behind lips pressed tightly closed.

Still waiting for any response from his subjects, Benison reached over and removed the hood so that all might look upon the transgressor. Standing bound among the Kindred was Albert. The prince did not look at his fellow Malkavian, at the once-long beard cut short and ragged, at the dried blood that had run from his ears, at the scrapes and contusions covering his face, no doubt from the hands of the Brujah enforcer. Albert's head hung low, his jests beaten out of him.

"Let this one be a lesson for all those who would deny the truth," said Benison. "Are there any who seek leniency?" Again silence gripped the throng.

Owain wanted to whisk Albert away. How long had he known the Malkavian, one hundred years, two hundred? Owain felt certain that Albert would not stand by while a friend was wrongfully punished. Owain could speak on his behalf, but to do so would be to mark himself, and how many secrets would be unravelled then?

Damn Benison. Owain clenched his fists at his sides. *Damn him for Albert's sake. Damn him for destroying…for destroying beauty.*

"Very well," the prince concluded. "The time for mercy is past."

Benison held out his hand, and again Kline came forward, this time carrying a three-foot wooden stake. The prince took the stake but still did not look at Albert's face, as if the condemned were not worthy to be gazed upon. "Do you have anything to say?" Benison asked.

With effort, Albert raised his head. His eyes were swollen and bloodshot. A hint of smile upon his battered lips, he slowly turned his head, taking in all those around him. Many refused to meet his gaze. Some glared accusingly at him. Owain was squeezing back into the shadows again, but the Malkavian's look came to rest briefly on him regardless. *"What would Angharad say?"* Albert whispered.

"May God have mercy on your soul." As Benison slammed the stake into Albert's heart, Owain almost stumbled, as if he himself had taken the blow. His knees buckled, and he felt himself stagger into someone.

What would Angharad say?

From where he lay on the floor, Albert's motionless eyes stared blankly at Owain.

What would Angharad say?

Owain felt ill. He fought down bile and blood. *Angharad.* How had Albert known? There were a host of questions Owain needed answered, but no way to ask them.

For an instant, Owain thought he heard a trace of the siren's song. Or was it the lullaby that Angharad had sung so long ago? Or were they one and the same? But no. It was only a trick of his mind and the echoing acoustics of the empty factory.

The Kindred were shuffling about, anxious to leave. This was no victory over an enemy, no time to celebrate. Albert was one of their own, fallen and punished. None wished to dwell on the fact.

Even Benison, firm in his duty, took no pleasure in the task. He stood with splattered blood on his hand, in his beard, on his suit. "This one will be left out for the sun. May our Lord claim his soul."

The last two nights had been too much for Owain. First the murder of the siren, now this. *Angharad.* He needed to be away from the crowd, but he forced himself to walk slowly. Thankfully there was no small talk after such an ordeal. He could not have stomached it.

A cold hatred burned in Owain's breast. Toward Xavier Kline, the killer, for the relish he took in destruction. Toward Benison for not understanding, for handing down death sentences. Toward Albert for saying her name, for dying. Toward all Kindred for living such sadistic, perverted unlives. But mostly toward himself, for a list of sins more grievous by far than what could have been said of the siren and Albert combined.

FIFTEEN

If Kendall Jackson noticed Owain's fists trembling with rage as he got into the car, she conscientiously ignored the fact. "Homeward," he instructed her.

Adref.

There were hints and traces of the siren in everything Owain saw and heard. He could not escape her. He lay down in the back seat of the Rolls and covered his eyes. His ears were ringing again, not as badly as Kline's must be after the direct blast he had taken, but far from completely healed. Owain squeezed his temples, as if that could make the ringing, the pain, the memories go away.

For the second time in as many nights, he had

stood by and watched as a Cainite deserving better had met final death. He had not fought on the siren's behalf, he had not lobbied on Albert's. Never mind that Kline and his goons would most likely have cut Owain down at the church. Never mind that Benison had already determined Albert's fate and that not even Solomon the Wise could have swayed the prince from his plans. Still Owain was punished by waves of guilt.

For so long he had felt...nothing. No joy, no remorse, no pity, no guilt.

Then for a few short weeks the siren's song had touched him. It had reached out to him and drawn him in, reminding him of his mortal days, days when emotions had burned strong, for good and for ill. She recognized his loss and had shown him her own. But the seeds of loss are happiness, and that Owain had forgotten. Love, loss, longing. Humanity. Owain had searched for it once. The last time he had seen his love he had been searching for it, had given up that search.

Angharad.

What would Angharad say?

Adref. Homeward.

In a few short weeks the siren had torn down the walls of his secure castle. She had dragged him from the small safe chambers, the dull ache of existence, and thrown him to the chaos that is living with all its incumbent pain and grief. And again it was the joy that was stolen from him.

As sure as Rhys had stolen Owain's one love, and a dark shadow in Westminster his life, as sure as the Norman Ventrue had stolen Wales and the Inquisition his one friend Gwilym, Benison and Kline had conspired to steal his newfound joy.

To drive the point home as surely as any sharpened stake, they had sacrificed poor Albert, and so Owain was doubly guilty—traitor to his prince, traitor to his friend.

Enough!

Owain sat upright from where he was slumped in the back seat. He pounded the passenger seat before him, his claws raking through the leather and padding.

Jackson glanced nervously over her shoulder, but continued to drive, saying nothing.

Owain drew back a fist to smash through the window…but stopped himself. Anger, too, was a gift of the siren. Yes, he had raged at the chess board, but for years nothing else. And what he felt toward Benison and Kline was like the sun next to a candle compared to his frustration with the game.

They were not far from home. Owain brushed the bits of cushion padding from his clothes. He smoothed back his hair.

His emotions would serve him. They would provide him with that crucial edge, that sense of purpose that he had lacked for decades upon decades—as long as he did not subordinate his reason to his feelings. His anger could drive him, but he could not let it rule him.

His mistake, Owain realized, was that he had cared. Had he not cared long ago, then his loss would not have haunted him so over the centuries. Had he not cared about the siren, then he would have missed the sensations she offered, as he would have any common harlot in life, but guilt for not tossing away his own life would not have tormented him.

She had drawn him in, manipulated him as surely as she had manipulated the mortals who were her herd, *as surely as she had manipulated Albert*. What visions of rapture had *he* seen? What avenues of lost days had he traversed? It was *she* who had led the Malkavian to his doom. It was *she* who had beguiled Owain into betraying his prince.

And it was she who had paid the price.

It all fit together perfectly, yet still Owain harbored sharp resentment against Benison and his Brujah buffoon. Like all those before, they would lord over Owain. They would approve or condemn his every action, his every thought. No better than Rhys, no better than the Normans, no better than the Inquisition. Owain would throw off this yoke as well.

"Sir, there's someone by the front gate," said Jackson from the front.

Owain saw that it was true, and that the *some-one* was no random stranger. "Pull up beside him." Jackson followed the instructions, and Owain pushed open the door.

"*Buenas noches, mi hermano*," said the visitor. He was short and dark-complected and wore a black suit with dark red shirt and black tie.

"Get in," Owain responded tersely.

The man did so, but as he opened his mouth to speak, Owain gestured irritably for silence. The Spaniard busied himself with straightening his tie. They rode to the house without a word.

After Jackson was dismissed for the evening, Owain led his guest to the trophy room, and the moment the door was closed turned on him. "What are you thinking, showing up unannounced and standing out on the street in front of my home? Have you grown reckless over the years, Miguel, or merely idiotic?"

Miguel grinned a wide, sly smile. His teeth were dingy and crooked. "And there are those in this city who would recognize me, *hermano?*"

"Whether there are or not…" Owain threw his hands into the air. There was no point trying to convince this kind.

"And another thing, in case you had not heard," Miguel's smile vanished, "I am *sacerdote* now, priest, but you being a friend, you may call me *Fray Miguel.*"

Owain was running his finger along the edge of his sword that hung on the wall. He did not bother to face his guest when he addressed him. "I will call you no such thing. You have no authority over me, and furthermore, you endanger my position by even coming here!"

"Tsk, tsk, tsk." The wide smile was back. "We ask so much of you, don't we *hermano Owain?*" No longer waiting for Owain's invitation, Miguel took a seat in one of the large leather armchairs. "Is it not customary to offer your guest refreshment?"

"What are you doing here? You didn't come all the way from Spain just to catch up on old times." Owain turned from his sword, sat across from Miguel.

Taking his time, Miguel looked around the room. "Nice place you have here. You have not done poorly for yourself in America, but you never do poorly, do you, *hermano?*" He admired the pewter ashtray, ran his finger along the brass lamp, taking as much time as he could, baiting Owain.

But Owain waited. He denied his urge to throttle the man across from him.

Finally, deciding Owain wouldn't be drawn out, Miguel answered. "El Greco would see you."

El Greco. It was a name that, except in reference to the mortal painter, Owain had not heard spoken in over eighty years. "Impossible. He would never ask that of me. Is this some trick of yours,

Miguel?"

Miguel chuckled. "He said you would resist, that you had grown lazy and soft in America." The comment sounded much crueler, somehow, coming from Miguel than it would have from his master, Owain's acquaintance but not quite friend. Miguel reached into his jacket and produced an envelope which he handed to Owain.

The folded piece of parchment inside was familiar to Owain. Its yellowed edges were similar to the letter he had received just weeks ago from the same source, the letter that had contained only six words but still had managed to rouse Owain temporarily from his chronic ennui. This time, as well, the message was brief, and even more significant:

> Owain, I must speak with you.
> Come to Toledo with all possible haste.

As always, the same flowing script. No signature. None was needed.

Owain read the message once again. "Impossible. There is far too much going on here. I cannot be away."

Miguel was all smiles. He thoroughly enjoyed watching Owain squirm, luxuriated in turning the screws even tighter. "*Mi hermano*, it is not a request."

"*Damnation!*" Owain slammed his fist on the arm

of the chair. "Why is he doing this? Is he trying to destroy everything we have done?"

Miguel was through playing. He hissed fiercely, fangs bared at Owain. "You forget what you are, Owain. You have been here alone for too many years. I tell El Greco we should watch you more closely. The information you send is not so valuable that you may disregard your other responsibilities." Miguel sat back again, straightened his tie. "You forget what you are, *mi hermano*. Once Sabbat, always Sabbat."

Owain held back a snarl. It had been years and years ago that he had joined El Greco, but there were actions that once committed could never be escaped, no matter how much time intervened. He didn't want to deal with any of this at the moment. Even with his loyalty to Benison frayed to the point of severed, he wasn't ready to be torn away from the trauma of the siren's death, from his memories of Angharad.

A third time Owain read the letter. The price for freedom was being called due, and there was no alternative but to answer.

The wide open spaces helped. Somewhat, at least.

Blackfeather had told Nicholas of Kindred all over suffering from the curse. They ripped out each other's throats questing for blood. They raved, believing they were other people. Nicholas was afraid he had joined them.

It had been worse in the city, with the kine and their cars, the buildings and the roads. Everywhere he had gone there had been someone, or something.

Now he could see as well as feel the gentle curve of the earth, the acres and acres of winter wheat spreading out in every direction from horizon to horizon. The sky was open, the stars brilliant in the darkness, true darkness, not the pale pink that pretended to be night in the city.

And the visions.

They had been worse in the city, one coming on the heels of the last, leaving Nicholas so disoriented and confused that he had barely had a chance to recover for weeks.

Back in the wilds, the visions still visited him, but less often. Nicholas was better able to regroup and hold his own. Several times he had even fought off the waking dreams that he had felt coming on, just as he had held down the hunger. He drew strength from the outdoors, sustenance from the crisp air, vitality from the unspoiled earth.

Be that as it may, he could not hold off the visions this night. He had struggled for hours, but now he lay on the gentlest of slopes, staring up at the stars, surrounded by close horizons of wheat.

Exhausted by the fight, he could do no more.

And the visions came.

Darkness. Darkness and pain. Eyes slow to adjust. Lying on side. Trying to roll over but pain all over. *Change position…cannot.*

Cannot move at all.

The spear. Eyes adjusting at last. See what already felt. Spear through body. Strong oak. Halfway in, halfway out.

Day? Night? Dragging on in cave. Helpless. Pain. Hunger.

Pain.

Hunger.

Darkness.

Sight again. Cave. Sound. Footsteps coming closer.

Hunter of the blood standing over. Speaking. "It is a pleasure to meet you at long last, Blaidd. The villagers speak highly of you. Well, they speak often of you, at least."

Rip throat. Pain. Cannot move.

Kneeling. Leaning closer. Biting. Drinking.

The image faded to darkness, and Nicholas found himself looking again at the bright stars, not the wall of a cave. The visions were always difficult to grasp at first. Like water going down a drain, they fled. But after a few minutes of concentration— not a simple task with the hunger that gripped Nicholas after the visions—it came back.

Blaidd. Nicholas' great-great-grandsire. He had been little more than animal in mind, but Nicholas had felt the power of his blood, held in check by the spear through his heart. Diablerized by a hunter of the blood. And the more Nicholas remembered of the vision, the more clearly he saw the face of Blaidd's killer. It was a familiar face, one that Nicholas had seen with his own eyes.

Nicholas climbed groggily to his feet. The hunger tore at his body. He was weak, and dizzy...and enraged. The curse of the city had not only followed him. It had begun centuries before when a city-dweller had murdered Nicholas' ancestor and stolen his blood.

The hunger drove Nicholas this night. He could recapture the blood of his lineage. It was not far distant. There were still a few hours before sunrise, so he set off at once. Even the weakness could not stop him as he set a furious pace back to the city, back to Atlanta. There would be a reckoning. He swore on his ancestor's memory that blood would pay back blood.

Owain Evans, slayer of Gangrel, would answer for his crime.